Isabella's Baby

Agnes Alexander

A Wings ePress, Inc.
Western Romance Novel

Wings ePress, Inc.

Edited by: Jeanne Smith
Copy Edited by: Christie Kraemer
Executive Editor: Jeanne Smith
Cover Artist: Trisha FitzGerald-Jung
Images: Woman/Horse by willsantt from Pexels
Texas scene by Yinan Chen from Pixabay

All rights reserved

Wings ePress Books
www.wingsepress.com

Copyright © 2022 by: Agnes Alexander
ISBN-13: 978-1-61309-510-2
ISBN-10: 1-61309-510-4

Published In the United States Of America

Wings ePress Inc.
3000 N. Rock Road
Newton, KS 67114

What They Are Saying About
Isabella's Baby

Filled with layered, lovable characters with vivid personalities, *Isabella's Baby* tells the story of one woman's harrowing fight for independence in the 19th century wild West. Isabella Greeley, pregnant and recently widowed, runs into her deceased husband's brother, Kerley, while on the run from an arranged marriage set up by her cruel uncle and passive aunt. Forced to take refuge with her rough hero, she quickly realizes he isn't what he appears to be, and she falls for his heart of gold. But if she's going to find a happy home for herself and her unborn child, she's going to have to trust many people she meets along her journey—and, most importantly, herself. Told in an authentic voice and bursting with high tension and higher stakes, *Isabella's Baby* is an exciting, romantic, triumphant story.

—Bianca Orellana author of *We are Eternal*

Dedication

To Kerley Baker, my brother Gary's first friend.
Thanks for letting me use your name.
I hope you like the way I portrayed Kerley.

* * *

One

Kerley McFarland reined his palomino up on the knoll at the edge of the woods and gazed into the valley below. He pulled off his black Stetson and shook off the excess water. Raking his fingers through his shoulder-length black hair, he replaced his hat and turned up the collar of the duster he'd donned earlier to protect him from the sudden storm. Though the thunder and lightning had ended, the rain had continued off and on for a while. Sometimes at a steady pace, at others only a drizzle, but it hadn't stopped. Wet and uncomfortable, he was about ready to turn back and chalk this up as another dead end.

Not one to give up easily, he decided to take a closer look before he left. He pulled a spyglass from the saddle bag and trained it on the farm below. Scanning the valley, he stopped and studied the house. Though built of logs, it was larger than many of the regular cabins he'd seen in Nebraska. It had a second floor and the roof sported three chimneys. The porch spanned the front of the house and wrapped around one side. Green shrubs surrounded the porch and a cultivated garden filled with fall flowers grew between the two large oak trees in the side yard.

Moving his view to the right and toward the back of the house, he saw a vegetable garden, which offered little this time of year except some greens, which he thought probably topped turnips. Situated beside it was a chicken coop, though the chickens were missing. He figured they were sitting on their nests because of the rain. Back of the coop was a pig pen, housing two hogs and four little pigs.

He shifted his glass to the left and saw a couple of outbuildings and a barn. Connected to the barn was a corral with two horses. One looked like a workhorse. It stood close to the building as if it were trying to shield itself from the rain.

A slow grin crossed his lips as he rested his spyglass on the brown and white pinto pony that seemed to be enjoying the rain. He hadn't been told wrong, after all. There was no mistaking the horse. The mare's markings were too distinct to confuse her with any other filly. On her left side, near her hind leg, was a perfectly shaped star with the equally perfectly shaped crescent moon above it. He grinned and took a deep breath. After searching for seven months, he realized his search was finally over. This was where the woman had brought the horse.

Forgetting his uncomfortable state, he slipped the spyglass into the saddle bag, grabbed the reins, and guided his horse, Shadow, back into the trees lining the area where he knew he'd continue to hide from view. It wouldn't be the perfect place to make camp, but from there he could watch the farm until the time was right to make his next move. That was, after he decided what his next move would be, and the best way to pull it off. He didn't want to kill anyone, but if it came to that, he would. After all, they probably deserved it.

~ * ~

Isabella Greely stood at the window beside the rock fireplace in the sitting room of the large log house. She continued to watch the rain. It had been coming down for several hours, but now looked as if it might clear up. She hoped not. *At least let it continue until after dark,* she prayed silently, because she didn't dare say the words aloud.

She knew if dusk arrived before the rain stopped, there was a possibility Fenton Pyle wouldn't come to call. Though he'd told them when he visited on Sunday he'd be back on Wednesday, she thought the bad weather might deter him. She prayed it would, anyway.

"Don't fret, child," her uncle William said from his rocking chair in front of the fireplace. He turned to the last page of his newspaper and added, "You can count on Fenton Pyle being a man of his word. I'm sure he'll be here soon."

She whirled around and the full skirt of her blue calico dress didn't completely hide her still small, but slightly thickening middle. "I'm not concerned about Fenton Pyle, Uncle William. In fact, I hope he doesn't show up today."

"Now, don't be like that, Isabella." In a timid voice, her aunt Vassie joined the conversation from her matching rocking chair beside her husband. She was mending socks, and didn't slow down when she added, "Fenton is a good man and, as your uncle William says, you need to be thankful he's willing to marry you in the condition you're in."

Isabella tried to keep her voice calm. "Please listen to me. I don't want to marry Fenton Pyle or anyone else for that matter, Aunt Vassie. Why can't you and Uncle William accept the fact that I'm a widow? I've told you over and over I was married to my baby's father, and I don't need some strange man claiming my child as his."

Her uncle spoke again. His voice was calm, yet firm. "Don't start that kind of talk again, young lady. You know we don't believe the tale you told us about being married, and it's important that I found a man willing to marry you in your condition. Fenton might be a little gruff, but he is a respected citizen in this area and his name will cover the sin you've committed and the shame you've brought on the Greely name."

Though Vassie's eyes said she didn't believe what she was saying, she added, "William is correct. When you're married to Fenton, you'll be accepted among the decent people in the area and so will that child you're carrying."

"Your aunt is right this time, Isabella."

"I've told you both over and over that I don't want to marry anyone. I was married to my baby's father. I can't help that he was killed the night before I had time to let you know about our wedding. At least I sent you a wire after his funeral."

"I understand why you're saying that, dear, but your uncle says your baby needs a father." The tone of her aunt's voice was somewhat understanding.

"My baby had a father, so why can't you just tell people I'm a widow, and nobody will look down on you or me or the baby when it's born. They'll understand I was with child before my husband died, and there won't be any disgrace for anyone."

"You know we don't believe all the lies you've told us about your baby's father, Isabella." William looked over his paper at her. "That's why I'm determined to help you rectify the shameful thing you've done before anyone else learns of your horrible sin. I won't have my name associated with your wanton ways."

Isabella shook her head and bit her lip to fight back tears. "Why didn't you ask my friend, Kathleen, while you were in Omaha? She knew I was married. She would have told you the truth."

"I didn't trust her to be honest with me anymore than I trust you. That's why I asked some of his gambling friends. I believe they told the truth when they said the man lived at the boarding house with you, but as far as they knew, you were never married."

"Oh, Uncle William, they were wrong. I was married. I wouldn't lie to you about such a thing. Why won't you and Aune Vassie listen to me?"

Vassie looked over her glasses at Isabella. Again, there seemed to be sympathy in her eyes. "We listen, dear, but as William says, we don't believe you. He says we can't take part in spreading the lies you keep telling us about being married."

William nodded. "Listen to Vassie, Isabella. We would be committing a sin if we repeated your lies. You might be willing to take a chance with your mortal soul, but your aunt and I are not going to take part in such a thing."

Isabella felt disgust all the way down to her toes. She knew there was no reason to continue arguing with them. "I'm getting a headache. I'm going to my room and take a nap."

"Go ahead, child. Maybe a nap will make you feel better. We'll call you when Fenton arrives." Aunt Vassie gave her a forced smile, then returned to her mending.

William turned back to his paper and said nothing more.

Isabella climbed the stairs and entered the small room at the end of the hall, the one she'd occupied since she'd come to live with them when she was fourteen years old. She had thought her aunt would have turned the room into the longed-for sewing room when she moved away, but there had been no changes in the décor since she'd left. When her uncle William had brought her back from Omaha under protest, the room looked the same as before. She hadn't wanted to return to the farm with him. She wanted to stay at the boarding house her friend, Kathleen Wooten, ran with her mother, have her baby, and make a new life for the two of them there in the city.

A year ago, when she'd told them Miz Wooten had inherited a boarding house in Omaha and wanted her to go with her and her daughter to run the place, her uncle had at first said no. But after widow Wooten promised the Greelys she'd make sure the girls would always be under her supervision, her uncle had finally agreed to let her go. At the time, Isabella had hoped never to see the Nebraska farm or her aunt and uncle again.

But it didn't happen that way. Miz Wooten had insisted the only right thing for her to do after Dale McFarland was killed was to wire her aunt and uncle and let them know what had happened. She now knew that had been a terrible mistake because her uncle William had come rushing to Omaha and forced her to return home with him.

It wasn't that she'd actually lied to him when he arrived. She just didn't tell him the entire truth. She didn't say that her baby was the result of a made-up marriage, but she did tell him Dale McFarland was her baby's father. And he was. She only left out the part about the fake marriage. A fact she had learned after Dale's death.

Thinking back, she realized it had all started the day Dale rented a room at Wooten's boarding house. During his first night at the supper table, it seemed to be his goal to make Isabella, the shy, little, gullible woman from the country, fall in love with him. At least to the point she couldn't tell him no.

Though the minute she laid eyes on him, Isabella thought Dale McFarland was one of the most interesting men she'd ever met, although she soon learned he was a gambler and a drunk. She didn't want to get involved with a man like him. But she did agree they would be friends. After all, he was staying at the boarding house and they'd be seeing each other almost daily. What could that hurt? It was always better to be friends than enemies, wasn't it?

She now realized how dangerous thoughts like that could be. If she'd followed her first instinct, she wouldn't be in the situation she was now in. She'd still be the happy young woman helping her friends run a boarding house instead of the miserable woman she was because her relatives were forcing her to marry a man she could hardly stand to be in the room with for any length of time.

Shaking her head, she turned her thoughts to the week following Dale's funeral. It had rained for almost the entire week, making her more despondent over the situation. Then on the fifth day, her uncle arrived and practically dragged her back to his Nebraska farm, and she was too exhausted and upset to fight him.

She had been back at the farm only four weeks, though as soon as they arrived, her uncle began looking for someone to marry her. Someone that would give her baby a name and cover her sin. No matter how hard she tried to tell him her baby had a name and she had been married, he wouldn't listen, and her aunt went along with anything he said, as she always did.

In only a few days, Fenton Pyle entered the picture. He was a widower with four unruly children. After meeting Isabella and looking her over, he told them one more young'un in the household didn't matter to him. His oldest, a girl, was sixteen. Only four years younger than Isabella. His youngest, a son, was ten. She wasn't sure if the other two were boys or girls. He'd never said, and she hadn't asked. She immediately knew Fenton wasn't looking for a wife to love or to love him. He wanted someone to cook, keep his house clean, and look after his children. Of course, he'd make sure his wife graced his bed whenever he wanted her to. It wasn't important that he was more than twice her age and didn't love her or that she didn't even like him, much less love him. None of this seemed to matter to her aunt and uncle. Especially her uncle. He was only concerned about preserving the reputation of the Greely name, and he decided Fenton Pyle was the answer. No matter what she said, they ignored her pleas and continued to plan the wedding. The two men had a meeting and discussed the situation, then they set the date of the event to take place the last weekend of the month. No matter what she said against it, the plans proceeded.

"No need to put it off, since you need a husband as soon as you can get one," her uncle kept saying. "When your baby gets here, you'll be glad I made you marry Fenton. People will think the child came into the world earlier than they usually do because that often happens with a first baby."

The fact that she hadn't accepted this plan didn't matter. Her uncle had accepted it for her. But Isabella knew no matter what anyone said, she'd never be glad about marrying a man like Fenton Pyle. In fact, she knew she had to get away, because the way things were going, there was no way she could convince her uncle to stop the wedding. She couldn't see herself married to that horrible man. Somehow, and some way, she intended to escape what she knew would be a lifetime of drudgery, though the two attempts she'd already made at running away had failed.

That wasn't going to stop her from running again. The next time she left, she and her horse, Moonstar, were not going to head toward Omaha as they had the first two times. It was too easy to be intercepted before she arrived at her destination. When she ran again, she'd head west. Nobody would suspect she'd go in that direction, and there was a good possibility she could get far enough away they couldn't reach her and bring her back to the farm and force her to marry that awful man.

In her room, she moved to the bed. Kneeling on the floor, she ran her hand under the feather mattress and her fingers found the small cloth bag containing the necklace Dale had given her on their wedding day and the money she'd found in his belongings after his death. Her aunt and uncle didn't know she had those things. Instinct told her not to share the fact she wasn't destitute with them. She wouldn't put it past them to insist she give the money to Fenton, and Aunt Vassie had always liked jewelry, though she had little of it.

She got up and moved to the wardrobe. Inside, she reached behind the heavy winter cape and felt for the feed sack she'd packed with the things she'd need. She wondered if she should add the cape. Though it was late summer, fall would soon become winter, and she didn't know if she'd be able to find a job before cold weather set in, no matter where she ended up. *Yes. I'll add it to the sack before I leave. Maybe I'll put in mittens and a scarf. I just can't let it get too bulky to carry on Moonstar.*

She turned to the dresser where she checked to be sure her comb, brush, a small mirror, and hair pins were where she could snatch them and dump them into the sack. She also noted the crude toothbrush and can of tooth powder were handy. She didn't want to forget those. If there was one thing Isabella didn't like, it was going through the day without cleaning her teeth.

Satisfied everything was ready to go, she walked to the window. She wanted to see if it was still raining. She sighed when she saw it was clearing up, and her shoulders dropped when she saw Fenton Pyle hitching his horse to the post near the front steps.

Though Isabella wasn't a woman with a loose tongue, or prone to losing her temper, she couldn't help stomping her foot and muttering, "Damn! Why did he have to come over here in the rain?"

~ * ~

Vassie and William insisted Fenton join them for supper. "We've got fried chicken and all the trimmings," Vassie explained.

"I shore like fried chicken. That oldest gal of mine don't know how to get it crispy." Fenton looked at Isabella. "Are you good at frying up crispy chicken like this for a hungry man and a house full of young'uns?"

Aunt Vassie answered for her. "Oh, my yes, she is, Fenton. She had a hand in frying the very chicken you're eating."

Yeah. I turned it in the big iron frying pan while Aunt Vassie made the bread, then she pushed me aside, and told me to peel the potatoes. But she didn't explain this to him because when he was around, she said as little to the man as possible.

"Glad to hear it. Me and my young'uns shore can pack in a parcel of fried chicken."

There'll be a snow blizzard in hell before I cook for you and your brats. She shook her head, and thought to herself, *when did I start cussing like a saloon cowboy?*

"Is there something wrong with your head, dear?" Vassie asked.

"No. I was shaking away a fly," she lied.

Uncle William looked at her. "Why, Isabella, you know better. There are no flies in your aunt's house."

Fenton chuckled. "They's plenty of them in my cabin. Them young'uns of mine don't think twice about holding the door open too long when they go in and out, and they busted out most of the screens. I give up trying to make them mind me about such things." Again he looked at Isabella. "They'll be your job when we get hitched. I'm sure you'll be able to control them better than me."

She didn't answer, but thought, *I'll be damned. Oh, no. There I go cursing again. I've got to watch my mouth.*

"I'm sure she'll be good at it, and you won't regret marrying her." William gave their guest one of his rare grins.

Vassie asked, "Are you getting excited about the wedding, Fenton?"

"About that..."

"Oh, no. You're not going to change your mind, are you?" Vassie looked frightened.

Isabella hoped his answer would be that he had changed his mind because he'd found someone who could cook excellent chicken. She was let down when she heard his answer.

"No ma'am, I ain't. I was jist wondering if it'd be too much trouble for you if we get married this weekend, instead the last of the month."

"No!" Isabella yelled.

He laughed. "Ah, come on. Looks like to me the quicker you get a pappy for that bastard baby in your belly, the happier you'd be."

Vassie stiffened and William said, "Though it's true, I don't think you should talk like that in front of the women, Fenton."

"I guess you're right. I know you folks are trying to save your niece's name, but don't you think it's too late? Everybody already knows she's got a baby in her."

Isabella broke the silence. "Then if everybody knows about my child, why should I have to marry you?"

"You know good and well everybody doesn't know about the child, Isabella. Besides, you need to give your child a name as well as find a good daddy for it," William said in an irritated voice. He turned back to Fenton. "If you're serious, we can probably have everything ready by this weekend, don't you think so, Vassie?"

"I'm pretty sure we can do it." She looked frightened but turned to Isabella. "I hope you'll help me."

"Of course, she'll help you." William's voice was firm, then he turned to Fenton. "I still intend to hold you to your promise about the five acres."

"I'm a man of my word, William. You should know that."

When the men began a conversation about the land, Vassie gave Isabella a slow grin and whispered. "I know this isn't what you want right now, but like William said, eventually you'll realize it was the best thing for you and your baby. You'll have a large and loving family when you bring your child into the world where it will already have brothers and sisters."

Fenton must have heard her because he stuck a fork full of potato in his mouth and said, "That's right. The young'uns are looking forward to you coming and taking some of the chores off their backs. 'Specially the oldest one. She don't much like to cook and clean, and she knows when you get there that'll be your job."

He took another bite and added, "Besides, who knows. We might have a couple more young'uns after a while."

Vassie gave her a smile. "Oh, Isabella, that would be wonderful. Your baby would have a brother or sister its age."

Isabella couldn't listen any further. She tuned them out as she let her mind conjure up what to do. The pressing question was: should she run away tonight or wait until tomorrow night? It was awfully wet and damp, but if she waited until tomorrow, something else might stop her. This thought made the decision for her. It had to be tonight.

Two

Fingers of dawn clawed their way upward in the eastern sky as Kerley rolled over and grunted. The nights he'd spent sleeping on the ground on this trip were beginning to catch up with him. Having been a Texas Ranger for over six years, he'd spent a lot of nights on the ground—and he hadn't always had the comfort of the soft pine needles he'd found in these woods last night. But since his disastrous decision to leave the Rangers, marry Betty Lou and settle on the ranch, it had never occurred to him how much better sleeping in a bed would be. Now, he wondered if he was getting soft. No! He couldn't let that happen. After all, he was only thirty years old. Much too young to think about being old.

To find a place where the water on the wet ground wouldn't soak through his bedroll, he'd had to back a good distance into the woods after the lights had gone off in the cabin last night. But he didn't figure it mattered. He'd watched when a rider had come to the door. He decided the family below knew the man, because he didn't leave until around nine o'clock, which was late for a visit to a working farm. Less than thirty minutes later, the cabin was dark. He knew everyone had gone to bed. He decided there was no need to watch further. He'd get his sleep and figure out what his next move would be. He hoped to be able to get the horse, make the dame who took it confess how she'd swindled his brother out of it, then give her a scare about how he was going to have her arrested, then he'd be on his way back to Texas to buy back his family ranch.

Though the sun was shining this morning, it was still damp and he wished he could build a fire and boil coffee, but he knew that wouldn't be wise. He made do with some hard biscuits, jerky and water from the canteen. After taking care of his personal needs, he walked back to the front of the woods where he would have a good view of the house.

The sun had appeared above the eastern horizon, and he heard the faint crow of a rooster below. In a few minutes, he saw an older man come out and head toward the barn. Probably to feed the stock, but the man wasn't in the barn long enough to feed anything. In a matter of minutes, he came dashing out and ran toward the house. He must have been yelling because an older woman appeared on the porch. He wished he could hear what they were saying, but it was impossible at the distance between them.

It then dawned on him the pinto mare wasn't in the corral with the other horses.

He snapped into action. In a matter of minutes, he saddled Shadow, threw his bedroll and saddle bags on his back, and climbed atop the horse.

"Let's go, Shadow. I want to see if we can find out what's going on down there. I've had too much trouble finding that damn woman and I don't want to lose track of her and Moonstar again."

As he approached the farm, the older man led the large workhorse to the front of a wagon sitting beside the barn. He was hitching it when Kerley walked Shadow up beside him.

"Hello, sir," Kerley said, trying his best not to sound as if he had an ulterior motive.

The man turned and nodded. "Howdy, stranger. How can I help you?"

"I was just passing through and thought you might spare a man a cup of coffee and some water for my horse."

"I'm in kind of a hurry, but I reckon I can take the time to give you that."

"Thank you, sir. By the way, my name's Kerley McFarland."

"Seems I've heard that name before, but I don't know where. Anyway, my name's William Greely and I hope you don't mind me asking if you came from the direction of Omaha."

Though Kerley had been to Omaha, something about the way the man asked the question instinctively told him not to tell him the truth. "No, sir. I came from the North Platt area."

The old man shook his head. "I was hoping you might have come from the direction of Omaha."

He wrinkled his brow. "May I ask why you'd want to know?"

Greely didn't seem to hesitate. "I hoped you'd met our niece. She ran away last night and I'm sure she headed that way. She's a strong-minded girl, but I can usually tell what she's thinking. Besides, she always tries to go to her friend's boarding house in Omaha when she runs."

Kerley lifted an eyebrow. So, somebody had run away, and they probably took the pinto. "Wasn't she supposed to leave?"

"Not at all. The little gal is supposed to get married Saturday, though she don't much want to marry the man. This ain't the first time she's got on that horse and took off in the middle of the night."

"Oh. What kind of horse was she riding?"

"It's one of those brown and white pintos. She brought it from Omaha. That's why I figure she's trying again to go back there. That's where her friend lives."

"I assume you're going after her?"

"I most certainly am. Like I said, she's supposed to get married on Saturday and she's got to do it." He shook his head. "I swear. Sometimes, no matter what you do, you can't knock sense into a woman's head. They think they're smart enough to make their own decisions about what's important in life. But most of them don't have no idea what's good for them. In this case, it's important she marry the man before he changes his mind."

"If I wasn't in a hurry, I'd be glad to help you go bring her back."

"I appreciate that, but I'm going to get Fenton Pyle. I'm sure he'll go with me. He's the man she's going to marry."

Kerley nodded, but before he could say anything, a woman came out on the porch. She was also up in years, so he figured she was the man's wife.

"Vassie, bring this man a cup of coffee." He looked back at Kerley as she turned and stepped back through the door. "Sorry, I can't invite you in, but I've got to get on my way. I want to get to Fenton's place before he goes out to work on his land. I'm sure he'll be interested in getting Isabella back, since he wanted to push the wedding up to this weekend. They was supposed to get married at the end of the month, but for some reason he wanted to do it sooner."

Kerley tried not to smile because the man was continually repeating himself. He did say, "I understand. I'm sure you want to catch up with her as quickly as you can. No man would like to be stood up on his wedding day."

"It probably won't be a problem to catch her. I don't think she wants to wear that little horse out. Every time she takes off, she tends to stop and rest it a lot."

Kerley didn't tell Greely he was glad to hear the woman wouldn't be running the horse into the ground in her hurry to get away from her impending wedding.

The woman returned with a cup in her hand. Steam rose from the top. She came down the steps and Kerley dismounted.

He took the cup from her and said, "Thank you, ma'am. It smells great." After taking a sip he added, "This is a really good cup of coffee." He wasn't lying.

In a minute, he handed her back the empty cup. "I appreciate that very much, Mrs. Greely."

She gave him a shy smile. "I'm glad you liked it."

Kerley turned and took hold of his horse's reins. "Don't let me hold you up, Mr. Greely. I'll just walk my horse down to the trough and let him have a drink. Then I'll be on my way."

"That'll be fine, 'cause I'm about ready to go get Fenton."

"Find her as quick as you can, William. We need to get busy planning the wedding." The woman looked worried. "I can't believe she's done gone and run away again."

"Don't worry, Vassie. I'll get her back, just like I always do. I'll sure be glad to get her married to Fenton. Then we won't have to worry about something like this happening ever again."

Kerley ignored them and walked toward the barn. For the first time, he was thankful for the rain. Without being obvious, he paid close attention to the horse tracks in the mud around the corral and the front of the barn. He noticed they led out of the yard in the opposite direction from which the man was going. He probably should tell them what he saw, but he'd learned it always paid to listen to that little voice in his head, and it told him to keep his mouth shut.

As he studied the ground, it looked to him like their niece probably had gone in the opposite direction of Omaha. He decided when he caught up with her and got his horse back, he'd bring her home in time for her wedding. He didn't need the bother of William Greely or anyone else going with him, because he'd make better time on his own.

Shadow drank water then slung his head back and forth. Kerley led him away from the trough and climbed into the saddle. He tipped his hat at the woman who was still in the yard, and he nodded to Greely. He rode off toward the woods where he'd spent the night. He'd hide there until the man was gone, then he'd head out and follow the tracks he hoped would lead him to his horse, and also to the runaway bride. He only hoped the intended groom knew what he was getting into. Of course, the fool probably didn't. If he did, he'd realize he was marrying a horse thief, among a number of other unlawful crimes the dame had probably committed.

~ * ~

Isabella reined her horse up under a tree and slid out of the saddle. She needed to take care of her personal business, and then, because she was hungry, she wanted to eat a bite. Wrapping the reins around a low hanging branch, she left enough slack in them so the horse could graze on the soft grass growing there.

She gave the horse a pat on the neck and said, "I'll be right back, Moonstar." She walked a distance away where the grass was taller so she could have privacy. Though she knew there was nobody around, it made her feel better to have a place where she felt nobody could spy on her if they were here.

Finished, she returned to her horse, used a bit of water from the canteen to wash her hands, then took a biscuit and a chicken thigh from the sack she'd tied on her saddle horn. She knew she had to be sparing with her food because there weren't many leftovers from last night's supper and she figured it was at least twenty miles or maybe more to the next town. When she'd packed to leave the house, she'd managed to find five pieces of chicken and six biscuits, and from the bowl on the table she snitched three apples. By being careful, she knew this should last her at least until she got to a place large enough to have a store where she could buy a few supplies for her continued journey.

Taking the food she'd selected to eat, she sat on a rock that protruded from the ground near a pine tree. It wasn't hot enough that she felt she needed to sit in the shade. After a bite of the chicken, she let her mind replay her escape. She didn't think of it as running away, but as escaping from a future life she knew she could never tolerate.

Her aunt and uncle had gone to bed as soon as Fenton Pyle left. She'd gone to her room and intended to stay awake until time to leave. But after taking the time to sew the money and necklace into the hem of her cape, she was exhausted. As she waited until she was sure they were asleep, she became drowsy. She lay back on the bed to rest her eyes for only a few minutes, but in spite of everything she could do, she fell asleep.

It was late when she awoke, but she wasn't sure how late because it was still dark. She jumped up and began gathering all the supplies she planned to take. She slipped out of her nightgown and donned the riding skirt she'd kept hidden since coming back from Omaha. Each time she ran, her aunt had tried to get rid of the skirt, but she'd always managed to find it and return it to its hiding place.

Slipping quietly downstairs, she'd gathered the food and eased out the back door. Not knowing how much time she had before daybreak, she hurried to the barn, saddled Moonstar, and tied on the food and her belongings. She knew her uncle would be mad when he saw she'd taken his bedroll, but she felt she had to have it. She might be lucky enough to stay in some hotels, though she figured she'd have to sleep on the ground before she got far enough West that they couldn't find her.

She'd led the horse out of the barn and glanced at the house. Still dark. Climbing into the saddle, she turned Moonstar toward the back of the barn and in a western direction. She wasn't going to get caught on the road to Omaha again. And now she was several miles from the farm.

Her aunt and uncle usually got up early, so she figured they'd probably missed her by now. She hoped they'd head for Omaha looking for her. Hoping she was out of their reach, she finished her chicken and biscuit, drank from the canteen, and moved back to her horse. She wouldn't tarry here any longer, just in case.

"Well, girl." She rubbed the horse's neck. "Are you ready to get started? I want to get as far as I can before dark. I have no idea what I'll find in this direction, but we might come upon a village that has a general store before we get to the next town. If so, I can buy more food. If not, I have plenty of chicken for today. I'll even share an apple with you at supper."

Moonstar snorted and Isabella smiled, patted her neck again, then mounted and turned the horse to the west.

~ * ~

It was mid-afternoon when Kerley caught a glimpse of a rider in a distance. He pulled out his spyglass and smiled when he saw a woman's back. She was riding the pinto. He grinned as he started to plot how to approach her, when, seeming for no reason, two riders came at her from the trees along the side of the road. He didn't hear her scream, but he was sure she did.

Kerley had no choice. He spurred Shadow into a gallop and raced toward the group. As he closed in on them, he saw they'd pulled her from the horse and one of them was in the process of ripping off her blouse while the other one held her with her hands pinned behind her back. They were so intent on what they were doing they didn't hear him approach. Drawing his gun, he fired over their heads.

The man holding her arms shoved her to the ground and they both pulled their guns. A bullet whizzed by Kerley's head.

He didn't hesitate. He fired his pistol and one of the men went down.

Another bullet knocked Kerley's hat from his head as he leaned over Shadow's neck, and he fired again. The second man hit the ground, screaming.

Kerley dismounted and rushed to the woman, who still lay face down on the ground. He knew she was still alive because he could hear her crying. He could also hear more horses coming in the distance.

He took hold of her shoulder. "I think these two men had friends and they're headed our way. We've gotta get out of here."

Isabella pulled away from him. "Don't touch me."

"Look, lady. I don't want to touch you, but if you don't get on your horse, there are going to be men here who will be glad you're already on the ground."

She gave him a hard look but said nothing.

"I'm getting out of here. Are you coming or not?"

Isabella nodded and started struggling to her feet.

Knowing they had to hurry, Kerley reached down and picked her up. She let out a little scream. He ignored her and sat her on Moonstar. He grabbed his hat and mounted Shadow. In seconds, they were racing down the road. He could tell the horses behind them had stopped. He knew they had discovered the bodies of their friends and would be coming after them. He wasn't sure how many more were in the gang, or if he could fight all of them off. He did know it probably wouldn't be a problem if he and the woman had gotten away before the gang had seen them. But did they?

In front of them, he noticed a cloud of dust. It then hit him that this was probably the stagecoach route. The men who'd attacked the woman must have been the lookouts waiting to rob the stage, but when they saw her come along, they couldn't resist a pretty woman. He had to let the stage driver know what he'd be facing, so he sped up Shadow and the woman followed. He hoped the driver would recognize they were no threat and would stop.

He did stop. "You want a ride?" The driver glared at them.

"No. Just wanted to warn you. There's a gang about a mile behind that attacked us, but we managed to get away. I figured they plan to hold you up."

"How come she's the only one messed up?"

Isabella gasped and grabbed the front of her shirt.

"I'd gone to look for food and the two lookouts grabbed her. I got back in time to kill both of them. Then I heard several horses, and I wasn't sure I could fight them off."

"Well, I don't think we'll have that problem." He nodded toward the man beside him. "Not only do I have my guard, but there are two army officers and three enlisted men inside."

A man's voice came from the coach. "We heard him and we're preparing for a fight."

"I was going to hide her and offer to go back with you, but it doesn't look like you'll need me."

"I think we can handle it, but I appreciate the offer." The driver nodded and slapped the reins over the back of the horses. "Thanks for the warning and good luck to you."

As the stage rumbled away, Kerley turned to Isabella. "I think we should go on in case one of the outlaws gets away and comes after us. I don't want to kill anyone else today."

"Do I have time to get another shirt out of my bag?"

He nodded and discreetly turned in the other direction, though he knew there was no need. He'd already seen the shapely woman beneath the rips in her shirt, yet she'd somehow managed to pull it together to cover herself. Maybe it was something he could take advantage of before he took her back to the couple on the farm and her impending wedding.

In a minute she said, "I'm ready."

He didn't say anything, but only nodded as they turned their horses west on the stage road. He knew he'd have to confront her about Moonstar later. He had to keep her with him for a while. As bad as she probably was, he wouldn't abandon her there in this lonely area.

Three

Isabella didn't know why she didn't protest when the stranger who had rescued her continued to ride along beside her. He hadn't said a word since they'd left the stagecoach, not even to introduce himself, and it had been at least an hour or more since the encounter. He hadn't asked where she was going or why she was traveling alone. He hadn't even looked at her.

But she had looked at him. She couldn't help it. His looks would draw attention anywhere he went. At an inch or more over six feet tall, he towered over most men. His build was that of a hard worker with powerful arms and wide shoulders that tapered to a slim waist and muscled thighs. His dark hair and striking blue eyes were compelling, and the beard and mustache were neatly trimmed and accented a square chin and shapely nose.

She decided she'd have to break the silence. "Thank you for saving me from those horrible men."

"You're welcome."

Silence again.

After another ten minutes, she asked, "Why did you do it?"

He glanced at her. "Do what?"

"Rescue me."

"I didn't figure you could get away from them on your own."

Now what was she going to say?

She didn't have to come up with anything because, in a flat voice, he asked, "Where did you get that horse?"

This question startled her. Why would he be interested in her horse? Whatever was behind his thinking, she saw no reason not to tell him. She also decided to tell him she was a widow. Though she'd done this with her relatives, and it hadn't worked to her advantage, this man had no reason to think she wasn't telling the truth. Besides, in a way she was a widow. If the people she would come into contact with in her new life accepted this fact, it would work out better in the future for her and her child.

She glanced at him and said, "My husband gave her to me."

His eyes looked like icy cold shards of frozen water as he glared at her. "You're married?"

She dropped her head and swallowed. Lying didn't come easy for her. "I was."

"So, you ran out on him?" His voice wasn't kind.

She glanced up and muttered, "Of course not. I'd never do that."

"But you said..."

"My husband is dead." She looked down again, but explained nothing further and was glad he didn't ask any more questions.

They rode another mile without speaking. Then out of the blue he asked, "Where are you headed?"

"West."

"Where in the west?"

She glared at him. "Does it matter?"

"Of course it matters. How will you know if you're heading in the right direction if you don't know where you're going?"

Was he trying to trick her? Had her uncle sent him to bring her home? No. How could he? She knew all their friends, and this man wasn't one of them. Besides, Uncle William would never ask for the assistance of a stranger. He'd more than likely send Fenton Pyle or would come himself to get her, as he had done in the past.

She decided to say the first town that came to her mind. "San Antonio."

He frowned at her. "If you want to go to San Antonio you're headed in the wrong direction. You need to go south or at least southwest."

Confused by his words, she muttered, "I was going to turn that way later."

"I see."

She realized he knew she was lying because he half smiled, or was it a smirk? It had happened so fast she wasn't sure, but more than likely it had been a sneer. Maybe he was making fun of her. If so, she figured it didn't matter. She had gotten away from her relatives, and it didn't look like he was going to force her to go back. At the moment, that was all that mattered.

After a few more miles, he nodded toward a patch of woods. "The sun's going down, and I'm sure the horses need a rest. I know I could use a break. Let's go over there and we can talk. Then you can tell me more of why you're headed to San Antonio."

She didn't want to, but something compelled her to follow him to the trees, though she had no intention of telling him anything about her plans to go to San Antonio or anywhere else. He didn't have a reason to know she didn't really have any plans, except to get as far away as she could from her uncle and the man she was being forced to marry. Besides, she didn't even know her rescuer's name or why he'd want to know anything about her.

Once they got inside the woods and looked behind the trees, they discovered a small creek. "It'll be good to get some fresh water," Isabella muttered to change the subject.

"I'll take the horses and fill our canteens if you like. In the meantime, I have some jerky if you're hungry."

"I have some chicken and biscuits. I'll share with you since you're watering my horse." She felt she at least owed him that for getting her away from the men who had attacked her.

He raised an eyebrow. "That sounds good. I haven't had chicken in a long while."

She removed the food sack and found a place for them to sit in the soft grass.

When he returned from the creek, he handed her the filled canteens, then moved the horses to a grassy area outside the trees so they could graze. Coming back, he glanced at the food she'd arranged on the napkin she'd put on the ground. "It looks good."

"I have apples for dessert, but I promised Moonstar I'd give her one."

"I assume Moonstar is your horse."

"Yes. If you'll look at her left hip, you'll see a perfectly shaped moon and star. I think it was logical to give her that name."

"Did you name her?"

"No. My husband did."

"I see." He picked up a piece of chicken and a biscuit. "Do you have a name?"

"Of course, I have a name. It's Isabella McFarland or Mrs. Dale McFarland. What's yours?"

He raised an eyebrow and stared at her but said nothing.

"Well, are you an outlaw or somebody you don't want to admit to being?"

He cleared his throat. "It might upset you if I tell you who I am."

"Unless you're Jesse James, I can't think of a reason it'd upset me."

He almost snorted. "No, I'm not Jesse James. Whatever made you think of him?

"I read in my uncle's newspaper about him being an outlaw who was wanted for robbing trains and stagecoaches."

"I see."

She took a deep breath. "Then will you tell me what your name is?"

He became serious, and his eyes narrowed as he stared at her. In a flat voice, he said, "My name's Kerley McFarland. I'm Dale McFarland's older brother.

~ * ~

Kerley watched as the hand she held the biscuit in began to shake. Her voice was a whisper when she glared at him. "You can't be."

"I assure you, I am." He wondered what kind of story she'd come up with, because he was sure his half-brother would never marry a woman like her. She looked too much like a woman most people would consider a lady. The kind of woman most men wanted to marry. But Dale had always gone for the flashy kind. The ones who hung out in saloons and dressed provocatively. He was more likely to use a woman like this one, then walk out on her instead of marrying her.

Of course, Kerley realized she was probably trying to fool him. She could be very good at hiding her real identity. But it didn't matter. This woman had unwittingly admitted she'd met his brother, or she wouldn't know his name or be in possession of his horse.

When she only stared at him and didn't say anything, he added, "My brother was not the marrying kind, so why don't you tell me how you came up with the idea of claiming him to be your husband?"

She turned her head from him. "That's between Dale and me."

He reached out, took hold of her chin, and pulled her head back around so he could glare at her. "You do know that Dale is dead, don't you?"

She slapped his hand away and stood. "Of course, I know my husband is dead. You don't have to be such a brute."

Before he could stop her, she jumped up and ran toward the creek without saying anything else.

"Oh, hell," he muttered and finished his chicken. He then got up and followed her. He knew he'd said the wrong thing, but sometimes he couldn't control his temper or his tongue. It had always been his habit to say whatever he was thinking. But in this case, he knew he should be more careful how he handled her. How was he going to find out the answers to any of his questions if he kept treating her like the lying young woman he knew her to be? If he kept it up, he'd never find out what she had to do with Dale or how she had come into possession of his brother's horse.

He found Isabella sitting on a rock beside the creek. She still had her biscuit in her hand. He noticed she'd put the chicken inside it, but she hadn't taken a bite. She was staring at the rippling water, and she looked as if her thoughts were a thousand miles away.

He spoke in a soft voice so he wouldn't scare her. "I owe you an apology. I shouldn't have been so blunt, but it was a shock to hear you claim to be married to my brother."

She turned toward him and said something he wasn't expecting to hear. "You're nothing like Dale. He had his faults, but he was at least a gentleman when he talked to me."

He bit his tongue as he tried not to say something that would upset her again. "You're right. I've always been blunt, and direct. I'm considered the more serious one in the family. The one who often speaks before he realizes how his words will be taken."

"Dale was seldom serious."

Maybe she did know his brother. At least she had a grip on this aspect of his personality. "I hadn't seen Dale in some time, but he was my brother and I cared for him."

She whispered, "He told me about you."

Kerley chuckled. Now, he knew she was lying. Dale would never tell some woman about him. "I can't imagine what he'd say about me."

She glanced at him. "Though I don't understand why, he said he wished he could be more like his older brother."

He didn't reply, but took a seat on a rock facing her. "Why don't you finish your food, and we'll see if we can have a discussion without making each other mad?"

She gave him a tentative nod and took a bite of her biscuit.

He was anxious to hear her reaction to his next statement and he watched her closely. "I stopped at your uncle's farm this morning to water my horse."

Confusion filled her eyes. "How do you know it was my uncle's place?"

"He told me he was getting ready to go look for his runaway niece. I assume that is you."

She started to get up. "I better...."

"Relax. He's not coming in this direction."

Though she looked scared, Isabella sat back on the rock. "How do you know?"

"He told me he was going to Omaha because that was the way you always ran. I tracked you out of the yard coming this way, but I didn't tell him."

"Why not?"

"I wanted to know why a woman would run away from home and from a man she was supposed to marry in a few days."

"Mr. McFarland, I didn't just run, I actually escaped from my upcoming wedding. If you had ever met Fenton Pyle, you'd understand why I had to get away."

Kerley lifted an eyebrow. "Then why did you accept his proposal?"

She looked ready to hit him. "I didn't accept any proposal from him. Uncle William accepted it for me, and Aunt Vassie went along with him, just like she always does. I knew I could never marry a man like Fenton Pyle, and I was determined to get away before they forced me to do it."

"He must be pretty bad."

"He's an old man with a house full of unruly children. He doesn't want a wife. He wants a slave."

He raised an eyebrow. "And you didn't want to be a slave?"

"That's right. I didn't. Besides, I can't stand the awful man."

"I can't help being a little confused. Why were your folks determined you marry this man, since you don't seem to like him?"

She had no intention of telling him the truth. "I think it was because I had been living in Omaha on my own. They thought it would mar my reputation if I didn't marry somebody who they considered respectable."

"And this man you say is awful is respectable?"

"Yes. He's a member of their church and everything."

"Didn't you tell them you were married?"

She nodded. "They didn't believe me."

He wanted to tell her he didn't believe her either, but he decided to hold that information until he found out more about her. There had to be a more compelling reason for their wanting her to marry this Fenton Pyle person. He'd discover it because he had plenty of time and, though he wanted answers, he wouldn't rush her in the process of getting them.

He stood and decided to change the subject. "We still have a couple of hours of daylight. How about we move on? We can get another few miles forward before we camp for the night."

She gave him a questioning glance but didn't speak. Instead, she stood and walked toward her horse.

When they reached the animals, he turned and offered her his hand to help her mount Moonstar. She took it and mumbled a thank you to him.

As she mounted, he was stunned. Did he see what he thought he saw when she turned sideways? *No.* It must have been the way her clothes pulled around as she straddled the horse. It had to be his imagination. But was it? Could this pretty young woman be expecting a child? Was this the real reason for her rushed marriage? If so, why was she fighting the nuptials? Most women in this condition, and without a husband, would be happy somebody would marry them.

He walked around his horse without speaking. Things were getting more confusing. Not only did he think he saw a protruding stomach on the lady, but the touch of her hand had sent a jolt through him. Something he hadn't felt in a long time. He didn't like this and hoped when they made camp for the night, he could find the answers to the questions running through his head. Then he could take Moonstar and hurry this lying female back to her uncle and her unwanted groom.

Four

Isabella didn't say anything as they started down the road. She had a feeling Kerley was keeping something from her, but she wasn't sure what. She'd play his game for a while and see if she could discover what secret he was hiding, because she was sure he had one. She only hoped he wouldn't try to pry all her secrets out of her. Especially the one about the baby. After the way he acted when she claimed to be married to his brother, she didn't know how he'd accept the fact that he was going to be an uncle. She decided it was best to keep quiet about it for a while.

They'd gone a short distance when he pulled beside her. "I'm hoping there'll be a settlement with a general store in a few more miles. We could use more supplies."

"That sounds good. I have enough food so we can eat tonight, but there won't be anything left for tomorrow."

"The chicken was good, and I wouldn't mind having another piece tonight. I would like to pick up some bacon and coffee to make breakfast. I really need my Arbuckles in the morning, and I've run out."

Was he planning to still be with her in the morning? She didn't dare ask at the moment. She'd save that question until later. "How will we be able to cook those things?"

"We'll build a campfire. I've been on the trail for a long time, and I've learned how to eat pretty good when I travel by horse."

She decided to see if she could get him to admit what he was thinking. In a soft voice she said, "You sound like you intend to accompany me all the way to my destination."

His voice was flat when he answered. "You said you were married to my brother, and I think that kind of makes you my responsibility."

"I don't see why."

"If you're family, I wouldn't feel right deserting you. As I've always believed, family members look out for each other."

Isabella knew she couldn't argue with this statement. If she did, he'd think she wasn't telling the truth about being married to his brother. After all, she could tell he already suspected she was lying. An argument would only confirm it to him. She bit her lip and looked ahead, hoping he wouldn't say anything else.

Nothing else was said, but a short time later, he rode his horse up beside her. "I see somebody coming toward us. I don't think it'll be anybody who means us harm, but we need to be prepared."

Looking ahead, she could see only dust, but she decided to take his word for it. "What should I do?"

"Just act casual and let me do the talking."

She nodded and watched as he adjusted the gun on his hip. She hoped he wouldn't have to use it, but she knew he wouldn't hesitate if he felt he needed to. She remembered how quickly he'd taken care of the men who had attacked her.

As they drew closer, she saw they were going to meet two men on horseback. In spite of herself, she began to feel apprehensive. Though she knew she was safe with Kerley, she couldn't help remembering what had happened before.

When the two riders drew closer, Isabella could see it was a man and a young boy of about twelve. She relaxed. Surely a man with a child had no intention of attacking them.

As the four of them met and reined up their horses, Kerley said, "Hello, folks."

"Howdy," the older man said. "Don't know if I've seen you folks around here before."

"We're on our way to North Platt to visit my wife's relatives there."

"I see. Where are you from?"

"We're from Omaha."

Isabella knew the man was suspicious of them when he said, "I'm surprised to see you riding horses. The stage comes through here."

Kerley didn't hesitate. "The rocking of the stage makes my wife sick and she's a good horse woman, so when we go somewhere, we often travel by horse. We decided it would be better to do so on this trip."

Isabella was a little surprised he'd passed her off as his wife. He could have said his sister or some other relative, but wife seemed a little off center for him to say.

The man nodded. "That makes sense. Women have their own ways, don't they?"

"They sure do."

The man chuckled. "I'm Walter Judson. This here's my son, Eli. What's your handle?"

"Kerley McFarland. Wife's name is Isabella."

The man nodded at Kerley and then tipped his hat to her. "You folks been camping out?"

"We have. I guess I was lucky to marry up with a woman who doesn't mind sleeping on the ground now and again. Of course, we'll sleep at a hotel when we come to a town that has one. How far is it to the next town anyway?"

"Gomer is about six miles ahead." The man laughed. "Be careful you don't miss it. It's not a very big place."

"They ain't no hotel in Gomer." Eli spoke for the first time.

"Boy's right. Ain't no rooming house neither."

Kerley pushed back his hat. "Would there happen to be a store where we could buy a few things? We're a little low on supplies and were hoping to buy some as soon as we could."

"Yelp. There's one. Ain't very big, and they may not have everything you want, but you'll be able to find enough to get by on until you get to a bigger place."

"Thanks, Mr. Judson."

He nodded. "You folks be careful. Gomer ain't a very friendly town. I don't go there no more than I have to."

"Thanks for the information. We'll keep our eyes open." Kerley nodded as Judson and Eli moved to leave. Without saying anything, he urged Shadow forward. Isabella followed.

The sun was falling behind the horizon when they entered what she figured was the town the man had told them about. Walter Judson had been right. There wasn't much to the place. A small building sat on the left side of the road. It had the words *'Ollie Miller's General Store'* in faded black letters painted across the front. On the right, and a little way down from it, was an even smaller building that didn't have a name on it, but dirty looking curtains that had once been light blue or maybe green, hung limply out the open windows. Three other buildings stood away from the rest and completed the village. Other than the store, she had no idea what any of these businesses were, and she didn't care. There was something about this place called Gomer that frightened her, and she wanted to move on. She didn't even want to stop for supplies. She was about to tell Kerley this when he stopped his horse in front of the store's hitching post and started to dismount.

He glanced at her. "Aren't you going to come in with me?"

"Let's not go in there, Kerley. I don't like this place."

He settled back in the saddle and looked at her. "We need supplies, Isabella, and this looks like our only chance to get them anytime soon."

"I'll not eat any of the food we have left, and then I'll have enough for you until we get someplace else. Let's keep going."

"Don't be ridiculous. I can't eat and see you not eating anything. We're here, and we might as well buy some supplies." He got off the horse and moved beside her.

Though she didn't know why, she was frightened. She looked into his eyes and muttered, "Please keep your gun ready."

He gave her a sly look. "Honey, it's always ready."

~ * ~

Kerley was surprised when Isabella stayed close to him as they went up the two steps to the door of the store. He wondered what she was frightened of, but for some reason, he knew she wouldn't explain it to him now. He automatically reached down and put his hand on her shoulder. Again, he was surprised when she didn't pull away. What was up with her?

Opening the door, he moved his hand from her shoulder to the small of her back and ushered her inside the dusty and musty smelling store. He felt her tremble, but again, she didn't move away from him.

A heavyset man with slicked back black hair and a handlebar moustache glared at them. "Howdy." His voice was more curious than friendly. "I didn't hear the stage come up."

"We're on horseback," Kerley said.

"Oh, I see. What do you want?"

Kerley lifted an eyebrow. "Need some coffee and a couple pounds of bacon."

"I got the coffee, but ain't got no bacon."

"Then we'll take the coffee." He remembered Judson had told him they probably wouldn't have what he wanted. He glanced at the shelf behind the storekeeper. "Give us four cans of those peaches behind you."

The man nodded and set the cans on the counter with the coffee he'd taken from the lower shelf. "Anything else?"

Kerley glanced at Isabella. "Need anything?"

In a soft voice, she said, "If he has them, how about a small bag of flour and a couple of cans of beans?"

Kerley nodded at the man. "Add that and a jar of that blackberry jam I see on the shelf."

The man added up their purchase and after paying, they headed out. Two poorly dressed young cowboys were standing between them and their horses when they went outside. The boys looked to be in their late teens.

The hair on the back of Kerley's neck stood up and without saying anything, he shoved the package of supplies into Isabella's hands.

"That there's a mighty purty woman that man's got with him. Don't you think so, Cousin Billy Joe?"

The taller one nodded and looked embarrassed, but he didn't speak.

The shorter one went on. "She looks a little tired out to me. Probably needs to rest." He turned his eyes to Isabella and waved toward the building with the open windows. "Want to come over to Moll's place and rest a bit before you go on your way?"

"No, thank you." Her voice shook.

"We need to move on." Kerley took hold of her elbow with his left hand and urged her toward the street.

The short guy shook his head and grinned a silly grin. "Ah, mister. Why do you want to be so unfriendly? You probably need a drink. Why don't you go enjoy a bottle at Sam's place down the road whilst your woman is resting?"

"As I said, we're leaving and we're in a hurry to go." Kerley saw the young man's hand sliding toward his gun.

It didn't clear the holster before Kerley had his pistol out and pointed between the young fellow's eyes. "I think you better let us pass before somebody gets hurt." Kerley's voice was deep and there was no doubt he meant for these two to get out of his way so he and Isabella could get to their horses.

The shorter one, who seemed to be the leader and the bravest, looked shocked but held up his hand. "Don't look like these folks want to be friendly, Billy Joe."

The tall young man spoke for the first time. "Let 'em go, Spike. They said they was in a hurry."

"I don't see why they have to go. I was just being neighborly." He again moved in front of Isabella with another grin on his face. It disappeared when a bullet landed in the dirt in at his feet.

He jumped back. "Damn you! You could've killed me."

Kerley's eyes bored into his. "Not this time, but if I have to shoot again, I won't shoot into the ground. And you will be a dead man."

The shopkeeper came to the door. "What's going on?"

"I didn't do a damn thing, and he shot at me, Pa. Then he said he was going to kill me."

"Is that what happened, Billy Joe?"

"I guess so, Uncle Ollie," Billy Joe said. "Spike said he was just trying to be a good neighbor to them, but I think they just wanted to be on their way."

"He's right, Pa. I tried to be friendly, but this fellow ain't the friendly type."

Ollie shook his head. "Some people ain't friendly. Let them go, Spike."

"Ah, Pa."

"I said, let them go." He eyed the gun in Kerley's hand. "I don't want no trouble, mister. Put your gun away and I'll see these boys go on about their business and leave you alone."

The boys moved, and without speaking and without holstering his gun, Kerley walked Isabella to her horse. He kept his gun on them because he wasn't sure if the shopkeeper had a firearm in the hand under his apron. When she was in the saddle, he swung up on Shadow. Looking at the men, he said, "If any of you follow us, be ready to fight."

He and Isabella started their horses back down the road the same way they had come.

She frowned and shouted. "Aren't we going the wrong way?"

"Just keep going. I'll explain later." He was glad she didn't argue with him.

Kerley looked back and saw the store owner giving them directions. In an instant, they headed to some horses that were hitched in front of one of the other buildings. He knew he'd been right to start this way. They planned to follow. Probably intended to rob him and it was no telling what they'd do to Isabella if they got their hands on her.

Glancing at her, he saw she was clutching their supplies to her chest and holding the reins with her other hand. As soon as he could, he holstered his gun and opened his saddle bag with one hand. He then reached for the supplies and jammed them inside.

"Let's speed up."

She nodded and kneed Moonstar. Her horse was soon in a full gallop. Shadow kept pace beside her.

It wasn't long until they came to an area where there were trees on each side of the road. He pulled back on the reins, and she did likewise.

"Why are we stopping?" There was fright in her eyes.

"I have a plan. I want you to walk Moonstar to the right and hide in those trees. I'm going to the left, but I'll join you in just a few minutes." When she looked as if she was were going to ask questions, he added, "I'll explain later. There's no time now."

She nodded and turned Moonstar into the trees.

Kerley kicked Shadow into a gallop to the left. As soon as he reached the trees, he stopped and ran him back to the road. He then slowed his horse and walked him toward the area where Isabella was waiting for him.

She gave him a puzzled look. "Why did we do that?"

"To confuse them. Now we'll continue through these woods in this direction. We'll be able to circle around Gomer this way."

She shrugged, then moved her horse to follow him.

An hour later, he found what he thought was a safe place to stop. He moved back beside her. "There's a sheltered area over here to the right. I think we should make camp."

"Good. I have a million questions."

"I'm sure you do, and I'll try to answer them as soon as we get the horses settled and get set up so we can sleep ourselves."

"Do you want me to gather some sticks to make a fire?"

"As bad as I'd like a cup of coffee, I don't think we should build a fire. I don't want to advertise our whereabouts to anyone."

"I understand. I still have some biscuits and a couple of pieces of chicken." She touched his arm. "If you'd like, we can open a can of peaches."

"Sounds good. I'll unsaddle the horses, then we'll eat."

When they settled down with the chicken and peaches, she turned toward him in the moonlight. "Will you please explain things to me now? Why did we come back in the direction we had come and why did you run into the woods on the other side of the road and send me to hide this way?"

He couldn't help smiling at her curiosity, but he knew she probably didn't see it in the fading light. "We came back this way because I remembered these woods were on both sides of the road and knew it would give us a way to escape those men without running our horses too hard. I've used the trick before and, as I said earlier, I wanted to confuse them. I felt sure they'd follow us, and the reason I sent you into the woods in this direction was so I could stir up enough dust with Shadow to make them think we turned in the other way. It was a gamble I hoped would work."

"It makes sense, so I'm hoping it did work." She took a bite of her food and after swallowing she asked, "What do you think will happen if they catch us?"

"Nothing good, that's for sure."

"I don't know why, but I had a strange feeling something would happen in that town."

"Is that why you didn't want to go into the store?"

"Yes. I was scared for some reason."

"You have good instincts. I didn't get the bad feeling until we were inside."

"But you got us out of it."

He didn't say anything. He wasn't sure what to say. All he knew was that at the time, he knew he had to get Isabella away from the danger they were in. Though he was sure what the shorter ones one's intentions toward her were, he hoped she didn't suspect what the guy had in mind, and he didn't think she did. In fact, he was beginning to think Isabella was more naïve than he'd thought. But how could she be? She'd not only lied about being married to his brother, but she'd also stolen his horse.

Finishing with his half of the can of peaches, he stood. "I'll spread out the bedrolls. You need to sleep over there near those rocks. Can you shoot a gun?"

"I've shot Uncle William's shotgun a couple of times, but it always knocked me backward and I decided guns weren't for me."

He raised an eyebrow and took a small gun out of his boot. Putting it in her hand, he said, "You probably won't need this, but in case you do, just point it and pull the trigger. It won't knock you down." He didn't tell her the gun had belonged to Dale. It was one of his brother's few possessions Kerley had been able to collect while he was in Omaha. But there was no need for Isabella to know that.

She took the gun, and her voice shook when she asked, "Do you think I might have to shoot somebody?"

He didn't want her to be afraid, but he thought she should be prepared. "Not tonight, but you never know what we'll face in the future."

"Okay." She sat on the bedroll he laid out. She still had the gun in her hand.

"When you lay lie down, put the gun beside your shoulder. You can grab it if you need it, but I don't want you to accidently shoot yourself, or me either, for that matter."

He knew his words made her angry because she plopped down and put the gun near her right shoulder. She asked in a terse voice, "Where do you intend to sleep?"

He threw down his bedroll beside her. "Right here. I have to be close enough to protect you if the need arises."

"So, you do expect trouble." Her voice had calmed a little.

"I hope not." He lay down. "Now let's get some sleep. We need to get an early start in the morning."

She turned her back to him and didn't answer.

Five

It was beginning to get light when Isabella opened her eyes. She turned over and noticed Kerley's bedroll was no longer beside her. For a moment, she felt deserted and thought she would panic, but she couldn't let herself do so. She bit her lip and sat up. It then hit her that she not only felt stiff and sore, but she had to relieve herself.

Getting to her feet, she looked around, but still didn't see Kerley. She couldn't waste time worrying about him. She had to take care of nature. She'd look for him later.

Starting to step away, she noticed the gun he'd given her. She picked it up and stuck it in the pocket of her brown riding skirt. Moving behind the rock, she saw a secluded area and decided she'd go there to tend to her business.

Finished, she moved back to where she'd slept and saw her bedroll was gone. Again, there was a minute of panic. A noise to her left made her jerk her head around and reach into her pocket to make sure the gun was still handy.

She relaxed when Kerley stepped into the clearing. He had a can of peaches and the last of her biscuits in his hand. "Good morning."

She nodded and greeted him with a good morning.

"I've loaded the horses so we can be on our way as soon as we eat a bite."

She didn't answer but nodded.

He sat on a downed log she hadn't noticed and handed her the biscuits. Pulling a knife from his belt, he jabbed it in the top of the peach can.

Isabella couldn't help thinking how proficient he was in taking care of himself. She wondered how many cans he'd opened with his knife. She couldn't help smiling to herself.

"Something funny?"

She shook her head. "Not at all. I was just thinking that you're good with a sealed can and that knife of yours.

"I was a Texas Ranger for several years and I had to eat out of a lot of cans. Got pretty good at opening them."

She was surprised at his statement. "I didn't know you were a lawman."

"I'm not now, but I used to be. Gave it up a few years ago."

She took a seat on a small section of soft moss and pine needles. "Why?"

He handed her the can to take out some peaches. "My father and Dale's mother were hurt pretty bad in a riding accident, and I moved home to help take care of things at the ranch."

"What about Dale? Since his mother was hurt, did he come to help, too?"

"He came for a while, but he didn't like living on the ranch. He said he was a born gambler and I guess he was. Besides, he knew I'd take care of everything, just like I always have." He looked at her. "Didn't he tell you anything about his family?"

She gave him a slight smile. "He told me about you. He was proud of you and said he wished he could be more like you."

"So, you've said, but I never saw that side of him." He picked up the empty peach can and abruptly stood. "We need to get started."

"I'm ready." She didn't want to hold him up because she wasn't sure what he'd do if she did. Especially since he had such a quick temper and he seemed to be in a hurry to get away from there.

~ * ~

Kerley decided to lead the way. He'd followed her enough to know what a tempting sight she made in the saddle when she rode in front of him. From under the floppy hat she wore, her long blond hair hung in a braid down her back. Her backside was one a man couldn't help noticing the way it molded into the saddle, and her delicate features were the kind any man wanted to caress and protect. That was, any man except him. He'd learned his lesson well and he had no intention of letting go the way Betty Lou had seen to his learning.

Seeing Isabella from the back was distracting enough, but when she looked at him with her soft green eyes, it almost melted the hard feelings he felt toward her. Was that why he was putting off stopping? They'd been on the trail all morning and, from the position of the sun, he was sure it was noon or a little after. He had to hand it to her, though, she wasn't a complainer. In fact, she hadn't once asked when they were going to stop for a rest.

"Damn it," he muttered to himself. "I'm not being fair to me, her or the horses either."

He reined Shadow in and waited until she was beside him. "Let's stop over there near that small knoll. We'll rest a bit, make some coffee, and eat a bite. Then we'll decide where we're going from here."

She nodded and turned Moonstar in the direction he'd indicated. He followed.

After taking care of the horses, he came to the clearing where she was searching in the food bag. She looked up when he said, "I can't wait to get a cup of coffee in my hand. How about you?"

"It would be nice, but do you think it's safe to build a fire?"

"Yeah. I'm sure if those fellows were going to catch us, they'd have done it by now."

She placed the food bag down. "Are you sure?"

"Yes, I'm sure."

She sighed. "Then, do you want me to gather some sticks?"

"That would be helpful. I'll find some rocks to build a pit while you do that."

It wasn't long until they had the coffee pot he'd pulled from his pack sitting on hot flames. In minutes, the coffee began to boil. A can of beans sat on the hot rocks warming.

She looked at him. "The chicken is gone, but we have a couple of biscuits left. Or if you'd rather, I can make some pan bread with the flour we bought."

"I'd like to have some of your pan bread." He moved to the bag he kept tied to his horse. "I have a frying pan for cooking and a pot you can mix the dough in. I also have some baking powder and a couple of spices, if you want to use them."

"That's great. It'd be nice to have milk, but I can make do with water."

He studied her as she sat on a blanket in the grassy area nearby and began mixing the bread. Again, he was struck by her beauty. He could see why his brother was attracted to her, though she didn't appear to be the flashy kind Dale usually went for. Of course, maybe she was flashy when she wasn't on the Nebraska farm with her folks and where she'd keep it well hidden. Though he didn't want to, he couldn't help finding her more attractive than he usually let a pretty woman's looks get to him, even if she was nothing like Betty Lou.

Betty Lou had been a bit taller and had long black hair. Her eyes were as blue as the sky on a sunny April morning, and her skin as soft as silk. Though she didn't spend much time working hard on the ranch, taking care of the house, or caring for his pa and his stepmother when he had to be on the range, she was never too tired to spend time with him because she loved him. Or so he had thought. He learned later it was his money she liked, and it was other men with whom she wanted to share her love.

He looked away for a few seconds to push thoughts of Betty Lou out of his mind. When he looked back, Isabella had stood to put the bread in the pan and set it on the rocks to cook beside the beans.

He frowned, as he again noticed the shape of her belly. She was too small in the shoulders, arms, and hips to have her stomach stick out this much. He was sure this woman was going to have a baby, but how was he going to ask her if she was with child? Had she really been married to his brother and was this child of his brother's seed? How did a man approach a subject like this with a woman in a way to get the right answers?

He had to know, and there was no way to find out except to ask. He opened his mouth just as she let out a little scream and jumped backward.

"What is it?"

"A snake," she cried.

He came to his feet and grabbed his gun. He then shook his head, returned the gun to the holster, and watched as a small harmless rat snake slithered a foot beyond the fire. "It's fine, Isabella. It isn't poisonous. Besides it's already several yards from here."

"Oh, Kerley." She grabbed his arm and moved close to him. "I'm so afraid of snakes. When we were children, one bit my baby brother, Gary, and he died. I've been terrified of them ever since the day that awful thing happened."

Without thinking, he slipped his arm around her shoulders, though he didn't expect it to feel so right. "Don't worry. If there are any more around, the fire will keep them away."

"Thank you." She glanced at the fire. "Oh, my goodness. I've got to turn the bread. I don't want it to burn."

He let her go, but for some reason he didn't want to. Berating himself for having such a feeling, he watched as she leaned down and flipped the bread. He could get used to watching her cook like this. *Hell, man. Where did that thought come from? You thought you had the love of your life. Why are you having these feelings about a woman who is no more than a bed partner for your brother or some other unknown man? Get a grip on yourself.*

She gathered her skirt in her hand and lifted the coffee pot. "Ready for a cup?"

"I sure am." He held out the tin cups she'd already set out.

She dipped beans into the two tin plates and cut them a piece of bread. "I'm glad you opened the beans before we heated them. That can is hot."

"Did you burn yourself?"

"No, but I almost did." She sat on the blanket and picked up her coffee. "This is a simple meal but it's tasty."

"I think so, too." He took a bite of the bread and forced himself to smile at her. "I'm surprised at how good this bread is. It's hard to get good bread with so few ingredients."

"When I was helping my friend, Kathleen, and her mother at their rooming house in Omaha, she gave me some pointers on how to make things taste good when you didn't have a lot to work with."

He decided now was as good a time as any to get into a discussion with her. "Was that where you met Dale?"

"Yes." Her voice wasn't very loud. "He had rented a room there."

Kerley knew he had to tread easy if he wanted to find out about her time in Omaha with his brother. "If you don't want to talk about it, we'll drop the subject."

She shook her head. "He was your brother, and you have a right to know what happened, yet it's hard for me to talk about."

"Take your time."

"I can tell by your actions you've figured out Dale and I weren't suited to be married to each other."

When she said nothing else, he said, "I didn't think so. Dale wasn't the marrying kind."

"Maybe not, but I'm telling you the truth when I tell you I truly believed we were married. I never got to confront him about the marriage being a scam because I found out it was on the same night when they came to tell me he'd been killed. They said he was shot because he cheated at cards." She sighed. "I don't know if he cheated or not, but I don't think he would have. He seemed to be more honest, especially when I learned he'd decided to tell me the truth about our marriage."

He wanted to ask her more about the marriage, but he knew if he rushed her, she'd clam up. Instead, he said, "I couldn't say either way, but I never knew him to be a cheater. He was good at cards, and he won often enough without resorting to cheating."

She was silent a moment, then said, "Would you mind if we don't talk about it anymore right now? I promise you I'll tell you the whole story when we stop for the night."

He wanted to prod her to go on talking, but he was afraid if he did, she'd never tell him what had happened. If she'd really open up to him later, he could wait for the answers. He just hoped she was being honest when she said she'd tell him the entire story. He knew there was a lot more to it. He just wasn't able to figure out what, but he intended to find out.

~ * ~

William Greely looked at the shopkeeper. "Are you saying there was a man with the woman, and they stopped here for supplies?"

"Shore was. Tall man that looked like a gunman. The woman was mighty pretty. My son took a liking to her, but she weren't much friendly toward him and the man was downright hostile."

The door opened and a skinny cowboy with stringy hair and dirty clothes walked in. Another cowboy, a little taller, followed him in.

The shopkeeper said, "Hey, Spike. Do you remember that couple who stopped in here a few days ago? The one with the pretty woman you liked."

"I remember them," the tall skinny one said. "Spike liked the woman and wanted to take her to Moll's place, but her and her man weren't too friendly to us."

Spike added, "I think me and the woman could've been friends, but that man with her didn't want me to have nothing to do with her, did he, Billy Joe?"

"I thought Spike could handle him, but he threatened him with his gun," Billy Joe said. "Spike said we needed to foller them, and we got our horses and took off after them, but they got away and we didn't see them no more. I'm glad because I didn't want the man to shoot us."

"Which way did they go?" Fenton asked.

"I was outside by then," Ollie said. "They must have been as dumb as Billy Joe, 'cause they went back the same way they come."

Spike nodded. "We thought that was strange, but we went about a half a mile looking for them. We would've kept after them if Clem hadn't stopped us. That's my friend who went with us. He said they weren't no need to keep going 'cause they'd gone in the woods. We did search the woods for a while, but we didn't find them."

"Clem's a good tracker and he said they probably doubled back through the woods and went around Gomer. We decided to give up and come on back." Spike scratched his chin.

Billy Joe added, "I'm sort of glad we didn't catch them. I didn't want the man to shoot Spike for bothering his woman."

Spike laughed. "It was a shame we lost them, 'cause I shore would've liked to get to know that pretty little gal. I know she would've liked me."

In a haughty voice, William said, "I assure you, if she was my niece, and I think she probably was, she would never want to take up with a stranger."

William didn't give him a chance to answer but looked at Fenton. "That means he must have forced her to go with him and they must have continued on the way we're headed. We know they didn't go back the way they came because we would've met them."

"Damn! I was hoping we wouldn't have to go no further than here. I'm gettin' tired. Besides, I need to get back to the farm. It ain't no telling what my young'uns have done to the place since I've been gone."

"Why're you after them anyway?" Ollie asked.

"Me and William's got a deal. I'm gonna marry that niece of his and give that baby she's carrying a name and I'm going to let him have five acres of my land he's been wanting."

The shopkeeper frowned. "So that man she was with weren't her husband?"

"No. She don't have no husband, though she keeps trying to say she was married to a gambling man in Omaha," William explained.

"Did that man with her take her away from you?" Spike asked.

William answered. "As I said, he must have forced her to go with him. I can't believe my niece would take up with a strange man and then travel with him unless she had no choice."

"She seemed to like him," Billy Joe said.

The shopkeeper said, "I don't know about that. I do remember the man kept her awful close to him while they was in here gettin' supplies. I guess he was afraid she'd tell us he'd kidnapped her and all the time she was trying to get away."

Spike looked angry. "I knowed she wanted to go to Moll's place with me and he wouldn't let her. I wish I'd kept on their trail, no matter what Clem said."

"Well, Fenton. Since we have to keep going to see if we can catch them, we better buy some supplies and hit the trail. They've got a good head start on us already."

Spike laughed. "You ain't gonna never catch them in that wagon you're traveling in. They had two good looking horses and they could be almost to California by now."

"Surely not," William said.

Fenton nodded. "I think he's right, William. I'm about ready to give up and go home. We ain't gonna catch them."

Ollie raised an eyebrow. "Maybe these boys could help you fellows get her."

William frowned. "How?"

"They're pretty good trackers and, for the right price, they could catch up with them two and get the woman back for you. 'Course, it'll cost you a little."

"I don't think we should do that," Billy Joe said.

Everyone ignored him.

"How much will it cost?" Fenton asked.

"Fifty dollars for each of us. If Clem goes with us, that'll be a hundred and fifty dollars," Spike blurted before anyone else could say anything.

"That's a lot of money, but I guess it does sound fair," William said.

"I think so, too, but all I got on me is twenty dollars," Fenton said. "How much you got on you, William?"

"After I pay for the supplies, I'll have around ten dollars, but I took Vassie's egg money, and I told her I wouldn't spend all of it. She expects me to bring some home, but if I don't, she knows better than to say anything to me."

"Vassie's smart enough not to say anything about what you do with the money. Besides, she don't have to know how much you've spent, and it'd shore save us a lot of time not to have to keep huntin' them. Why don't we give these here boys what we've got and when they get the woman back, we'll give them the rest?"

William frowned. "I don't know if we should, Fenton. You know I don't like spending money when I don't know if I'll get something out of it or not."

"We got no choice, William. You want your niece back and I want to make her my wife so I can get some help with them young'uns of mine. I need a woman to take care of them." He grinned. "Besides, I'm kind of looking forward to getting her in my bed and it don't look like we're gonna be able to catch her by ourselves. She's done got too far ahead of us."

"You got no need to talk about her going to bed with you, Fenton."

He shrugged. "Well, married people do sleep together, you know."

"I guess you're right." William fumbled with his wallet and shelled out ten dollars. "I hope we're doing the right thing."

"We are." Fenton gave them his twenty and looked at Ollie. "Now, what should we do?"

"Why don't you give us your names and then go on back home? Spike here will send you a wire when they get your niece back, then you can decide if you want them to bring the woman to you and collect the rest of the money you owe them, or if you want to bring the money to them and get her yourself."

"That sounds good to me. Let's get a few supplies and head home, William."

William frowned. "What if'en you don't get her?"

"Then we'll let you know that, too," Spike said. "If'en we fail, you won't owe us any more money."

"That sounds fair," Fenton said.

The shopkeeper put in. "I'll even give the boys the supplies they'll need on credit, and they can pay me when they collect the rest of the money from you. If they don't get her, I'll just take the loss on the goods they take."

"I guess that'll work," William mumbled, then turned to them with a glare. "My niece is going to have a baby and I will tell you this: if either of you touch her in any way, I'll have you arrested, and I won't give you a dime when you come back with her. Do you understand that?"

Spike started to say something, but Fenton butted in. "I agree, and don't think you'd be able to get away with messing with her. She has a big mouth and she'd tell us right away if any of you touched her."

Though Spike looked like he wanted to argue, his father said in a voice that left no room for doubt, "For that kind of money, you fellows will behave with the woman, won't you?"

Though he didn't look like he agreed, Spike said, "You're right, Pa. We'll treat her like the lady I'm shore she is."

"I think he means it, William. Let's make the deal, and head home. As I said, it's no telling what kind of mess my young'uns have made since I left."

After the two men went out the door, Spike turned to his papa. "Good thinking, Pa. We shore fooled them, didn't we?"

"You boys done good."

"Yeah. Easiest money I've ever made. Here's your share, Billy Joe" Spike handed his cousin a dollar and crammed the rest in his pocket. "Are we going to foller them two old coots out of town and take what they have left?"

"No, Spike," Billy Joe said. "You made a deal with them, and you should stick to it."

"For once the idiot's right. There ain't no need to follow them, Spike. I watched as the one called William paid me. He ain't got but a dollar and some change left. I'd say it's best to forget it." He looked at Spike. "I can see you've got somethin' on your mind. What is it?"

"I was just thinking. Maybe we should go after that woman. No matter what they say, not only will I get to have my way with her, but if I take her back to them men, we'll get the rest of the money and maybe we could demand more." He grinned. "What do you think, Pa?"

"I think that's a good idee. You could ask for the extra for what you had to put out on her and I'm shore those honest men will pay you for her even if she is messed up a little."

"Let's do it, Billy Joe."

Billy Joe shrugged. "I don't know. He said she was going to have a baby and..."

"Look, you idiot. A baby in her ain't gonna make a difference. I'll do all the thinking and like always, all you'll have to do is listen to me and do whatever I tell you to do."

"He's right, Billy Joe. All you have to do is listen to him."

"Then I guess I ain't got no choice."

Ollie laughed out loud. "That's right, If you want a place to live, you ain't got no choice. Now, why don't I get you some supplies together and you go make shore your horses are ready? If you want Clem to go along, I'm sure he's at Moll's place."

"Come on, Billy Joe. Let's see if Clem wants to come. He's a better tracker than we are, and I think I'd like for him to go with us. I'm shore he'll like the idee of making some quick money. I just want him to know I'm in charge of this plan and he has to listen to me."

"Bring him back by here and I'll tell him he has to listen to you."

"We'll do that, Pa," Spike said, and the two boys went out of the store, but only Spike was laughing. Billy Joe had a frown on his face.

Ollie turned to the shelves and started filling a bag with supplies. *It'd sure be worth a sack of items to get the boys out of town and out of my hair for a while. Besides, if they did pull the deal off, the money will be nice to get. I'll only charge the boys half of it as the cost for the supplies. After all, Spike might not be no good, but he is my son, and my nephew, Billy Joe, didn't matter no how.*

~ * ~

Most of the afternoon, Kerley and Isabella rode in silence. After a few hours, the sun disappeared behind the gathering clouds and Kerley was sure rain was on the way. Yet, he wanted to get as far as they could before it set in. He didn't like riding Shadow in the rain and he figured Isabella wouldn't want to keep going either. He wanted to find a place they could camp for the night and get out of the falling weather if possible. He figured they had moved into Kansas and there weren't a lot of trees on the open range. He couldn't help wondering why Isabella hadn't asked why they were still heading south. She hadn't said a word of where they might be going. It was as if she didn't care, and he thought that a little strange.

Before he could continue to ponder, he noticed what seemed to be an abandoned cabin in the distance. Of course, he felt they had to be careful. It could be anything from a lazy farmer's home to an outlaw's hideout. The closer they got, the more deserted it looked. If that were the case, they could get out of the bad weather for the night.

He pulled up beside Isabella. "It's going to rain in a little while and I think we need to take cover. If that cabin ahead is unoccupied, I think it'll be a good place for us to stay. There's even a barn where we can stable the horses."

She nodded.

He continued to speak. "Stay behind me. We have to make sure there's nobody around."

She nodded again and he took the lead. Guiding Shadow into the yard, he saw the front door was standing ajar. One side of the porch sagged but didn't look as if it were going to fall any time soon. The growth in the yard was knee high and there were no animals around. Domesticated ones, anyway. There were probably plenty of wild ones nearby.

He stopped and dismounted at the front steps. "Wait here, Isabella. I'll make sure it's safe to go inside."

"Can I dismount and move around a bit to unstiffen my legs?"

"I'd rather you stay on your horse in case we have to leave in a hurry."

"I understand."

He gave her a quick nod and stepped through the open door.

It wasn't as bad inside as he thought it would be. There was a stove in the end of the room and a couple chairs—one with a broken ladder back and the other with a missing leg. He pushed open the door in the other side of the room. He ducked as a bird flew over his head and out the front door, giving him a start.

He had to chuckle. "Man, you're getting jumpy."

In the bedroom, there was a built-in bed on the far wall, but there was no mattress. The rest of the room was empty. The window in the side of the room was missing. "Thus the bird," he muttered and closed the door.

Stepping out on the porch, he looked up at Isabella and offered her his hand. "It seems to be safe. Get your bedroll and the food and come on in. I'll get the horses settled in the barn and be right back. There might even be some old leftover hay for them."

"Good." She gathered the supplies and went through the door.

When he returned, he dropped their saddles to the floor. "I didn't want to leave these outside because it's beginning to rain. There wasn't much of a place to store them in the barn."

Isabella had the stub of a broom in her hands and was sweeping the floor. She looked up at him. "Did you find any hay for the animals?"

"A little. They seemed glad to get it."

She nodded at her broom. "I thought if we had to sleep in here, I wanted to get rid of some of the dirt on the floor."

He grinned but didn't tell her they'd been sleeping on the dirty ground every time they'd slept. Instead, he said, "I'm going to check the stove and see if it's safe enough to build a fire in, then I'll go gather some wood before the rain gets any harder. That way we can have some coffee and heat our food."

"If you can't find any dry, you can finish breaking up those chairs and use them as wood if you like. They're beyond anyone ever sitting in them again and I know they're good and dry, and should burn well."

"Good idea."

The stove checked out fine and, though he couldn't find a lot of dry wood, he was able to turn the chairs into an armload of firewood before the soft rain began to fall harder. By the time he had the fire going, it was as if the bottom had fallen out of the clouds and spilled all its water at once.

Turning from the stove, he saw Isabella struggling to close the front door. He moved over to help her. They pushed hard, but it didn't shut completely, though it came close enough to keep the rain from coming inside.

After putting the coffee pot on the stove, he looked at her. "What have we got left to eat?"

"There's some of the pan bread I made for dinner, the blackberry jam, two cans of peaches and one more can of beans. There's also an apple in our food bag. While you were out, I found a few potatoes in a pan on the shelf on the back porch where I found the broom. They were a little wrinkly, but not rotten. I decided I could fry them if I can have your knife to peel them."

He grinned. "Sounds good and I'll be happy for you to use my knife."

Thirty minutes later, they ate the beans, potatoes, bread with jam and drank steaming coffee, then topped it off with peaches. Setting his plate aside, Kerley said, "It was good, Isabella. You'll make some man a good wife someday."

"I don't intend to ever get married again."

He raised an eyebrow. "Why not?"

"Marriage is not what it's made out to be. I thought I had married Dale, but later learned that had been a farce. Then my aunt and uncle tried to make me marry Fenton Pyle. I decided I had to get away so I'd never have to marry him. Now I don't figure marriage is in the stars for me and I'm content with that idea."

"If you meet the right man..."

"I don't want to talk about it." She stood and picked up their plates. Carrying them to the shelf on the side of the room, she turned to him. "Do you want some more coffee?"

He decided not to push her any further about marriage at the moment. "Sure."

She took his cup and hers to the stove and filled them again. "The fire is going out and it's not going to be able to keep this coffee hot much longer."

"The coffee's fine and it's plenty warm in here without a fire. We have enough wood left and I'll build it again in the morning so we can make coffee before we get on the trail."

Returning, she sat on the bedroll and looked at him. "I'm surprised you haven't asked me about the discussion we were having earlier today."

"I thought you'd bring it up when you were ready to talk."

"I was waiting for it to get dark."

He lifted an eyebrow. "It's almost dark now."

"I know."

"Take your time, Isabella."

She sipped her coffee and didn't say anything for several minutes and he waited.

When she broke the silence, he was surprised when she said, "I'm going to have a baby in four or five months, Kerley."

So, she was admitting what he suspected. Now would she tell him the baby belonged to his brother or some other man? He still had doubts it belonged to Dale, but he wouldn't indicate this thought to her at this time. He wanted her to keep talking. He simply said, "I thought so."

There was another space of silence. Then she said, "Before you ask, yes, Dale was the father of my child."

He bit his lip to keep from denying his brother would ever get a woman pregnant and then marry her. He knew Dale would more than likely leave town. But Kerley didn't voice that; he decided to say nothing for the time being.

She sighed. "It happened a little over six months ago. As I told you, Dale rented a room at the boarding house. He said he was a gambler by profession, but he didn't like staying in the saloon when he came to a new town. Kathleen had rented to gamblers before, so she let him move in. Dale seemed to like me right away and I admit he was charming and, though I was leery of him, I liked him, but I kept my distance and intended to keep it that way."

She paused for so long Kerley didn't think she was going to say anything else.

But she did. "I guess he saw me as a challenge, but at the time I didn't realize it. He spent time talking to me about things I thought were interesting. He told me about the ranch in Texas that he grew up on and about his big brother who he idolized. He never told me about you being a Texas Ranger, though." She paused and asked. "But you said you were no longer a Ranger?"

He shook his head. "That's right. I resigned some time ago, even though they've told me I could come back anytime I wanted to. I've been thinking about doing it."

"He didn't tell me any of that." She shifted positions. "When I rebuffed all of Dale's attentions, he began to push harder. At the time, it didn't occur to me that he was giving me all this attention just to get to sleep with me. I guess he took my pulling back as a greater challenge, because he began bringing me little gifts. Flowers, chocolate, and now and then he'd bring a trinket of some sort. Of course I was flattered. I'd never had a man give me that kind of attention and I liked it. Still, I held out and he began telling me things like he'd never met a woman like me and he never thought a woman would capture his heart and even that he never dreamed he'd fall in love, but he had and with me. He also gave me elaborate gifts. One was a beautiful necklace he said belonged to your grandmother. By the way, I still have it and of course, I'll give it to you. This he presented to me when he asked me to marry him. At first, I thought he was kidding, but when he bought me a ring, I believed him. After that, things moved fast. The day before our wedding, he took me to the stable and presented me with Moonstar because he knew how much I loved her. He'd often let me ride her when we took rides. He said he'd made all the arrangements for the wedding and the next day we were married in the parlor of the boarding house. He said he was afraid if he went into a church, the roof would collapse on us." A small laugh escaped her lips. "Believe it or not, I was a happy bride. For almost six weeks, we lived at the boarding house. He would go to the saloon to gamble at night, and I'd help Kathleen and her mother. Then the bottom fell out of my world."

She paused for so long he thought the confession was over. Then he realized she was crying. He forced himself to ignore it as he waited.

She dried her eyes. "One day I hadn't felt well and went to my room early. My stomach was upset, and I began to throw up. It was then I realized I was pregnant. When I finished throwing up, I decided to go down and see if I could find something to settle my stomach. As I approached the kitchen, Kathleen was talking to a couple of boarders and her voice stopped me. She said, 'Are you telling me that Isabella and Dale are not really married?' Then Stacy, one of the men who often gambled with Dale said, 'That's right. Everybody at the saloon is surprised he's stayed with her as long as he has, since he only pretended to marry her to get her in the bed.' He went on to say the man who married us was a gambler friend of Dale's who happened to be in town and thought it would be fun to take part in the scheme your brother had thought up to get me in his bed."

She paused again. "After I heard that, I turned around and ran back to my room and cried and cried. Then when I dried my tears, I decided what I was going to do about the situation. I planned to wait up for Dale to come home and I was going to demand an explanation of why he'd do such a thing as to say he loved me, then go so far as to pretend to marry me just to get to sleep with me. I didn't get a chance to ever talk to him again because that was the evening they came to the door to tell me Dale had been killed by a man who accused him of cheating." She stopped abruptly.

Kerley didn't know when he had changed his mind about Isabella's honesty. He only knew in his heart that she could've never made up a story like she'd told him. It had to be true.

He touched her arm. "I'm so sorry this happened to you, Isabella."

She nodded.

"So your aunt and uncle found out you were going to have a baby and tried to marry you off to a man you didn't want to marry?"

"Yes. I don't know how they found out about the baby unless Kathleen told them. I just know when Uncle William came to get me, I didn't put up much of a fight. I was too hurt and confused, so I willingly went home with him. When I told him I was married to Dale, he didn't believe me. He even pulled my so-called wedding ring off my finger, and I never saw it again. I guess he either sold it or gave it to Aunt Vassie. We had only been back on the farm a few days when he told me I was going to marry Fenton Pyle, a farmer who lived next door to him."

"But you couldn't go along with this choice of husband for you, could you?"

"Never." She shook her head. "Fenton Pyle is an awful man. He only wants a woman to take care of his terrible children and to cook and clean and I don't know what all else. He said he'd raise the baby as his own, but I knew he wouldn't because he's a cruel man. It would have been an awful life for both me and my baby."

He swallowed. "I know it's a little late, but I apologize for my brother, Isabella."

"That's not necessary, Kerley. He must have thought what he did wasn't so bad. Besides, he's gone and there's nothing that can be done about it. I've accepted what happened to me. I'll get through it, and I will make a good mother. I know that. I just hope you don't mind me pretending to be your brother's widow. Even if he wasn't the kind of man I thought he was, I want my baby to have its father's name."

"A child should have its father's name." Because he couldn't think of anything else to say, he stood. "Thank you for telling me. I know it was hard for you and you must be exhausted. Why don't we both try to get some rest and we'll talk again tomorrow."

"I am tired. Telling you everything did wear me out." Isabella lay down on her bedroll and he moved to the back door to see if the storm was getting better. He found it had slowed, but he saw lightning flash in the distance. He guessed there was another storm on the way.

Going back to his bedroll, he figured he'd have a hard time going to sleep with what she'd told him replaying in his mind. It was such a sad story, not only about her, but about his brother, too. He was wrong about his need to sleep, though. As soon as he lay down, he drifted off.

Six

They made breakfast at the cabin then went to the barn to saddle their horses. Isabella looked at him as he was tightening the cinch around his horse's belly. She decided now was as good a time as any to ask him the question that kept running around in her mind.

"Why are you still keeping me with you?"

He didn't look up but continued his work. "I told you, family looks after each other."

She took a deep breath. "But I'm not really part of your family. I told you the truth last night when I said Dale and I were never legally married."

"If you told me the truth, as you say, that child you're carrying is family."

Tears came to her eyes, and she muttered, "It was the truth."

Finished with his saddle, he moved closer to her. "I didn't mean to imply that I doubted you because I don't. I believe it happened just like you said it did." He took hold of her saddle. "Let me do that. It's heavy and you probably shouldn't be lifting it."

"I can do it, Kerley. I'm not helpless."

He paid her no attention but took the saddle and lifted it to Moonstar's back. She'd already placed the saddle blanket there. "Sorry

I made you cry. If you haven't already, you'll soon learn I'm a direct person. Sometimes my words come out sharper than I mean for them to."

"I didn't mean to tear up. I've heard women in my condition tend to be emotional."

He didn't say anything, but as soon as he had the saddle in place, he gave her a half grin and turned to help her onto her horse. He then climbed atop Shadow. "Now let's see how many miles we can put behind us today. I hope to get there in a week, but I don't want to rush you."

They had been riding in silence for over an hour. Isabella had been thinking about his remark about getting *'there'* in a week. She couldn't help wondering where *'there'* was.

Her curiosity got the better of her and she rode up beside him. "Get where, Kerley?"

He frowned. "What are you talking about?"

"You said you wanted to get there in a week. I was wondering where *'there'* was."

"I was talking about the old family ranch in Texas."

She was shocked. "You mean you're taking me home with you?"

"You didn't think I'd desert you out here in the wild, did you?"

"I...I...well, I didn't know."

He shook his head. "Don't worry, Isabella. Dale is gone, but I'm here. I'll make sure you and your baby are taken care of."

She couldn't speak as gratitude filled her heart. She only hoped Kerley was telling her the truth. It would be wonderful to have him to stand up for her and her baby. That way she'd never have to worry about Uncle William showing up and dragging her back to the farm and forcing her to marry Fenton Pyle.

Even with all those those pleasant thoughts, she couldn't help wondering what Kerley was going to tell the people on his ranch. Especially his wife. She knew he was married because Dale had told her he was. Maybe he would pass her off as Dale's widow. It seemed to be the best solution, but she didn't have the nerve to ask him if he thought so, too.

She glanced at the man beside her. Again, her thoughts jumped. *He is such a good-looking man. Even better looking than his brother, and Dale had been handsome. Kerley's wife is sure lucky to have him. Many of the men I've seen aren't nearly as well put together as Kerley McFarland. I hope his wife appreciates this.*

She continued to think as they rode for another hour or so. Then his voice broke into her thoughts. "I see cattle roaming around over there on the range. We must be close to a ranch."

"Is that a good thing or a bad one?"

"Depends on who the rancher is. I've found most people in Kansas are friendly."

"You mean we're not in Nebraska any longer?"

"Nope."

She didn't say anything for a minute, then asked, "I'm a little confused. Your ranch is not in Kansas, is it?"

"Nope," he said again. "It's in Texas."

She started to tell him she remembered Dale telling her that, but he stopped his horse and was standing in the saddle looking at something. She stopped beside him and asked, "What do you see?"

"I think it's the ranch house." He reached behind him and took his spyglass out of his saddlebag. Looking through it, he said, "Yep. I see the house and some other buildings."

She'd read about what a spyglass could do, but she'd never seen one. She wondered if he'd let her look through his, then realized she'd never know unless she asked. "I've never seen one of those before. Can I look through your spyglass?"

He lowered it and looked at her. "You've never looked through one of these?"

She shook her head. "I've never seen a real one, so I've not had the occasion to look through one."

He handed her the glass and showed her how to focus it.

"Oh, my," she almost squealed. "It makes things look so close. How does it do that?"

"I know it magnifies things, and I'm sure there's some other scientific reasons to explain how it works, but I'm not a scientist. I just use the thing when I need to check something I can't see by just looking with my eyes."

She moved the spyglass in another direction. "Oh Kerley, look over there."

"Where?"

She pointed to the trees some distance to the right. "I see a deer and her baby. Isn't it a cute little thing?"

Before he could answer, she pointed it upward. "And look at that bird flying over us. It's gigantic. It looks like it's right on top of our heads. This is wonderful."

After she pointed out a couple of other things he said, "Well, if you're through playing, we need to get on our way."

She lowered the glass and looked at him. Was he angry at her? No. He didn't look angry. He was grinning. She smiled back. "I'm sorry. I've never seen anything like this before. It's fascinating and I can't help being excited."

He reached for the glass. "You can play with it again sometime, but for now, let's get going. Since there's a ranch here, we can't be too far to a town."

She handed him the spyglass and, without replying, turned Moonstar to follow him.

It wasn't long until she began seeing scattered fields, some with horses and cows and always a ranch house. She moved closer to Kerley. "I think we're getting near a village."

"Looks like it."

"I hope we can find a nice place to sleep and maybe take a bath."

He half grinned at her. "They might have a nice hotel, but don't count on it."

She turned her head to the side and looked at him. "Why do you think this town won't have one?"

"I've been through a lot of small communities in my work, and I figure if you find any kind of hotel in them, you're lucky. Very few of the ones you do find seldom have bathrooms in them."

"Maybe they'll bring a tub to the room."

"Maybe they will." He grinned at her again.

Isabella wanted to hit him, but she turned her eyes straight ahead. How could he know what they had in the upcoming town if he'd never been there? Of course, he could have been there before, for all she knew. She didn't really know much about this man, but she thought he'd at least confess to her if he had visited the town before. *Well, I'm not going to waste my time wondering whether he knows what he's talking about. I want a bath and if there's a way to get one in this place, I'll get one.*

When they stopped their horses in front of a clapboard house that had a *Room for Rent* sign, she began to doubt her resolve to get a bath. She was sure this was one luxury they didn't offer. They probably didn't even have a bathtub they could or would bring to the room.

~ * ~

When Kerley left her in the small bedroom, Isabella knew he was right about the available accommodations in such a small town. A two-story house might serve as a hotel, but she wondered if it wasn't really a private home and the owners just wanted to pick up a little money by renting out this room. The place was clean but had nothing else going for it. Not even a comfortable bed. "I'm sure it'll be better than sleeping on the ground," she muttered and turned to place the small bag carrying her clothes on the bed.

There was a knock on her door.

Frowning, she moved to it. "Who is it?"

"We got your bathtub and some water," a gruff female voice said.

Isabella opened the door and watched as a rotund woman wearing a dirty white apron brought in what looked like a tin wash tub. A gangly boy followed with two buckets of steaming water.

"Where you want it?" the woman demanded.

"Over by the bed will be fine and thank you."

"Ain't no need to thank me. Thank your man. He demanded you get this."

She was surprised to hear Kerley had arranged for her to get the bath. "Well, I appreciate it anyway. I'm looking forward to a bath."

"You don't look nasty enough for one, but 'to each his own,' as my ma used to say." She placed the tub on the floor at the side of the bed and turned to watch as the boy emptied the buckets of water into it. She then said, "Go get them buckets full again, Ronnie. He said she had to have four buckets of hot water and two cold ones."

"Ah, Ma. I don't want to carry no more water. It's heavy."

"Shut up and do like I told you. That man give us a dollar to get this up here to his woman. He'll take back the money if'en we don't do it."

"But..."

"Don't talk back to me, you lazy young'un. Do what I said afore I bust your mouth with the back of my hand."

She started for the boy, but he grabbed the buckets, turned, and ran out of the room before she got close enough to hit him.

His mother followed.

Isabella stared after them, not believing a mother would talk to her son in such a manner. Or him to her. She vowed at that moment she'd raise her child with respect, then he'd respect her in turn. The way her parents had raised her before they had died.

A short time later, the boy returned with two more buckets of hot water, and his mother followed him with the last two, which were cold.

Afterward, they left without saying anything to her or to each other. Isabella locked the door, undressed, climbed into the tub, and leaned back in the warm water. Her thoughts were on Kerley McFarland. Though he was often gruff and bossy, he'd turned around and surprised her, just as he did with this bath. If the woman running this place hadn't said anything, she'd never know he'd paid extra for it, because she knew he wouldn't have told her. It felt wonderful and it was sweet of Kerley to make sure she enjoyed the luxury of a bath while he stepped out.

Where he stepped out to, she had an idea, and it really didn't matter. She appreciated the privacy of being in this tub. The only thing that would make it better was if the people in this house would stop shouting at each other. She felt if they kept it up, she'd have a hard time sleeping. Besides that, she couldn't help but wonder if this place was safe.

She finished her bath, dried with the cotton towel they had supplied, and slipped into the one nightgown she'd brought with her. Sitting on the side of the bed and rubbing her hair in the towel, she was surprised when there was a knock at the door. She jumped. Who in the world would be coming to her room now?

Seven

The knock came again, then a voice said, "It's me, Isabella. Let me in."

She recognized Kerley's voice and frowned. Why was he coming to her room? Didn't he rent one for himself?

After the third knock, she moved across the room and opened it a few inches. "What do you want, Kerley?"

"I want to get in this room."

"But…"

"Give me enough room to get through this door or I'm going to shove it open, and you might fall. You don't want that, do you?"

"Of course not." She jerked it open, and surprise filled her face. "I didn't expect you to come back here tonight, and why do you have your bedroll with you?"

He lifted an eyebrow and gave her a half grin. "Are you saying you intend to share the bed with me, so I won't have to sleep on the floor?"

"Of course not!" Her voice was indignant.

"Didn't think so." He chuckled and tossed the bedroll to the floor. "Did you enjoy your bath?"

She ignored his question. "Surely you don't think you're going to sleep in this room with me, do you?"

"Yes, ma'am, I am."

"You can't."

"And why not? We've been sleeping together on the ground and in a cabin on the way here. What difference does this room make?"

"But people will think...I mean, it's not proper."

"My dear Isabella, it's more than proper and people will not think a thing about it."

"How do you know what they'll think?"

"I know because I registered us as husband and wife."

"Oh." She gasped. "Why?"

"I took one look at this place and decided you wouldn't be safe in here alone."

"But..."

"For heaven's sake, Isabella, relax and let's try to get some rest. You may not get another chance to sleep in a bed for some time, so you need to take advantage of it."

Still not sure, she moved back to the bed, sat, and watched as he spread the bedroll at the foot. He sat on it to take off his boots. Glancing at her, he laughed his deep half-laugh. "If you're going to sit on the side of the bed all night, how about switching places with me? I'll crawl in and make use of the whole thing."

She jumped up and straightened the covers. "I'm going to bed now."

"Good. Get in and cover up because I'm going to blow out the light."

"Do you have to?"

"Unless you want to watch me take my pants off, I have to."

Isabella turned all shades of red as she jumped in the bed and pulled the covers over her head. She heard him laughing quietly when he walked up beside the bed and blew out the lighted lamp on the bedside table. The floor creaked as he moved back and lay on his bedroll. She felt a little guilty that she had a bed and he had to sleep on the hard floor. But only a little.

~ * ~

When Isabella opened her eyes the next morning, it took her a few seconds to remember where she was. When she did, she jerked the covers up to her neck and looked around. The feeling that she shouldn't be here with Kerley McFarland was as strong as it had been last night.

Again, it took a few seconds to realize she was the only one in the room. Also, his bedroll was no longer at the foot of the bed. She wondered if he had deserted her, but didn't dwell on it.

Jumping up, she made a quick job of her morning routine, including getting dressed. She was pinning up her long hair when the bedroom door opened, and Kerley stepped inside.

He raised an eyebrow. "Glad to see you're up. I thought you were going to sleep all day."

Ignoring his remark, she asked, "What time is it?"

He pulled a gold watch from his vest pocket. "Seven forty-five."

"That's not so late." She jabbed the last pin in her hair and turned to face him. "How long have you been up?"

"A while and I'm getting hungry. Are you about ready to go?"

"Yes, I'm ready." She didn't bother to ask where they were going. She figured he'd already decided and there was no use to suggest they eat before getting on the road.

It surprised her when he said, "I saw a small restaurant down the street and decided we should eat before we leave town. Hope that's all right with you."

"It's very much all right. Like you, I'm a bit hungry."

"Then shall we get out of here and head for the eatery?"

"I'm happy to do that."

He picked up her small bag and opened the door. "Let's go."

~ * ~

After a breakfast of flapjacks and sausage, they went to the general store and replenished their supplies. They then mounted their houses and left the little town in silence because each seemed to be lost in their own thoughts.

Kerley sure was. He had done a lot of thinking as he tried to go to sleep at the foot of Isabella's bed last night. He knew he hadn't told her the real reason he was headed to the old family ranch in Texas, or the ranch that used to be. The ranch he had an idea he might be able to buy and build back up to the way it was when his grandfather, Gary, was alive. He didn't tell Isabella that when his father died, his stepmother had inherited the place, and how, when she found out she owned it she told him to leave. She informed him he was no longer needed because she was going to manage the ranch herself. He then learned the woman had let the ranch go down so much she lost it to the bank for taxes. And he definitely hadn't told Isabella about his marriage to Betty Lou and how it had ended. He had almost decided he never would.

But in the wee hours of the morning, when he thought about Isabella and her situation, he came to a conclusion of what he felt should be done. Now, all he had to do was pick the right time to tell her, and if need be, convince her it was the only thing they could do.

That time came when they took a break at midday. "I think we should stop, Isabella. I'm not very hungry, but I think the horses need to rest for a while."

"I'm not much hungry either. I think I'll only have a bit of the bread and cheese we bought." She dismounted, handed him the reins, and took their sack of supplies. "Let's sit over there on that soft grass."

He handed her the canteens and a blanket. "I'll take care of the horses."

When he had the animals watered and hobbled at a grassy area, he came back to her. She had the blanket spread on the ground and had set out the bread and cheese and a can of peaches. "I know how good you are with opening these cans with your knife and I thought you might like a little dessert."

"You're a smart lady. You've already learned about my weakness for sweets."

She laughed and he was surprised at how good it sounded to him.

In a minute she said, "Well, get out that knife of yours and do your part."

He chuckled, took out his knife and she handed him the can.

"I can see right now that you can be a bossy little lady when you want to be."

She giggled, passed him a hunk of cheese and bread, and said, "Well, somebody always has to be in charge and sometimes I like for it to be me."

"I think I'd already figured that out about you, Miss Greely."

She frowned. "Don't you think you should refer to me as something other than Miss Greely?"

He grew serious. "You're right and that's something I wanted to talk to you about."

"Oh?"

"I've been thinking of what we should tell people when we get to the ranch in Texas."

"By the way, where is this ranch in Texas?"

"About forty miles from Lubbock. Now, stop interrupting and let me finish. At first, I thought we could pass you off as Dale's widow, but I'm not a fan of telling lies. Besides, eventually one of us could slip up and people would know we hadn't told them the truth. I know the people in the area, and the fact we had lied wouldn't set well with them. In the end, it could not only hurt you, but hurt the baby as well."

"I hadn't thought of that. But if you don't say I'm Dale's widow, what will you tell everyone?"

"I think I've come up with the perfect solution, if you're willing to go along with it."

"What solution is that?"

He looked directly into her eyes and said, "We could get married."

~ * ~

Kerley knew she would be shocked, but he was surprised at the anger that filled her eyes when she snapped, "What did you say?"

"You heard me. I said we could get married."

Her anger came out in her voice. "Don't you think your wife would have an objection to your bringing another wife home with you?"

He then realized Dale must have told her about Betty Lou. He knew he had to let her know that was all over, though he had no intentions of giving her the details. "My wife is dead, Isabella."

He watched as the anger in her green eyes turned to sympathy. "I'm sorry," she whispered. "Dale didn't tell me, and I didn't know."

"He may not have known, but I'm reconciled to it, though I don't like talking about it." He took a drink of water and hoped she'd drop the subject.

For several minutes they were silent. Finally, he broke it. "Well, what do you think?"

She frowned. "About what?"

"Us getting married."

"I still think we could just say I'm Dale's widow. If we're careful, people would probably never know it wasn't true. They'd understand you wanted to bring your sister-in-law home with you. Especially if you tell them she has no family of her own."

"It'd never work. As I said before, one of us could slip up and give the secret away. Besides, the neighbors would be the first to doubt the story."

"Why?"

"Too many people knew Dale's habits. They'd know he'd never marry a decent woman unless there was a reason he had to. If some of them did believe the story, they'd wonder why I insisted on my brother's attractive widow live with me. It would not only hurt your reputation, but it would be hard for the baby to understand when it got older."

"But..."

"Also, there's always the off chance that your uncle could eventually show up and demand you return to Nebraska and marry that Pyle man. Since you were not married to anyone in Texas."

"Oh, no!"

He lifted an eyebrow. "The only other choice is if you tell everyone what really happened. Are you ready to do that?"

She dropped her eyes. "Of course not."

"I didn't think so." He stood. "You think about it on the way to the next town. If you agree with me that our getting married is the only answer, we'll find a preacher and get hitched when we get there."

"Why so soon?"

"We've crossed into Texas and when we get to the ranch, we have to make people think we've been married for a while. Since your condition is beginning to show, we want them to think I married you sometime during the many months I've been gone. The McFarland name is known all around the area. Therefore, we need to do the deed in a town far enough away from home where none of the family or the name is known."

When she only stared at him, he reached for her hand and said, "Let's get started. There's still enough time to get a few miles further today. That'll give you enough time to decide that I'm right and we should get married. If your answer is *yes*, there's something else I need to tell you."

"What?"

"That'll come later."

~ * ~

Two days later, they reached the town of Edisonville and had stopped early and checked into the hotel. Isabella couldn't believe that after she'd thought it over, she'd told Kerley she'd decided she would marry him. It had made sense at the time when she decided it. But did it make sense now? Now that he'd told her the other fact he thought she had a right to know: the fact that not only would she be taking on a husband, but she would be going to a ranch that no longer belonged to the McFarland family. A ranch that, after his father's death, his stepmother had let the bank repossess. A ranch he intended to buy back and start running again.

Though Kerley had given her a chance to change her mind about the wedding, she said she would still go through with it and now, here she was on the way to the preacher's house with him. She couldn't help wondering if marrying a man she hardly knew was the wrong decision. What if he was as bad as Fenton Pyle? What if all he wanted was somebody to work hard in the household to help get the ranch on its feet again? What if the neighbors thought she was wrong for him? He hadn't told her much of anything about them.

Even more important, what if Kerley turned out to be a terrible husband? He could be the type to beat his wife, or he could be the kind to spend his nights getting drunk in a saloon or spend time there with loose women, the kind of women his brother had liked. He could be the thoughtless kind and never consider her feelings. He could even turn out to resent the baby he'd sworn he'd raise as his own child. Maybe even be mean to it. Though he'd been mostly nice to her since they met, she didn't know him well. How long had it been? A week? Two weeks, or maybe three. She couldn't remember.

Was it too late to change her mind? If she did change it, what would she do? She had very little money and she knew raising a child on her own would be hard, if not nearly impossible. Should she have married Fenton Pyle like her uncle had wanted her to do?

She glanced over at Kerley. Absolutely not. Marrying Fenton Pyle would have been much worse than marrying this man. If she wasn't sure about anything else, she was sure about that. No matter what her marriage to Kerley McFarland held, it couldn't be as bad as being married to Fenton and raising his brood of children.

At least Kerley had been thoughtful enough to rent a room at the hotel so she could bathe, change into her one good dress, and rearrange her hair while he'd gone to the bathhouse and had a bath and a shave. Of course, he kept his mustache, which made her happy. She liked it on him.

Kerley spoke and brought her out of her thoughts.

"This looks like the place," he said. "The man at the hotel said it was a little white house beside the church and this is the only house anywhere near the house of worship."

They dismounted and tied their horses to the small hitching post as the door opened and a smiling, rotund woman with her gray hair tied with a blue ribbon on the back of her head, stepped outside. "Hello, folks."

"Howdy, ma'am. I'm Kerley McFarland and this is my wife, I think. But you can say she's my fiancée, Isabella Greely. We'd like to see the preacher, please."

She grinned. "I'm Martha Jane Hall, Reverend Noah's wife, and why do you say you think she's your wife?"

"We were married in Omaha a few months ago, but I found out later that the man who married us might not have been a real judge, so we want to make sure our marriage is legal."

"Well, isn't that one to talk about. I bet you've come to have Preacher Noah hitch you up so there won't ever be a question about the first marriage."

Isabella blushed and Kerley chuckled. "We sure did. Is he around?"

"He's at the church. We got the new hymnals one of our generous members donated and he's over there putting them out so we'll have them for service Sunday morning. I was just headed to get him to come to the house for supper. When he gets busy at the church, he forgets how long he's been gone."

Isabella spoke for the first time. "Oh, if he could, do you think he'd marry us in the church? It's so pretty, I think I'd like to get married there."

"Well, I don't see any reason why he can't." Her eyes sparkled. "Let me go back and grab the papers you need to sign, and he can perform the service before he comes to the house. Have a seat here on the porch swing. I won't be long." Without waiting for an answer, she turned and went back through the door.

After they were seated in the swing, Kerley looked at Isabella. "So you want to get married in the church?"

She nodded. "I hope you don't mind."

"I don't mind at all. In fact, I think it's a good idea." He smiled and took her hand. "Somehow it might make up for the fact that you're not having the fancy wedding I've been told most women dream of having one day."

She blushed and ducked her head. "I guess you're right about that."

"At least you look like a bride in your pretty yellow dress."

"Thank you, Kerley. It's the best dress I have and I'm glad I brought it with me when I left Uncle Williams's house."

"I'm glad you brought it, too."

She blushed again.

It wasn't long until the woman appeared again. Isabella was surprised to see she had changed her dress to a pretty light green one and put her hair in a neat bun on the top of her head, using pearl combs to hold it in place. She had some papers in her hand and what looked like a robe across her arm. "Shall we walk over to the church?"

They stood and followed her down the steps. She paused at a flower garden at the end of the walkway and looked at Kerley. "A bride needs to have flowers for her wedding, even if it is her second one. Why don't you pick your bride a bouquet, Mr. McFarland? Be sure to get some yellow ones to match her dress and throw in a few other colors to make the bouquet pretty."

At first, Isabella thought he would refuse, but he bent to pick some flowers. When he handed them to Isabella, his eyes twinkled as he looked at her. "I hope you like the ones I picked out."

"They're beautiful, Kerley, and I love them."

It turned out the Reverend Noah Hall was as delightful as his wife. After a short conversation, he put the robe she'd brought him on over his casual clothes and the ceremony began. For some reason, Isabella felt better about the entire marriage as soon as he pronounced them man and wife. One of the highlights to her was when Kerley put a ring on her finger and leaned over and whispered, "If anyone ever tries to tear this one off your finger, he'll answer to my gun."

To their surprise, the preacher and his wife insisted they join them for supper, and it turned into a lovely marriage celebration. One she knew she'd remember no matter what happened in the future.

Eight

Dawn was creeping through the hotel room when Isabella opened her eyes. For a few seconds she didn't know where she was, then it all came back to her. She closed her eyes and remembered. She and Kerley had been married yesterday and had spent the night here in this hotel room together. At first, she thought it would be like it was when they slept in the other hotel room. She would sleep in the bed, and he would sleep on the floor in his bedroll.

But this time she had been wrong. There was no bedroll and no sleeping on the floor. As soon as they arrived, it was obvious he was now her husband, and he would expect his wife to be his in more than name only.

She didn't fight because she knew she wouldn't win. Besides, she was sure he wouldn't be as brutal as Fenton Pyle would have been. At least she hoped not.

She shouldn't have worried. Though there had been no romantic words of love between them, Kerley had been as gentle and respectful as she'd always dreamed the man she married would be. He'd treated her as if they were in love, although she knew there was no love involved. Then it crossed her mind there was the possibility love could happen someday. Maybe she was already a little in love with him. If and when it happened for him, she knew she'd be a happy bride. Though her eyes were still closed, that thought made her smile.

"Are you having a nice dream?"

Startled, her eyes flew open. "I...uh..."

He laughed. "Sorry. I didn't mean to scare you."

She blushed. "How long have you been awake?"

"Not long." He stretched. "How about you?"

"Just a few minutes."

He gave her a quick smile. "How are you feeling this morning?"

"I'm fine."

"Good." He leaned over and looked at her. "If you didn't know already, you might as well learn right off that I'm longing for coffee as soon as I wake up. How about you?"

"That would be nice."

"I'm glad you agree." He rolled over to the side and sat up. "How about I put my clothes on and sneak down and get us a cup from the dining room? I'm sure they'll be open, and I hope that'll give you time to get ready to go."

"That should give me plenty of time."

He donned his clothes and went out the door without saying anything else.

Isabella sighed. Maybe last night hadn't been as good as she thought it was. This morning, he was sure acting as if nothing special had happened between them.

Knowing she didn't have time to dwell on it, she jumped up to get ready. It didn't take her long to take care of her morning rituals. She decided to wear her buckskin riding skirt and her white blouse. She figured that since they'd taken most of the afternoon off yesterday getting ready for the wedding, then going through the nuptials, they'd spend a long day in the saddle heading to the ranch he kept talking about. The one he wanted to get back on its feet so it could start showing a profit again.

She was braiding her hair when the door opened, and he came through it. He smiled at her and set the teacup on the dressing table beside her. "I remembered you said you liked tea better than coffee when you could get it, so I took the liberty of bringing you some this morning."

She smiled and meant it when she said, "Thank you, Kerley. That was thoughtful of you."

"You're welcome and by the way, you look pretty this morning."

"I thank you again." She sipped her tea. "If you keep saying and doing nice things for me, I might run out of thank-yous to say back to you."

He winked at her, then turned to pack up their belongings. "I thought we'd eat breakfast downstairs before we head out, if that's all right with you."

"I'd love that."

It wasn't long until they were seated in the dining room of the small but nice Edisonville Hotel. They were in the middle of breakfast when Kerley broke off his sentence and frowned.

"Is something wrong?" Isabella asked.

"I've seen those two young men who just came into the restaurant before. I'm trying to figure out when and where it was."

She looked at them and raised an eyebrow. "I think I might have seen them, too."

The two fellows took a seat at a table across the room from them and ignored everyone except the pretty young waitress who walked up to serve them.

Kerley shrugged. "Though I'm not usually, maybe I'm wrong this time. They don't seem to be interested in anything but the waitress and the coffee she's pouring."

"I'm often wrong about people. Maybe you are this time."

"I'm sure you're right, but for some reason seeing them feels like a warning to me."

"A warning of what, Kerley?"

"I don't know, but I don't usually forget faces. I guess it's my Ranger training. I never forget one that belongs to someone who intends to give me trouble or cause me harm."

"Sitting over there in the corner, it doesn't look like they're going to harm anybody."

"You may be right, but I still have a feeling we need to get out of here. Since we've finished eating, will you go to our room and get our belongings while I go to the livery and pick up the horses?"

"If it means that much to you, of course I will."

"Good. I'll meet you out front with our mounts in about twenty minutes." He paid for their breakfast and walked with her to the lobby, then stopped at the bottom of the steps leading upstairs. "I won't be gone long, but take your time."

"There's not that much to do. I'll be waiting by the time you get back."

He surprised her by leaning over and kissing her forehead. Without saying anything, he walked out the front door.

Isabella turned to go up the stairs and noticed the desk clerk smiling. She blushed and hurried ahead. His attitude didn't keep her from being thrilled that Kerley had kissed her right there in public. Maybe things would work out for them to end up happy together, after all. Maybe her marriage would turn out to be the kind she'd always wanted.

She hurried to their room, gathered up the saddlebags and the small bag she had brought her clothes in. She tossed her hairbrush and other personal items on top of her clothes and looked around. She was sure she had everything and wanted to be waiting on the front porch when he came back with the horses like she'd said she would be. Even if he didn't say anything, she was sure he would notice if she wasn't waiting there.

Satisfied, she went out into the hall, but she didn't get far. A hand reached out and grabbed her arm, making her drop everything. She let out a scream, but before she could call out again, a gag made from a smelly kerchief was tied across her mouth. She began to fight, but it was no use. The assailant didn't hesitate. He grabbed his gun from the holster and slammed it against her head. Instantly, everything went black.

~ * ~

Kerley was surprised when he didn't see Isabella on the porch when he rode up on Shadow and leading Moonstar. It dawned on him she was probably in the lobby. He hitched the horses and went inside to get her.

Frowning, when he saw the downstairs empty except for the desk clerk, he turned to the man. "Have you seen Mrs. McFarland?"

The chubby man almost giggled. "I saw her when you kissed her and left. She went up the steps, grinning like a happy possum."

Kerley ignored the remark about a possum. "And she hasn't come back down?"

"No, sir." He giggled aloud this time and winked. "Don't tell me there's already trouble in the marriage."

Kerley gave the man a hard look and without saying anything else, he went up the stairs two at a time. The first thing he saw when he rounded the corner at the top of the stairs were the scattered bags in the hallway and their room door standing open.

He recognized their belongings and hurried into the room. "Isabella, what's going on?"

The room was empty and in order. He instantly knew whatever had happened occurred when she went into the hall. But what could it have been?

Surely, she didn't decide to run away as she had from her uncle's place. She was impulsive, but not enough to do that. Last night, he'd thought she was accepting of not only the marriage, but of him, too. Would she have given up on him after only one night together?

He answered his own question as he turned and headed downstairs. "No," he mumbled, "She might leave me, but she would never leave Moonstar. She loves that horse. Besides, those are our belongings. She was heading downstairs with them."

On his return to the lobby, the desk clerk frowned when he saw Kerley's face. "Is something wrong?"

"Something's happened to my wife. Are you sure you didn't see her?"

"I'm positive, Mr. McFarland."

"Then who else has gone up those stairs since she did?"

From the tone of Kerley's voice, the clerk must have known better than to make light of the matter. "I don't think anyone else went up."

"I want a definite answer. Did anyone else go up those stairs or not?

"I'm not sure."

Kerley gave him another hard look. "Think back, man. Tell me everything that happened after my wife and I came down this morning."

Nervous, the clerk said, "Let me think. After you and Mrs. McFarland came down for breakfast, it was quiet for a while. Then these young men came in. They were talking loud and being a little too obnoxious. I told them I would have to ask them to leave if they didn't settle down. It kind of surprised me when they listened. They went into the restaurant, and it wasn't long until you and the missus came out. She went upstairs and you left."

The two men Kerley had noticed in the dining room came to mind. "How many men were there?"

His eyes darted around. "I'm sorry but I'm not sure. At first, I thought there were three, then I only saw two enter the dining room. I guess there were two."

It became clear to Kerley. Two of them distracted the clerk while the other one went upstairs unnoticed and abducted Isabella. It was the perfect set-up. Now he had to see if the two who had kept the clerk's attention were still in the dining room. He'd worry about why they had wanted to take her later. Now he had to find her before they could get very far.

~ * ~

Isabella didn't think she'd ever been more miserable than she was at that moment. Her head throbbed and the bounds around her ankles and wrist were so tight her hands and feet were numb and turning purple from lack of blood. The gag around her mouth kept her from calling for help. Not that anyone would or could hear her if she could yell. Not if she was where she thought she was—an abandoned one-room cabin, from the looks of it from the inside where she lay on an uncomfortable straw mattress on a bunk bed.

There was at least an inch of dust on everything she could see from her huddled position on a bunk. The only window was so coated with grime there would be no way to see from it, even if she could get up and go to it.

Taking a deep breath, she closed her eyes. Had Kerley missed her yet? What would he do when he did? Maybe he would search for her, or maybe he'd think she'd run off. But how could he after the blissful night they'd shared? Surely, he hadn't been pretending just to get her to sleep with him like his brother had. No. Reverend and Mrs. Hall were real. There was no pretend preacher this time. She was married to Kerley McFarland. He was her husband and she tried to think he would look for her and find her, sooner or later. That was, if she couldn't figure a way to escape on her own.

She refused to let negative thoughts about their marriage sink into her consciousness. She was sure Kerley wouldn't have fooled her in the way his brother did. She didn't know a lot about the man, but there was no doubt in her mind that he was an honorable, man and an honorable man would look for his wife. She decided, yes, Kerley would look for her, but would he find her? Was this cabin somewhere he'd be able to seek it out?

The door squeaked as it opened, and she looked around. The young man who walked through it looked familiar, but she wasn't sure where she'd seen him before.

He walked over to the bed and removed the gag from her mouth. "I don't see why he left this gag on you 'cause you can't make nobody hear you out here."

She decided to let him keep talking and he added, "How are you feeling?"

"I don't feel very well." She glared at him. "Why did you kidnap me?"

"I ain't supposed to tell you nothing about what's going on. Clem told me to tell you not to take it personal, 'cause you'll know why you're here soon enough."

"Why do you have to keep my feet and hands tied? They're hurting."

"They said you might try to run if we didn't keep you tied up, but I don't see how you could ever find your way out of here. It took me a while to find how to get back in."

She wondered what he meant by that, but decided she'd question him later. "Could you at least loosen my bonds a little? They're so tight it's cutting off the blood flow to my hands and feet."

He looked at her hands. "They do look a mite blue. Let me have them." He loosened the rawhide around her wrists. "Is that better?"

She wanted to tell him it would be better if they weren't tied at all, but she didn't know what he'd do, and thought she better not rile him. Though he seemed to be more reasonable than the man who had brought her here, she had sense enough to be careful. She took a deep breath. "Yes. Thank you. Now, would you do my feet?"

"They said you might run off if I didn't keep you tied up."

"You said that before, but could you at least loosen them like you did my hands?"

"I guess I can do that." He untied her feet and frowned. "I don't care what Clem said. I don't see no need of tying them back since I'm here. I could catch you if you tried to run."

Again, she tried to be careful about what she said. "Thank you."

"Damn, if'en you ain't polite. You done said *'thank you'* to me two times."

"I always try to be polite to people who are kind to me, and you were nice enough to loosen my bondage. I don't think the other man cared how much I was hurting."

He ignored her remark and moved toward the stove. "I think I'll make some coffee. You want some?"

"Do you think that stove is safe enough to build a fire in it?"

"It shore is. We done used it to make coffee when we got here last night. It looks like Clem drunk what was left over."

She'd already figured he wasn't the only one who had been in on her kidnapping, but she wasn't going to tell him she'd caught him mentioning someone named Clem. She'd just bide her time and see if he mentioned anyone else, so she answered his question. "In that case, yes I'd love a cup of coffee. Maybe it would help this awful headache. My head feels like it's going to fly off."

He frowned and picked up a stick of wood and crammed it in the stove. "Why does she have to be so nice? It makes me wish Clem hadn't hit her so hard."

Though he'd mumbled, she'd heard him. She didn't want him to know she'd understood his words. "Did you say something?"

He looked startled. Then he must have realized he'd said his thought aloud. He shook his head. "No, ma'am. Sometimes I think out loud. I was just wondering if there is somethin' in these supplies that'll make us a good dinner."

"I hope there is. I'm sure I'll be hungry by then." She forced herself to give him a smile. "As you may have guessed, I'm eating for two people."

He frowned again. "What do you mean?"

"I mean, I'm going to be a mother."

He looked scared. "Are you sure?"

Isabella couldn't help it. She laughed. "Of course, I'm sure."

He put the coffee pot down and rushed to her. "He said you was going to have a baby, but I forgot about that."

"Who said that?"

"Spike said I can't tell you nothing."

Isabella now knew a third person was involved. Sighing, she closed her eyes and moaned.

The man's voice sounded frightened. "Are you gonna be all right? Can I do somethin' to make you feel better?"

"I appreciate the offer, but all I need right now is to go to the privy."

"I'll take you right away."

"Please, uh...what's your name?"

"It's Billy Joe. Oh, no. I weren't supposed to tell you that. Don't tell Spike."

"I won't. I also don't need you to take me to the privy. A woman needs her privacy."

Again, he blushed. "It's all growed up around here. I'm not even sure there is a privy. You could step on a snake or fall over one of the rocks or roots if you go by yourself."

"You mean we're not in town?"

"No. But don't worry. I know you need privacy, as you said. I'll turn my back."

And maybe I'll hit you in the head and run away as soon as your back is turned. But she gave up on this idea as soon as she saw how overgrown everything around the cabin was. There was no way she could find her way out of this jungle. She'd bide her time and think of a way to escape later.

Nine

Kerley only had to take one look at the outside door to the back stairs to realize this was the way the kidnapper had left the hotel with Isabella. Since the culprit did not have a key to get in or out, he'd broken the lock to give him an easy escape after taking her.

In his mind, Kerley could imagine him dragging Isabella down those stairs and he seethed inside. What was the fool's intention in grabbing the woman? A string of questions filled his mind. How did he know Isabella was alone upstairs? Had he watched her go up by herself as her husband went out the door? Did he have a nefarious reason for taking her? Was his plan to have his way with her and then kill her? Had he harmed her baby in any way?

He shuddered. Isabella could be in a danger she doesn't realize, and though he'd only known her a little while, he felt sure she'd try anything she could think of to escape. She'd also try to do it in a way the child she carried wouldn't be harmed. He had to help her, and as quickly as he could come up with a plan.

He didn't want the baby to be hurt either, but he had to admit his main concern was for Isabella. He'd only been married to the woman for a day, but he'd already discovered there was something special about her. He knew if she proved to be as honest as he now thought she might be, it probably wouldn't be long until she would be an indispensable part of his life. Though after Betty Lou, he never dreamed he could feel this way about a woman again. It had even crossed his mind that with Isabella, he might be able to live a life that would eventually become a happy one. One they would build together once they got the ranch back and settled into a simple life where they could get to know each other better.

But to make this happen, he had to find her.

After checking around outside, he realized that whoever took her carried her off on his horse. A horse that had been tied to a tree at the edge of the vegetable garden behind the hotel. It didn't take him long to pick out which way they'd gone. He decided he had to get his own horse to follow them. It would be foolish and waste time trying to track them on foot.

Hurrying back inside, to save time he thought he'd leave Moonstar hitched to the hotel post instead of returning her to the livery. He did wonder if he should head out to find Isabella on his own or if he should alert the sheriff.

This problem was answered for him when he reached the hotel lobby. The sheriff was talking with the desk clerk. "Mr. McFarland, meet Sheriff Amos Reynolds. He came in to get his morning coffee and after I saw what had happened upstairs, I thought I should tell him what was going on."

"I appreciate it." Kerley shook hands with the sheriff. "I found the latch on the outside back stairs door has been broken. That's the way he got out with my wife. I also found his tracks headed out behind the buildings. I came back to get my horse to go after them."

"Do you have any idea why someone would kidnap your wife, McFarland?"

"I don't have a clue. We were remarried here in town yesterday and we planned to leave today."

"What do you mean remarried?"

"There was some question about our first marriage, so we decided to do it again to make sure everything is legal."

"I see."

"We don't know anybody in the area, so I don't have any idea who they were or why they would choose her to take."

The sheriff nodded to the left of the hotel. "The livery is in that direction. Let me pick up my horse and I'll go with you to track her. Since it hasn't been that long, hopefully we'll find her quickly and she'll be all right."

"I appreciate it. In fact, I left my wife's horse tied outside. I'll take it back to the livery and you can get yours."

"Won't she need it when we find her?"

"She can ride with me."

The sheriff grinned. "I see. Let's go."

The sheriff's horse was waiting for him when they got to the livery stable. Samuel, the livery owner, said he had seen them coming and saddled the horse for the lawman. He must have known they were in a hurry because he also said he'd be glad to unsaddle Moonstar and take care of her for McFarland.

Kerley decided Reynolds was good at his job as sheriff because it didn't take him any time to pick up the signs of where the horse had headed from the hotel. "Looks like he decided he had to keep away from the main street. Let's just hope these tracks continue and he didn't veer into the creek that's in this direction."

"My thoughts exactly, Sheriff."

"Say you and your wife are strangers in town, McFarland?"

"Yeah. We're on our way to my ranch in Texas. Was going to get remarried there, but I decided I didn't want to wait."

"Any reason for that?"

Kerley chuckled. "After you see my wife, I think you'll know the reason."

Amos laughed. "Couldn't keep your hands off her, huh?"

"Something like that, plus the fact she's going to have our baby."

"Congratulations. My wife's pregnant, too." Before Kerley could reply, Amos grew serious and slowed his horse. "Oh, hell. He went into the creek right here."

"He sure did. Why don't I cross over and ride down that side while you continue this way for a while? Maybe he didn't stay in the creek long."

The sheriff lifted an eyebrow. "You ever been a lawman?"

"How could you tell?"

"Your actions. You look for clues like a lawman and I noticed you were about to point out the exit into the creek at the same time I saw it. That gives me a clue. You either were or are in the profession."

"I was a Texas Ranger for a while."

"I see. I guess that's why you're good at this. Why'd you quit?"

Kerley didn't see any reason not to tell him. At least part of it. He wasn't going to bring in his first wife. "There was an accident on the ranch. My father and his wife were badly hurt. My half-brother had come home to help, but he wasn't a rancher. I left the Rangers to see if I could help save the place." He didn't give the sheriff time to answer when he added, "The culprit went out here. It looks like he headed toward the open country. Do you know what's in that direction?"

"Some farms and small ranches. I can't think of anything that would entice the kidnapper to take your wife this way, but I think we should head in that direction and see what we find."

"I agree."

~ * ~

Isabella woke when she heard voices on the porch. She couldn't believe she'd fallen asleep, but she had. She must have slept for a long time because she could tell from the shadows through the grimy window it was getting close to sundown. Looking around the room, she wondered who had come to talk with her abductor and why they had elected to talk outside instead of talking here in the cabin. She then remembered him saying *they* had used the stove without any trouble. It must be one of his friends. Either the one he called Spike or the one called Clem.

Deciding it didn't matter, she shrugged and stretched. She then discovered, not only where her hands tied again, so were her feet. At least they weren't as tight as they had been before, and whoever had tied her had left the mask off her face. Though it would be embarrassing for her, she knew she was going to have to ask him to untie her so she could walk to the privy, though she hated the thoughts of going out in those weeds and bushes again. She had hated it the first time she went outside, and she shivered as she thought of it, but it couldn't be helped. She had to go.

She started to call out to him, but a few clear words came through the open door and stopped her. A man's high-pitched voice was saying "...therefore, you need to do whatever I tell you to do to her, Billy Joe."

"But she's been nice, Spike. I don't want to hit her in the head like Clem did. I feel bad he done that to her when he grabbed her, and there ain't no reason to do it now."

"You fool. We don't want her to know that man she's traveling with is running around with the sheriff and trying to find her, do you? If you do, just remember you'll be in just as much trouble as we are if they were to catch you here with her."

"He ain't gonna find her here. That farmer said it was so growed up around this place you had to know it was here to find it. Besides, what will keeping her knocked out do? She can't make enough noise to let anybody know she's here and she ain't going nowhere on her own. She was scared to death of the growth around here when she had to go to the privy."

"You let her go to the privy by herself?"

"No, Spike. I went with her, but I did turn my back so she could have privacy. A woman needs privacy, you know."

The one called Spike laughed. "The way you're making up excuses for her sounds to me like you're stuck on the woman."

"That's foolish. She's a nice married lady. Ain't no way she'd ever look at somebody like me or you either, for that matter."

There was the sound of a slap.

"Damn it, Spike. Why'd you hit me?"

"Cause you're talking foolish. Who's to say she wouldn't want a handsome man like me? Besides, you need to remember what her uncle said, if you get to feeling too strong for her. He'll probably try to kill all of us if she comes back sullied. Besides that, we won't get the money he promised us for finding her."

"What do you mean by that?"

The high-pitched laugh came through the door again. "If you was smarter, you'd know exactly what I mean, Billy Joe. She's a mighty pretty dame and it'd be awful easy to take advantage of her on that little bed. 'Specially since she's tied up. It'd be even easier if she's knocked out and can't fight back, then she wouldn't know what I'd done to her."

"You shouldn't do something foolish like that, Spike. Like you said, you'd never get paid if you done something like that to her. Besides, you know she wouldn't have nothing to do with us when they stopped in Gomer for supplies."

"I think she liked me then. It was that man she's with who wouldn't let her even talk to me."

"I'm not so sure about that. Remember how he shot at your feet. If he was to find her and learn you'd hurt her, he might just kill you."

It then dawned on Isabella. These were the young men in that awful little town of Gomer where she and Kerley had stopped for supplies. Not only that, but they were the two who had come into the hotel restaurant this morning. Kerley had been right to be suspicious. She should have listened to him.

The talking outside continued.

"Though I hate to think you're smart enough to think of all that, you're probably right." There was movement, then he said, "Now, I better get back to town. I'm supposed to meet Clem at the saloon."

"You better watch yourself at that saloon. Don't get drunk."

"I won't, but I admit the liquor in the saloon is shore better than what Pa makes to sell. It's not as strong as Pa's, though. But don't worry about it. I leave most of the drinking up to Clem. I'm in charge and I have to keep a clear head so I can make good decisions."

"Does Clem drink too much?'

"Nah. He's too busy trying to get one of them saloon gals to set in his lap." He laughed. "'Course they only do it when he buys them drinks. I keep telling him they do it so he'll put out money for the liquor, but he thinks they do it because they like him. At times I think he's almost as stupid as you are."

"I ain't so stupid."

Spike laughed. "You've always been stupid, Billy Joe. You know that."

Billy Joe must have ignored the remark because he asked, "When are you coming back?"

"After I find out what her man decides to do when he don't find her. If he gives up on getting her back and moves on, we won't have to keep her hid till we hear from the wire I sent her uncle. Then we can go to town and wait to hear from him telling us what he's going to do. But if that man's still in town, we might have to find another place to hide out for a while. You know that farmer said we can't stay here more than a few days. I saw a couple of empty houses in town. We might move there, or we could go to one of the towns we come through to get here. I ain't decided yet."

Isabella's heart leaped. *What did these men mean about her uncle? Was he going to come here to get her? Would Kerley let her go back with him? No! She wasn't even going to think that. If Kerley was looking for her like they said, he'd not let her go back to Nebraska.*

The conversation went on. "How will you know what her man will do?"

"There's always somebody in the saloon running their mouth. That's why I hang out there. Earlier today, everybody was talking about how somebody had stolen the man's wife right out of the hotel." He laughed. "I gotta say, Clem done a good job getting her, though I know she's not really his wife."

"When I got here to relieve Clem from watching her, Clem said it weren't so hard to grab her and bring her out here. I just wish he hadn't hit her so hard. She's had a headache all day."

"There you go again, feeling sorry for her, and you can't do that. I've sent you to watch her, you need to do a good job of it and forget worrying about how she feels."

"I'll try, Spike, but you know I didn't want to kidnap her in the first place."

"You better do more than try. You better do it, and it don't matter what you didn't want to do. She's done been grabbed and we have a plan. Now, I gotta get going so I can find out what's going on in town. I'll come back to let you know what to do as soon as I hear from her uncle."

"Thanks for the supplies."

"If you ain't going to keep her knocked out, why don't you let her cook for you? I bet she's a good cook and you shore ain't as good at doing it yourself as Pa and me let you think you are."

"I might just think about seeing if she can make us somethin'. A hot supper I didn't have to cook would taste mighty good tonight."

The other man didn't answer, and Isabella heard a horse neigh and then walk off, probably with the other outlaw on it. As steps came inside, she closed her eyes. She knew she couldn't let Billy Joe know she'd heard him talking to his friend. At least it seemed he kind of liked her and she intended to take advantage of that. She would worry about what connection they had to her uncle later. Now she had to convince him she was still asleep without them giving him a clue that she remembered them from the town of Gomer.

~ * ~

As the sheriff questioned the stubborn man standing on his ramshackle porch, it was all Kerley could do to keep his mouth shut. He knew the old farmer was lying and he wanted to dismount and beat the truth out of him.

Sheriff Amos Reynolds said, "So you're telling us that a man and a woman didn't stop here and ask you for anything?"

"That's right." The man eyed Kerley.

The sheriff went on, "Then I don't understand why we followed the horse's tracks right up to the edge of your yard."

"I don't know nothing about that. I done told you, I ain't seen nobody, and I'll say it again if'en you want me to."

"Then you have no objection to us looking around on your farm, do you?"

"Ain't no need of looking. I done told you what you want to know."

Reynolds glanced at Kerley. "You have anything you want to ask to him, Ranger?"

The old man's eyes got big. "Is you a Texas Ranger?"

"He called me a Ranger, didn't he?"

The man's voice shook a little when he said, "I still don't know nothing."

"I hope you're telling the truth, because if we find the kidnapper and my wife on your land, and he says you hid them, you'll be just as guilty as he is." Kerley's voice became more threatening when he asked, "Do you know what the penalty for kidnapping is?"

"No."

"It means you'll hang by your neck until you're dead, right along beside the man who took my wife."

"She's your wife?" There was surprise in the man's voice.

"She sure is, and I'll make sure the person who took her and the one who helped them hide with her pays the full penalty for their crime."

The man swallowed and looked at the sheriff. "Is he telling the truth?"

"He sure is."

"Well...uh....maybe somebody did come by."

"When did they come and how many were there?"

"It was night before last and there was three of them."

"What did they say to you?" Reynolds demanded.

"They said they had come to town to get their sister who had run away, and they needed a place to stay for the night and a place where they could sober her up where nobody would find them. Then this morning I seen one of them come back by, and he had a woman on a horse with him. I figured it was their sister, but I didn't go out and ask them nothing."

The sheriff joined the conversation. "Why didn't you go out and ask them anything?"

After a slight hesitation, he said, "Like I told you, the men said their sister had run away from home and their pappy had sent them to bring her back. So I figured that was what he was doing. Taking her back home."

"Then you didn't go out and invite them into your cabin?"

"No, sir, Sheriff. I had told them there was an old, abandoned cabin on the back of Newman's property where it joined mine, and if'en they could find it, they might find it decent enough to stay in for a day or two. I told them they better not stay longer than that, 'cause Newman might not like them being there. Newman owns the farm next to mine and ever-body around here knows about his old cabin."

"Where is this cabin?"

He gave them directions, and Kerley said, "You better hope we find them, and that my wife is all right. If anything happens to her, I'll come back for you."

Though he saw the fright in the man's eyes, he didn't wait for an answer. He turned his horse and paused beside Amos Reynolds's mount. "Think we'll be able to find that cabin before it gets dark?"

"We're going to try, but if we don't, we'll know where to start looking in the morning."

Kerley nodded, and they rode away without further talk.

Ten

The next day, Isabella was not only uncomfortable, she was angry. She glared at the man riding beside her, who she'd learned was the one called Spike. "It's bad enough that you and these men kidnapped me. Why in the world didn't you bring me a horse to ride instead of an ornery mule?"

"Shut up, woman. I ain't got to tell you nothing."

"Ah, Spike, don't be so hateful to her. What will it hurt to tell her you rented the mule 'cause it was cheaper than a horse, and you was trying to save money?"

"You shut up your stupid mouth, Billy Joe. Jist 'cause she cooked you a good breakfast don't mean I have to coddle her. She didn't cook nothing for me."

"I bet she would've cooked for you if'en you'd been there to eat it."

"Well, I weren't, and I ain't gonna coddle her like you do."

Billy Joe frowned. "I didn't say you had to coddle her. Jist that you could be a little nicer to her. She's a nice lady."

Isabella broke in the conversation. "Why did you have to be so cheap? A horse couldn't have cost much more than this animal."

"He said your uncle told him not to spend no more money on you than he had to."

"Damn it, Billy Joe. Why can't you keep your stupid mouth shut? You baby her too much. She don't need to know none of our business."

Clem spoke up. "Will you all shut-up? We gotta to get out of this area afore that man catches up with us, and your mouthing is making us go too slow."

"What does my uncle have to do with you kidnapping me?" Isabell blurted.

"Woman," Clem said, "I told everybody to shut their mouth, and that meant you, too."

Though she wanted to say more, she could wait. She would ask her questions later, but she intended to ask them eventually, no matter what Clem or anyone else said.

She nodded to him. "I'll try to make this mule go faster." She prodded the animal gently, hoping he wouldn't hasten his space. She wanted to give Kerley as much time as she could to catch up with them if he was the man they were talking about being on their trail. The mule ignored her instructions and continued at the same pace he'd been going ever since they left the cabin half an hour earlier. She didn't let any of the kidnappers see her smile.

~ * ~

It was nearing noon when Kerley pulled back on the reins and stopped his horse. "It looks like the trail ends here. Somebody has been going in and out through the underbrush and weeds around this place."

"No wonder we were having such a hard time finding this old cabin yesterday." The sheriff looked at him and chuckled. "It's a good thing we didn't keep trying to find it last night."

"You're right. We would've never found it in this jungle. It's so grown up the only thing you can see is the tip of the chimney."

"In case they're watching, I think we should leave the horses here and go in on foot."

Kerley nodded. "I agree."

When they drew close to the ramshackle cabin, Kerley said, "I can tell by the way the brush is pushed aside and tree limbs are broken, somebody has been here, but it doesn't look like anybody is here now, or they would've come out and confronted us by now."

"I agree, but just in case, you stand to the side, and I'll see if anyone is here." He pulled his gun and rapped on the door. "Open up. It's the sheriff."

There was no answer to his knock, so Amos pushed the door open and stepped inside.

Kerley followed him and looked around. He moved to the small stove in the corner. "Somebody's been here. I can smell the fire that was recently in the stove."

"I smell it, too."

Kerley walked over and tapped the top of the stove with his finger. "It's still a bit warm and that tells me they were here this morning and left the fire to burn out on its own instead of putting it out."

"Do you think that means they don't plan on coming back?" the sheriff asked

"I do, and it relieves one of my fears about this."

"What's that?"

"It tells me my wife is alive, and they still have her with them."

"How do you know?"

"We've been following the tracks of more than one horse. I don't have any idea why they took Isabella, but if they planned to kill her, this would have been the place to do it because it would be a long time before her body was found. But since she's not here, I know she's alive, and that only means one thing."

"What's that?"

"It's up to me to catch them and get my wife back."

"I think I'll tag along with you, Kerley. I can tell from that look in your eye that you don't have arresting them on your mind."

Kerley sneered. "You know damn well I want to kill them with my bare hands."

"I thought so."

"What would you do if it was your wife?"

Amos chuckled. "Probably the same thing you're thinking of doing, but it's not my wife and as a sworn lawman, I don't want to have to arrest a former Ranger for murder."

"Since you seem hell bent on keeping me from committing murder, let's get started. We don't know how much lead they have on us, and I intend to catch them today."

Sheriff Amos Reynolds followed him out the door.

~ * ~

Isabella pulled the mule to a stop and turned to the man behind her. "I want to stop."

Spike said, "No. We need to keep going."

She ignored him and started to dismount.

"Damn it, woman! Stay on that mule," he shouted.

"No!" she shouted back and continued to climb down.

Clem whirled around and jumped off his horse. He grabbed her arm. "Spike told you to stay on the mule. Why ain't you listening to him?"

Though she was frustrated, she tried to keep her voice calm. "I said I need to stop."

Spike came up beside them and grabbed her other arm and shook it, almost throwing her off balance. "I don't care what you said. You can't do what you please. I'm the boss and you have to listen to me."

"You're hurting my arm, you brute."

Billy Joe walked up. "Don't hurt her, Spike."

Clem ignored Billy Joe, but he did let go of the arm. "Look, woman. We ain't got time to fool around. We need to keep going. Now get back on that mule."

Still in a calm voice but with anger in her eyes, she said, "If I get back on that mule, one of you will have to come up with some dry clothes for me. Nature won't let me go any further without relieving myself—and soon."

Billy Joe turned red, and Clem glared at her, then asked, "In that case, do you want me to walk her over to them bushes, Spike?"

Isabella put her hands on her hips. "You most certainly will not walk there with me. Don't you ruffians have any respect for a woman's privacy?"

Spike looked puzzled. "Well, I can't let you go by yourself."

"You can let her go by herself, Spike," Billy Joe said. "She don't need nobody to go with her. She ain't gonna go nowhere in these woods."

Clem turned and looked at Billy Joe. "How do you know?"

"'Cause she's scared of all the weeds. She's afraid she'll see a snake."

"Billy Joe's right this time." Spike frowned, then turned to Isabella and added, "You got five minutes."

"I'll need at least ten."

"Damn it, woman. Why would you need ten?" Spike spit out.

She whirled on him. "You men are so lucky. All you have to do is unbutton your pants, but for a woman it's different. What would you do if you had to contend with a dress, a bunch of petticoats while waiting for three foolish men who you've had to explain that a woman has a need to take care of her necessities in private and needs the time to do it?"

When Spike and Clem looked abashed and said nothing, Billy Joe said, "Go on, Miz. Isabella. We'll give you the time you need. Won't we, Spike?"

"I reckon we ain't got no choice. Go on and do what you have to do. Just hurry as fast as you can. We'll all wait here for you."

Isabella slapped the mule's reins into Spike's hands and walked away. She was glad they hadn't noticed she was wearing a riding skirt and not a dress. With Billy Joe's help, she felt she'd at least won a small battle against these men. Maybe she could push it and figure out how to use this small advantage to get away from them later. They were right about one thing. There was nowhere for her to go from here, but there might be a better place to run in the future. For now, she would keep her mouth shut and her eyes open.

~ * ~

William Kerby looked at his wife and frowned. "I'm trying to figure out what I should do, Vassie. The wire says they've found Isabella and have her stashed in a deserted cabin where that man she was with can't find her."

"That's good."

"Yes, it is, but when I told Fenton what they'd said, he told me he didn't have time to leave his farm long enough to go get her and bring her back home. That kind of worries me. We've got to get her back here as soon as we can."

"Are you saying you want me to go with you, William?"

"I hope you don't have to. This is a man's job and you'd probably just be a hindrance to me. You won't be going unless I can't do no better."

Vassie's mouth drew into a thin line and in a voice sharper than she usually talked to her husband, when she said, "Then if you don't want to take me and don't know nobody else who'll go with you, it looks to me like you'll have to go by yourself."

For once, William seemed to ignore her barb. "I can't believe Fenton turned me down. After all, he's the one who's going to marry her."

"It don't look like he's very interested in getting her back. Do you think he's changed his mind about marrying her?"

"Don't say that, Vassie. People are already talking about her running away from him, and it'll be a terrible disgrace if she don't have a husband when that baby gets here."

"I never dreamed we'd be disgraced in such a way by your niece. I sometimes wish you hadn't promised your brother on his deathbed you'd make sure Isabella was looked after until she got married. I don't know if the little dab of money he left you is worth it."

"Shut your mouth talking sassy to me, woman. I hoped when I let her move to Omaha, I'd never have to put up with her stubbornness again. She's just like my brother. You couldn't beat good sense into his head either."

"I know she's been a trial to you, William."

"I tried to do the right thing to cover her sin by finding a man who'd marry her in her condition. But did she appreciate it? She did not. I can't help it she took off to Omaha the first chance she got." He drummed his fingers on the table beside his chair. "I realize now that I maybe should have left her there in the first place. If I'd knowed she was going to have that gambler's bastard, I would have."

"I'm sorry, dear. I guess I'm just as upset as you are, and I shouldn't have said anything about her being your brother's child. My mouth gets the best of me sometimes." Vassie got up from her rocking chair, hoping there wouldn't be any repercussions because of her backtalking him. "I'm going to get a cup of coffee. Do you want one?"

"I might as well." He looked at the wire again. "I shore wish I could figure out how I could get her home without going all that way to get her."

"You're a smart man, William. I'm sure you'll work it out. You'll probably have the answer by the time I get the coffee." She left the room without looking back.

William frowned again as he kept looking at the wire. A sudden thought crossed his mind and he almost jumped out of his chair. Hurrying to the kitchen, he yelled, "Believe it or not, Vassie, you were right. I've got it."

She turned and looked at him as if he'd lost his mind. "What have you got, William?"

"The idee of what to do about Isabella."

Vassie turned so he couldn't see her smile. She was hoping he'd tell her he was going to forget the entire thing and let the woman stay wherever she was.

Instead, he said, "I'm going to wire them and tell them if they'll bring Isabella back here, I'll give them some extra money."

Disappointed, she said, "You do have a good idea. I just hate to see you put out more of your hard-earned money than you already promised them."

"Don't worry. I'll talk to Fenton. I'm sure he'll put in more money to get her back." He grinned. "Yep, it's the perfect answer. We won't have to worry any longer about being disgraced by her laying down with some no-good gambler and getting herself soiled. When she's married to Fenton, people will think she just had one of those babies that shows up early. Then the land deal will be sealed for good."

Disappointed in his answer, Vassie took a deep breath. Though she was seething inside, she still remembered how he'd spent her hard-earned egg money when he'd taken it with him and hired those men in the first place. But she knew she couldn't let him know she didn't like the idea of him spending any extra money. He'd only take his irritation out on her. He might even beat her like he did a couple of months ago when she spilled some hot soup on him.

Taking a quick breath, she said in the voice she always used when she wanted to placate her husband. "That sounds like a good solution, William. I knew you'd think of something. Now, let's take our coffee back into the parlor and drink it."

He grinned and followed her. He didn't think she had any idea that the fact they would be disgraced because of Isabella's coming baby wasn't the main reason he wanted her back to marry Fenton Pyle. It was because of the deal he and Pyle had made about the five acres of land. A deal that would take place as soon as Isabella became the wife of his neighbor. That land was of the most importance to him.

~ * ~

Isabella wondered if they were ever going to stop again. Not only was the mule an uncomfortable ride, the animal seemed to get more sluggish with each step. She was beginning to think she'd end up walking and leading it if they didn't reach their destination soon.

Almost as soon as she had this thought, Spike called a halt to their travels. He moved up beside Clem and said something to him.

She thought it might be worth hearing, so she eased up behind them. Spike was saying, "I think we need to blindfold her and maybe gag her before we get there."

"If somebody sees her, won't they wonder why she's blindfolded and gagged?"

"You may be right, Clem. But what else can we do? I don't want her to know where she's being held. She might figure out a way to signal that man of hers."

"Can't we just keep her hid in the woods till it gets dark?" Billy Joe butted in.

"That's not a bad idea, Spike," Clem said.

Spike looked as if he were thinking. "You may be right, but we can't leave her here alone. It's a good while till dark, but one of us will have to stay with her."

"You could leave Billy Joe here to watch her. He seems to like her, and I don't think he'd mind doing the job."

Spike grinned. "Is he right? Would you be willing to stay here with her, Billy Joe?"

"Yeah. She's a nice woman. She ain't give me no trouble since I've been watching her."

Spike glanced around and saw Isabella watching. "I like the idee you had about leaving Billy Joe here, but there's something else I need to tell you. Let's ride off to the side where we can talk in private."

Clem looked confused but followed.

In a minute they returned. Spike glared at Isabella and said, "Since you're so interested in what we've been planning, I think you need to get off your mule and rest a while. Me and Clem are going into town for a while. Billy Joe will stay with you."

She started to open her mouth to speak, but he shook his head. "Don't start arguing. I ain't got time to listen to you and your complaints. We'll tell you what's going to happen later."

She turned to Billy Joe. "What's going on?"

He shrugged. "I don't know. Let's just get off these nags and rest while we can, Miss Isabella. They'll tell us what they have planned whenever they want to."

She knew there was no need to ask anything else, but she hoped she wouldn't have to spend the night in these woods with no bedroll and nothing to eat. She also prayed silently that what she was enduring today wasn't causing any harm to her baby.

After watching Clem and Spike ride away, she turned to Billy Joe. "Why did they leave us here instead of letting us go into town with them?"

"I'm not sure, Miss Isabella. Maybe they didn't want nobody to see you in town."

"Please call me Miz Isabella, Billy Joe. I've told you before, I'm a married woman."

He blushed. "I'll try."

"Good. Now, tell me why they don't tell you everything they plan. Don't they trust you?"

He shrugged. "No, ma'am. I guess they think I'm too stupid to know what they're up to."

"Why in the world would they think that?"

He shrugged again. "I don't know why. They just do."

"Then maybe they have another reason."

"I don't think so. They tell me all the time I'm too stupid to know anything. They've always said I'm not as smart as they are." He changed the subject. "I got a blanket, Miss...I mean, Miz Isabella. I'll give it to you to put on the ground to sit on while we wait for them, then I'll go hobble the horses."

She laughed. "Good luck with my *horse*."

He laughed too. "I'm sorry Spike got you a mule to ride. I wouldn't have done that."

"It has been an experience riding him." She smiled at him and took a seat on the blanket he spread near a tree. Her thoughts were reeling. It did seem the other kidnappers didn't trust Billy Joe with anything except simple jobs. She was thankful they thought him capable of looking after her, because he was the nicest of the three. She couldn't help wondering if there was some way she could turn this to her advantage.

When he returned, he held a hardtack biscuit out to her. "I keep some of this in my saddlebag. I know it ain't much, but I thought you might be hungry. I got some water in the canteen, too, if'en you're thirsty."

"Thank you, Billy Joe. I thought we might not get anything more to eat today."

"I don't know if we will or not because I don't know when they'll be back. They didn't tell me."

"Have a seat, Billy Joe. I want to ask you something."

He hesitated a minute, then sat on the grass beside the blanket.

She nibbled on the hardtack, then asked, "Why do you let Spike and Clem push you around the way they do?"

He dropped his head. "I guess 'cause they're smarter than me."

"I don't know about that, Billy Joe. You seem to be pretty smart to me."

He blushed. "Thank you, Miz Isabella."

"It's true. The only thing I don't understand is why you helped them kidnap me."

"I didn't want to, but I had to."

"What do you mean?"

"Spike told me I had to do it."

"Do you do everything Spike tells you to do?"

He nodded. "Yeah. Pretty much."

"Why, Billy Joe?"

He shrugged. "I guess 'cause I've always been told I had to listen to Spike. He ain't as big as I am, but he's three years older."

She wrinkled her brow. "How old are you, Billy Joe?"

"Fifteen or sixteen, I think."

"You don't know?"

"Not really. When I come to live with Uncle Ollie, he said I was three years younger than Spike and I had to let him guide me."

"So, your uncle Ollie is the one who told you you had to listen to Spike?"

"Yeah."

"Has he always told you that?"

"Yeah," he said again.

"Why?"

"I guess 'cause he says if I don't listen to him and Spike, I'd have to leave Gomer and find somewhere else to live. I don't know where I could go. I've lived with them since I was six or seven years old."

"Why do you live with them, Billy Joe? Where were your parents?"

"Uncle Ollie told me my ma was a whore and she dumped me on him 'cause she thought I was dumb and she didn't want me no more 'cause I got in the way when she had customers. I don't know who my pa was."

Isabella couldn't help feeling sorry for this young man. Still, she knew she couldn't let him get away with what he'd done to her. When they were caught, she just didn't want him to be punished as harshly as Clem and Spike would be, and she decided she'd do what she could to help him get a lighter sentence. After all, if he was only fifteen or sixteen years old, he shouldn't have to be punished as much as the older boys were.

Eleven

Two hours later, the sheriff glanced at Kerley and noticed the relieved look on his face. "It looks like your wife is doing all right."

Kerley nodded. "I'm glad. It does look like that young fellow is trying to do what he can to make her feel comfortable."

"I know it relieves your mind." Amos stood from the hiding place they'd taken in the bushes surrounding the area where Isabella and her kidnapper were camped. "Shall we head in and rescue her now?"

"I'm ready."

They eased into the opening and Sheriff Amos Reynolds yelled, "Get your hands up."

Billy Joe started sputtering and stood, throwing his hands in the air.

Isabella let out a little scream, then she saw Kerley. Jumping up, she ran to him. "I'm so glad to see you."

He folded an arm around her. "Are you all right? Did they hurt you?"

"I'm fine now that you're here."

He leaned down and kissed her forehead.

"Don't you hurt Miz Isabella," Billy Joe shouted.

She glanced at him and saw the sheriff securing his hands behind him. "It's all right, Billy Joe. This is my husband."

He seemed to relax. "Then I guess it's all right if he touches you."

The sheriff frowned and Kerley lifted an eyebrow. They both looked confused.

Isabella smiled at him. "Billy Joe has been good to me. He's protected me from the others, and he's tried to make me as comfortable as he could."

"Where are the others?"

"I don't know. They left us here some time ago and rode off toward town."

"Do you know why they left you two here?" The sheriff asked Billy Joe.

"No. But I know Spike is gonna be mad at me for letting you come and get us. I hope he don't beat me up too bad."

"So your friends are coming back?" the sheriff asked.

"They said they was, and they told me to wait here with Miz Isabella."

Kerley pulled Isabella closer to him and whispered, "Is he slow or something?"

"Don't be too harsh with him. He's been told he's stupid so many times he believes it, and yes, I think he might be just a little slow, too. Of course they take advantage of him."

"You amaze me, Isabella."

"How do I do that?"

"You've been kidnapped and only you know what you've gone through, but what do you do when I find you? You're concerned about one of the kidnappers, not about yourself."

"I'm delighted you've found me, and I can't wait to get back to town, but besides being away from you, there are only two things that are really bothering me."

"What's that?"

"One is that I heard them talking and I learned Uncle William is somehow involved in my kidnapping. I don't know how, but I hear them bring up his name now and then."

"I'll talk to the sheriff about that, and we'll see if we can find out what's going on with him. What is the second thing that bothers you?"

She gave him a shy smile. "Spike made me ride a mule today and I'm sore."

Kerley chuckled. "If I'd been sure I'd find you today, I would've brought Moonstar."

"I'm just thankful you looked for me."

"Did you think I wouldn't?"

"I hoped you would."

"Then, let's head to town. It looks like Amos has his prisoner ready to go." He hugged her again. "If you want me to, I'll ride the mule and you can have my horse."

She looked up at him. "You'd really do that?"

"I would."

She shook her head. "You're a good man, Kerley McFarland, but you don't have to ride the mule. I've rode him this far and I can make it into town on him."

"I've got a better idea."

"What's that?"

He winked at her. "Since it feels pretty good to have you in my arms again, I think you should ride on Shadow with me, and we'll lead the mule back to town."

She looked into his eyes and smiled. "I like that idea, Mr. McFarland."

The sheriff cleared his throat. "If you two are through deciding where you're going to ride, let's head into town. I've got more kidnappers to arrest."

Kerley laughed and put Isabella in the saddle in front of him. "We're ready. Let's go."

They hadn't gone far when he looked down at her. "Are you riding all right?"

"Yes, Kerley. Now that you've found me, I'm fine. Of course, Billy Joe wasn't ever mean to me. In fact, he's only done what the others have told him to do."

He pulled her tighter to him. "You don't know how relieved I am that they didn't take advantage of you."

"I'm not so sure they wouldn't have if Billy Joe hadn't kept reminding them my uncle said he'd not pay them if they sullied me."

"And you don't know what your uncle had to do with this kidnapping?"

"I'm not exactly sure, but from what I picked up, I think he's either paying them to bring me back to Nebraska or to keep me hidden until he shows up here to collect me. I figure he's still trying to make sure I marry Fenton Pyle."

"He is sure determined to get you married to that Pyle fellow, isn't he? He's probably going to be mad when he learns it's too late for him to pull off his plan, since you're now a married woman."

"I've been thinking about his determination that I marry his neighbor. I know he told me he was pushing me into the marriage because he wants to save the Greely name from my sin of having a baby, but I'm beginning to wonder if there isn't some other reason behind it."

"What do you mean?"

"I'm not sure. It's just that if saving the Greely name was his real goal, he should've been satisfied when he learned Dale and I were married. At least I thought we were, and I figured nobody in Nebraska would question that fact when we returned. Uncle William had even seen Dale's grave, so he knew about his death."

"Most any reasonable man would have accepted your story."

"I thought so. It was like he actually had another reason for making me marry Fenton Pyle. I just can't figure out what that reason could be."

"Well, whatever it is, or was, it's too late now." He smiled down at her. "You're married to me and there's nothing he can do to change that."

She frowned. "Are you sure?"

"Positive."

"Thank you, Kerley."

He winked at her and pulled her closer to him, but he didn't say anything else.

~ * ~

The door to the jail opened and Kerley walked in. Amos looked up. "Did you get your wife settled in the hotel?"

"I did. At first, she didn't want to stay there alone, but when I gave her a gun and told her to shoot anybody she didn't know who tried to come through the door, she said she'd be all right."

"Think she will be?"

"Hope so, but I want to get those other two rascals behind bars, then get back to her as quickly as I can."

"I understand. Let's go."

Kerley followed him out the door. "Where are we going?"

"Billy Joe told me he was sure I'd find them in the saloon because they liked to hang out there when they were in town."

"He was that cooperative?"

Amos nodded. "I have a feeling Billy Joe only does whatever Spike tells him to do. The thing is, the guy stops at doing anything really bad. He even said he liked Mrs. McFarland and told the others they better not hurt her, or they wouldn't get paid."

"Isabella said something to that effect. I think she liked him better than the others."

They reached the door to the Pickle Barrel Saloon and stepped inside. "Say, you're sure you'll recognize those men?"

"No problem at all. That's them over there in the back corner. Looks like they're not paying any attention to anyone except those women with them."

"That's Apple Betty and Peaches on their laps. The owner has a thing about naming all his girls after fruit." Amos kind of laughed and added, "Shall we break up the party?"

"I'm ready."

They ambled over to the table in the corner and Amos said, "How about you girls beating it. We have a little business with these fellows."

The woman with black hair looked at him and smiled. "Sure, Sheriff. Anything you say."

"Aw, you ain't got to go nowhere. I wanna talk to you, not these men."

The blonde patted Spike's greasy brown hair. "Don't worry, baby. When you finish your business with them, Apple Betty and me will come right back to entertain you."

As the women walked off, Clem said, "Why are you bothering us, Sheriff? We ain't done nothing that should concern you."

"It doesn't concern me directly."

"Then why the hell are you here?" Spike blurted.

"I came to save your lives."

Both Spike and Clem frowned.

"What do you mean by that?" Clem asked.

"This quiet fellow standing here beside me is in a mood to kill you both. I tagged along with him because I didn't want a murder in my town tonight."

"We ain't done nothing to him," Spike snapped, but his eyes said differently.

Kerley reached out and grabbed Spike's collar, pulling him from the chair. "You kidnapped my wife, you good for nothing bastard. I may kill you, even if the sheriff is here."

"You ain't got no wife," Clem said. "Her uncle said she weren't married."

"I don't care what he said. She's married to me."

Spike looked confused. "But she's gonna marry that other feller."

"The hell she is."

"The bartender is giving us the eye. I don't think he likes the fact these guys are beginning to talk so loud. Maybe we better take them to my office where I can question them."

Clem leaned back and put his arms across his chest. "I ain't going nowhere."

"Then I guess I better put the cuffs on you."

"Don't do that." Spike looked worried. "We'll go with you. Come on, Clem."

"I don't want to go," Clem groaned. "Peaches is coming back, and I want to spend some more time with her."

"Forget Peaches," Amos said. "Now, stand up and let's go."

Kerley put his hand on his gun. "You'll either listen to the sheriff or I'll put a bullet in you right now."

"You better listen. I'm not sure I can control him much longer."

"But..."

"Damn it, Clem. I've seen this fellow shoot. Besides, it won't take long to answer their questions, then we'll come back here and get the women."

"Don't count on it," Kerley muttered, but he didn't say it loud enough for them to hear.

~ * ~

Isabella jumped out of the chair and eased to the hotel room door when there was a knock. "Who is it?"

"It's me. Kerley."

She opened the door and fell into his arms as he stepped through the door.

He pulled her close and kicked the door shut with his foot. "What's wrong, honey?"

"I was scared."

"I see you're still dressed, and you have the gun in your hand." He was gentle when he slipped it away from her.

She didn't notice. "I kept hearing funny noises and I was afraid something would happen to you, and I don't know what I would do without you."

"You don't have to worry about that, Isabella. I'm here and I intend to stay here as long as the Good Lord will let me." He eased her to the bed and sat, pulling her down beside him. "I didn't mean to be gone so long, but those boys were stubborn. It took a while to get the story out of them."

"Will they come back here?"

He smiled at her. "No, Isabella. They're all locked up in jail and they'll stay there until a judge gets here to hold the trial."

She sighed and relaxed a little. "Did they tell you why they kidnaped me, Kerley? I heard them talking about Uncle William. Did he put them up to it?"

"He hired them to find you. He's probably on his way here to get you now."

"Oh, no. I don't want to go back home with him."

"Don't even think such a thing. You'll not go anywhere except to the ranch with me."

She looked up at him. "Are you sure?"

"I'm positive." He kissed her forehead. "Now, why don't you put on your nightgown, and we'll go to bed. I'm sure you're exhausted."

"I am tired, but I'd like to get a bath before I go to bed if I could."

"I think I'd feel better with a bath, too. I'll go make arrangements for one a—"

"I don't want you to leave me."

"I won't be gone long."

"I know, but, well I guess it'll be all right."

He stood and took her hand. "Tell you what. Why don't you come with me?"

Her face brightened. "Thank you."

An hour later, they were in bed. He pulled her into his arms. "Are you feeling better?"

"Much better." She cuddled against him, then gave a sudden jerk.

"What's wrong?"

"I'm fine. I'm just having twinges in my stomach every now and then."

"How long has this been going on?"

"A day or two. It got worse while I was riding the mule today."

"I know one thing we're going to do tomorrow morning. We're going to find a doctor. I want to make sure you're really going to be fine."

"I don't think that'll be necessary, Kerley. I just need a good night's sleep and a little more rest than I've been getting. The bed in the cabin had an uncomfortable straw mattress. I actually thought I heard insects in it at times."

"I'm sorry you had to go through such a thing, Isabella."

"As I said, now that I'm back with you, everything will be fine, and we can head to your ranch in the morning."

"We'll not be going anywhere until the doctor says you can travel."

"But..."

"Don't argue with me. If you must, say you seeing a doctor is necessary for my piece of mind." He pulled her closer. "Now, relax and go to sleep. I know you need a good night of rest."

She obeyed him and in a matter of minutes she was sound asleep.

Twelve

Isabella stood by as Kerley thanked Doctor Basil Stoddard for seeing his wife, and paid the nurse, Emma, who happened to also be the doctor's wife. He then ushered Isabella out of the office. "I'm a little hungry. Would you like to try that little café down the street and see what they're serving for dinner?"

Isabella tried to smile at him and failed. "That will be fine."

He smiled at her. "Don't be upset, Isabella. "Everything will be fine."

"You're not mad?"

"No. I'm not mad."

She looked up at him. "I know the doctor came to talk to you after he examined me. I'm sorry to be so much trouble for you, Kerley."

"I had a feeling last night something like this would happen and I've thought of what we can do. We'll talk about it over our meal."

Isabella only nodded, but she couldn't help wondering what he meant. Was he going to leave her here in this town? Was he going to tell her that the marriage was a mistake, and he was going to divorce her so he could get back to his real life on his Texas ranch?

They reached the café and Kerley held the door for her. The place wasn't busy, and she wondered if it was because it was a little early for dinner or if the food here wasn't very good. It was too late to go back to the hotel to eat, so she let him lead her to a table near a window looking out onto the main street.

A young waitress approached them. "Hello, folks. My name is Liza and I'll be waiting on you. Our special today is beef, cabbage, mashed potatoes and carrots with biscuits or cornbread. Of course, all the coffee you can drink."

"That sounds good to me." He looked at Isabella. She nodded and he added, "Bring us two specials."

"All right. Can I get you some coffee to drink while your plates are being prepared?"

"I'll have that coffee you mentioned and I'm guessing my wife would prefer tea."

Isabella nodded again and the girl hurried off.

As soon as she brought their drinks and they were alone again, Kerley said, "It doesn't look like we can leave to go to the ranch for a while. The doctor told me it would be dangerous for you to travel in your condition."

"Maybe he was wrong."

He shook his head. "We can't take that chance. I know you don't want anything to happen to you or your baby and neither do I. So, if you agree, I've decided what we'll do."

She said a silent prayer, *"Oh, please, God. Don't let him say he's going to leave me here."* Aloud she said, "What's that?"

"When Amos Reynolds said we needed to stay here until your kidnappers are tried and sentenced, he also told me there was a boarding house on the street behind the general store. He said the lady that ran it was nice and he knew they had good food because he'd eaten there. He thought you might feel safer there than you do in the hotel, and I agree. But I want to know what you think."

"It sounds fine, Kerley." Her heart began to beat faster. *'If he's going to leave me, at least I know something about boarding houses.*

"I'm glad you like the idea. After we finish eating, we'll go look it over and if it's as nice as Amos said, we'll move there this afternoon."

"Does that mean you'll stay there with me?"

He frowned. "Of course. Did you think I'd leave you there alone?"

Before she could answer, their food arrived.

When the waitress left, she looked at him. "I'm sorry, Kerley. It's just that the only two men I've ever trusted have let me down."

"You're talking about my brother and your uncle, aren't you?"

"Yes."

"Then I guess it's up to me to prove to you there are men in the world you can trust, and I'm one of them." She blushed and he added, "I will tell you this. Believe it or not, you're one of the few women I've trusted since my mother died."

"Really. I thought you'd had a lot of good women in your life."

He shook his head. "I'll tell you my story sometime, but not now. Let's dig into this food and see if it tastes as good as it smells. Then we'll go check out that boarding house."

She was curious about his comment, but she only nodded and picked up her fork. The food turned out to be very good.

~*~

Isabella liked the looks of the Yellow Door Boarding house the minute it came into sight. "Oh, Kerley. Look. It has pretty flowers leading up to the front steps and there are rocking chairs on the front porch. It looks like such a homey and comfortable place."

He cocked his head to the side. "I don't think I've ever seen a yellow door on a house."

"I haven't either, but it's pretty."

"I guess it's all right. I just hope it'll be a better place to stay than the hotel. Not that it was bad, but I know you weren't comfortable there and the clerk sure liked to know what was going on all the time."

"I admit he was nosy, but I'm kind of glad. I felt a little safer when he made it clear he was going to make sure nobody got in my room after you rescued me."

"I don't want you worrying about that. All the men who wanted to kidnap you are behind bars and will stay there until the trial, then they'll be sent to prison."

She frowned. "May I confess something, Kerley?"

"What in the world do you need to confess?"

"I kind of don't want Billy Joe to go to prison. The boy said he was only fifteen or sixteen years old, and I don't think he's really a bad person. I believe that a little while in jail is all the punishment he needs. As I told you, he didn't have much of anything to do with the kidnapping, and he was good to me while he watched me. In fact, I think he was on the verge of letting me go when you and the sheriff found us."

He swallowed. "As much as I'd like to see them all hang for their crime, I think you could explain all of this to the sheriff or the judge when he gets here. One of them might be able to get Billy Joe a reduced sentence."

"Oh, that would be wonderful."

They reached the steps, and he took hold of her elbow and ushered her across the wide front porch to the front door of the pretty white house. "I see where this place gets its name, though, like I said, I don't think I've ever seen a yellow door."

"It's welcoming, isn't it?"

He opened the door. "If you say so."

"Hello there." The short little woman with graying hair greeted them with a warm smile. "I'm Willie Mae Monroe. How can I help you nice-looking folks?"

Kerley removed his hat. "I'm Kerley McFarland, and this is my wife, Isabella. We'd like to see about renting a room for a couple of weeks."

She smiled at them. "I can tell a happy couple when I meet them, and I have just the right room for you. Come this way and I'll show it to you."

"Thank you, Miz Monroe," Isabella said.

"Oh, honey. Call me Willie Mae. Everybody does." She waved her hand and came around the counter of the reception desk. "Now, please follow me. The room I have in mind is at the end of the hall at the top of the stairs."

"May I ask you something, Willie Mae?"

"Of course you can, young man."

Kerley smiled. "I kind of like your front door but I wondered why it was painted yellow."

She laughed out loud. "That's a simple question to answer. Yellow was my husband's favorite color and he painted it that way before he died. He said as long as it stayed yellow there would always be sunshine in our house. I keep it painted that color in his memory and when I turned my home into a boarding house, I named it for the door."

"That's a wonderful story, Willie Mae."

"Thank you, Mrs. McFarland."

"Now wait a minute. If you want me to call you Willie Mae, you must call me Isabella."

"Thank you, Isabella. Now, let's go see the room I think is the one for you."

As soon as they stepped into the large room, she knew Willie Mae was right. It was the perfect room with its high poster bed, white curtains, matching spread, comfortable blue chairs, and plush rug.

"It's beautiful, Willie Mae," Isabella whispered.

"I thought you'd like it, dear. Now, if you go through that door on the left, you'll find a private bath area. It has its own hip tub and water pitcher stand. There are some towels on the shelf beside the window."

"Oh, Kerley. Isn't it lovely?"

"It is nice. Do you think you'll be comfortable here?"

"Oh, yes."

"My wife likes it, so we'll take it, Miz Monroe."

"Willie Mae."

"Yes, ma'am. Willie Mae." He grinned. "I do have one question. Is there a stable around where we could leave our horses?"

"I do have one. It's in the back, but it isn't used a lot, so I don't know what condition you'll find it in. You're welcome to put your horses there, but I'm afraid you'll have to get your own supply of feed. Since my husband died, I don't keep it up like I should because most of my customers leave their horses at the livery."

"Feed's no problem. I'll get the supplies our mounts will need and move them to the stable later." Turning to Isabella, he said, "Since you seemed pleased, would you like to stay here while I go check out of the hotel and bring our belongings over?"

Willie Mae answered for her. "Of course she will. She's got no business traipsing around town carrying suitcases in her condition. You go on and take care of things and Isabella will come down to the parlor. I'll make her a nice cup of tea and we'll get acquainted."

He glanced at Isabella and she nodded. "Then, shall we go downstairs and let Willie Mae get us signed in?"

Willie Mae waved her hand. "We can take care of that when you get back. Now go on with you and don't worry about your wife. I'll see she's taken care of."

Without warning, he smiled at Isabella, leaned over, and kissed her forehead. "If it's all right with you, then I'll go. But I'll be back in a little while."

"I'll be fine, Kerley." She knew she was telling the truth. For the first time since the kidnapping, she felt as if she were in a safe place.

He left and Willie Mae laughed. "Honey, you've got yourself a good man there. You better hang on to him."

"I'm going to try to do that because I agree. He is a good man."

"Makes my heart want to pitter-patter to see a young couple in love like the two of you." She turned toward the door. "Now, come along and I'll brew that tea I promised you."

"You don't have to do that, Miz...I mean, Willie Mae."

"Don't mind doing it at all. Fact is, I'm looking forward to a cup of it myself. As I said, it'll give us a chance to get better acquainted."

Isabella smiled and followed the woman out the door. For the first time, she felt safe without Kerley by her side.

~ * ~

Only about an hour had passed when Kerley rode Shadow into the backyard of the boarding house and saw Willie Mae step out on the porch and toss a pan of water to the yard. He was leading Moonstar. He waved to the woman, and she motioned for him to ride near the porch. "Yes, ma'am," he said when he was close enough."

"When you get your horses settled, come in the back door. Isabella is in the kitchen with me, and you'll save me a trip to the front room to let you in."

"I'll do it."

She nodded and turned back into the house.

Kerley proceeded to the small but adequate barn. He was glad to find it clean. At least he wouldn't have to muck out the stalls before turning the horses in them. Glad the livery keeper had already fed and brushed the animals, all he had to do was to make sure they had plenty of water and a few oats for the evening and those he had stopped at the feed store and bought.

Finishing with the animals, he went out the door, picked up the bag Isabella's clothes were in and the saddle bags he'd stashed on the bench outside the barn. As he headed to the house, he wondered if he should knock before entering but decided not to. After all, Willa Mae had told him to come inside by the back door.

Opening the door, he stepped into the kitchen and saw Isabella standing at the worktable mixing dough in a big wooden bowl. "I hope that bread will be as good as the pan bread you fed me on our trek to Edisonville."

She smiled at him. "I hope these biscuits will be much better, because I didn't have to make them with water. Willie Mae had milk."

"I hope you like fried chicken, Kerley," Willie Mae said. "I'm fixing it because it's my son-in-law's favorite, and he and my daughter are coming to supper tonight."

"I love fried chicken and I'm sure yours will be wonderful."

She laughed. "Oh, my goodness. You sure are a flatterer, aren't you?"

He winked at her. "Only with pretty women."

"Lord have mercy, Isabella. I do believe you've going to have your hands full with him."

"You're sure right about that, Willie Mae." She looked at him. "Why don't you take our belongings to our room, and I'll come up as soon as I finish the bread."

He hesitated. "Maybe I should check us in first."

Willie Mae shook her head. "Go ahead. We'll take care of that later."

He waited only a minute, then said, "Do you mind if I come back and get a cup of coffee?"

"I figured you were waiting around for some reason." Willie Mae laughed. "Go on to your room and I'll send one up with your wife for you."

"That sounds good." He winked at her again. "You're a good woman, Willie Mae. I bet your husband was a happy man."

"He sure was. In fact, you remind me of him when he was young. Now, go on with you."

"I'm on my way and thank you for that compliment." He went out the door and hoped Isabella wouldn't be far behind with the coffee.

She wasn't.

Kerley smiled at her when she entered the room with a big mug of hot coffee. "That smells mighty good."

"Willie Mae said she keeps a pot on the stove most all the time and that you could help yourself anytime you felt the need to indulge."

"That's great. I'm sure I'll take advantage of it." He took a sip of the steaming brew. "Tell me something. Why were you helping Willie Mae with the cooking?"

"While we were having tea, she said she was having her family for supper. When I asked her if I could help her out, she wanted to know if I was any good at making biscuits. I told her I was pretty good, and I'd be happy to make some for supper."

"I sure am looking forward to the biscuits. Along with chicken, they're one of my favorite foods, too."

She smiled. "Is there any food you don't like, Kerley?"

He frowned. "To be honest, I can't think of anything right off."

She stood. "I better get my clothes out of the bag and hang them in the wardrobe. I'm sure they're wrinkled."

"Since Willie Mae is having company for supper, should we go to the café to eat?"

"No. She said she wanted us to meet her daughter and her husband."

"Did she tell you anything about them?"

"Nothing except that her daughter is an only child, and she likes her son-in-law. They've only been married about six months, so there aren't any children yet. But Willie Mae says there is one on the way and she can't wait to be a grandmother."

"She has one of the best attitudes I've ever seen. She must have always had a happy family around her to make her feel the way she does."

"I don't know, Kerley. She alluded to the fact something terrible had happened in her past but when I asked her about it, she changed the subject."

"That's odd, since she's so talkative about everything else."

"I know, but I guess we all have a right to a few secrets." She turned from the wardrobe. "I think I'll change from this skirt and blouse to my yellow dress. I want to make a good impression on Willie Mae's daughter and her husband."

"If it's that important to you, do you want me to change shirts?"

"No, Kerley. You look handsome just the way you are."

He sat his empty mug aside and stood. "Handsome, huh?"

She blushed. "Well..."

"Never mind." He smiled at her. "You look great to me, but if you want to change, go ahead. I'll go downstairs and get us registered. I want to sample Willie Mae's fried chicken before we get thrown out of here for not signing in and paying our bill."

She returned his smile, then headed to the bathroom to change her dress as he went out the door.

Thirteen

The back door to the boarding house opened and a female voice called, "Are you in the kitchen, Mama?"

Willie Mae came out of the pantry. "Come on in, Charlotte. I was hunkered down looking for my special cobbler pan."

"Did you find it?"

"Yep. I know how much you all like my peach cobbler, so I thought I'd whip one up." She put the big blue pan on the worktable. "Where's Amos?"

"He had something he had to clear up at the office, so I told him I'd meet him here."

"Well, have a seat. The baked beans are about ready to come out of the oven and you know it doesn't take too long to bake the cobbler."

Charlotte sat on one of the stools at the worktable. "Is there anything I can do to help?"

"No. You just rest. I know it probably tired you out to walk over here."

"I declare, Mama. You're just like Amos. You'd think I was the only woman in town to ever have a baby."

"Well, you are having my grandbaby and I want to make sure it gets here safely."

Kerley walked through the door. "I'm sorry to interrupt, Willie Mae."

"No problem, Kerley. Come in and meet my daughter." She turned toward Charlotte. "Honey, this is Kerley McFarland. He and his wife are going to be staying here for a while."

"Hello, Mr. McFarland."

Kerley nodded at her. "Howdy, ma'am."

"Where's Isabella?" Willie Mae asked.

"She decided she wanted to change clothes before supper. She'll be down in a minute."

Willie Mae laughed. "She didn't have to do that. We're pretty informal here."

"When did you check in, Mr. McFarland?"

He set his empty coffee mug on the table. "Actually, that's why I came down before my wife. We just got here this afternoon and I haven't yet signed us in or paid your mother and I wanted to do it."

"There'll be time for that after supper, Kerley. I don't want to leave the kitchen to get the paperwork done right now. Something might burn." She waved toward the parlor. "Why don't I get you another cup of coffee and you can wait in the parlor until supper is ready?"

Before he could answer, the back door opened again, and Amos Reynolds came into the kitchen. He frowned. "Kerley. I see you decided to come to the boarding house. Is your wife with you, or you just checking it out?"

"Actually, we're not officially checked in, but my wife is upstairs in the room we've been given changing her dress."

The women looked at them. "Do you two know each other?" Charlotte asked.

"Sure do. You know I told you I was helping a man find his wife because somebody grabbed her at the hotel."

"Don't tell me this is him?"

"It is."

Charlotte turned to him. "Oh, my goodness. She must have been frightened. Is she all right now that she's safe?"

Kerley nodded. "She's fine. Believe it or not, one of the outlaws made sure she was protected from the others. But she didn't want to stay in the hotel any longer. I'm glad Amos suggested this place because she likes it a lot."

Isabella appeared at the door and Charlotte jumped up and hurried to her. "Oh, Mrs. McFarland. I'm so glad you're all right. Amos told me what a terrible ordeal you've had."

Isabella looked stunned at the woman's concern, but managed to mutter, "Thank you for asking. I'm fine now."

Willie Mae took over. "All right, now. My kitchen is getting too crowded. All of you go into the parlor and get acquainted, and I'll call you to the table when supper is ready."

"Let's go, everyone. When my mother-in-law speaks, I listen."

Laughing, they left the kitchen and trooped into the parlor, where they fell into a conversation that convinced them they'd be well acquainted by the time they ate their meal.

~ * ~

Isabella sat at the dressing table brushing her hair as Kerley sat on the side of the bed to remove his boots. Turning her head to the side, she said, "I enjoyed supper with Charlotte and Amos."

"I noticed you and Charlotte seemed to become instant friends."

"Maybe it was because we're both going to be mothers at about the same time."

"That could have had a lot to do with it."

"I was surprised to learn you and Amos were such good friends."

"Though I like the man, I don't know if you'd call us friends. We got to know each other pretty well while we were searching for you." He stood and unbuttoned his shirt. "You about ready to go to bed?"

"I am." She laid her brush down and stood. "I didn't mean to hold you up."

As soon as she climbed into bed, Kerley blew out the lamp, removed the rest of his clothes, then climbed into bed beside her. "I didn't mean to rush you, Isabella. I guess I was only anxious to try out this bed we have yet to pay for."

She giggled. "Willie Mae doesn't seem to be in a hurry to take your money, does she?"

"Amos said she'd get around to it in her own time. He also said it shows she trusts us, and she doesn't always trust people who come here to rent a room. In fact, she doesn't rent to many people. If she doesn't like them on sight, she tells them she's full-up even if there are no guests at the time."

"She probably doesn't make much money doing that. In Omaha, Kathleen and her mother took most any guest who came for a room at their place."

"I learned Willie Mae only turned her home into a boarding house when Amos and Charlotte moved into the house behind the jail that the town furnishes for the sheriff and his family."

"In that case, I'm surprised he suggested we come here."

"He didn't tell me it belonged to his mother-in-law, but he is aware of her habits. He knew she wouldn't rent to us if she didn't like us and I'm sure he thought it better we not know he was related."

She yawned. "I guess he didn't want our feelings to be hurt if she turned us down."

"You may be right."

She yawned again. "Looks like I'm getting sleepy, so I'm going to say good night."

Kerley had something else he wanted to talk to her about and was a little disappointed she didn't want to talk longer. He decided he'd have to wait to tell her later, because this news was going to take a while. "Good night, Isabella."

~ * ~

Two days later, the stagecoach stopped at its usual place near Edisonville's only hotel. A middle-aged couple disembarked and looked around. "I'm glad that at least they let us out close to the hotel, such as it is. They say that doesn't always happen in these awful Western towns," the man said. There was a sneer in his voice.

"The hotel's not a very fancy place, sir," the driver said. "But I've stopped in towns where the accommodations are much worse."

"Is this the only place for a traveler to stay in this town?" There was a question in the woman's shaky voice.

The driver said, "There's a nice boarding house on a street down from here. You turn to the right at the general store, and you can't miss it because it has a yellow door. I've stayed there when I had a layover, and the hotel was full. You can't beat the food there."

"Would it be cheaper?" the man asked.

He shrugged. "I wouldn't know. The stage line pays when I have to sleep over, but as they say, you get what you pay for."

"William, if you don't mind, I'm too exhausted to walk very far. Why don't we go register for one night here so I can get a bath and see if I can get some of this dirt and grime off me? If you think we should change places, we can check that boarding house out tomorrow."

"I don't know about that." He picked up the luggage the driver had thrown down and asked, "Tell me again where this boarding house is."

The driver pointed him in the right direction and pulled away with the stage.

"Get your suitcase and let's go, Vassie."

She sighed but did as he told her to do.

~ * ~

Isabella followed Charlotte through the back door into the kitchen of the Yellow Door Boarding House. Willie Mae looked up and grinned. "Were you girls able to find what you needed to make Isabella a dress that isn't getting too tight on her?"

"We did. In fact, we bought her two pieces and me one." Charlotte looked around. "We sure would like a cup of tea if you've got the water hot, Mama."

"I always have hot water. Have a seat and I'll get you a cup."

"Maybe I should go put my material in my room first."

Charlotte sat at the worktable. "I'm sure Mama would like to see it before you do."

"Of course I would."

"All right." Isabella smiled and joined Charlotte at the table.

As Willie Mae poured the tea, the bell in the entry sounded. "Oh, my goodness. I wonder who that could be."

"It might be a customer you like, Mama. You go see and I'll get the honey for the tea."

"I'm not sure I want a customer today." She smiled at them. "I'll see the material when I get back, Isabella. In the meantime, rest up and enjoy your tea."

The little bell on the counter in the entry began to sound as if someone were in a hurry.

"I'm coming. Please quit hitting the bell so hard."

A man and a woman were in the desk area and the man looked around. "It's about time somebody came to wait on us. I'd like to speak with the proprietor about renting a room."

In the kitchen, fright filled Isabella's face.

"What's the matter?" Charlotte asked.

"That sounds like my uncle. Oh, Lord, please don't let it be him."

"Why?"

"I'm afraid he's come to take me away."

"Don't be afraid. I'm sure it'll be all right. Let's listen and see what he says to Mama."

"I happen to be the proprietor." Willie Mae's voice had an icy tone to it.

Charlotte grinned and whispered. "There's not a chance in million he'll rent a room here."

Isabella frowned and wondered why but she didn't say anything.

The man said. "I might have known this place was run by a woman. Why else would it have a name like Yellow Door Boarding House? Only a woman would give a place of business such a silly name."

"I'll have you know my husband liked the name."

"Never mind about that. My wife and I need a room until we find our niece. We may be here for a night or so. How much do you charge?"

"Three dollars a night for a couple. Two more if you take your meals here."

"Five dollars a night! That's outrageous."

"Then you should go to the hotel. I understand they only charge a dollar a night."

"That's still too much."

"Well, here and the hotel are your only choices in this town, unless you want to sleep on the street. Besides that, The Yellow Door Boarding House happens to be full right now and I don't have a room to rent you and your wife at any price."

"You wouldn't happen to know any good Christian family in town who would put up a Christian man and his wife for the night, would you?"

"No, I don't. Now, please leave. I have to get back to my kitchen and cook supper for the guests because they expect their meals on time."

"Then I guess I have no choice."

"I'm so tired, William. I don't know if I can walk all the way back to the hotel," his wife said. "Can't we rest a minute?"

"Don't be such a complainer, Vassie," he snapped. "Come on. We've got no choice but go back to the hotel." He turned and went out the door, and without a word, she followed.

"Oh, Charlotte. What am I going to do?"

"I don't understand, Isabella. What's going on?"

Willie Mae came back into the kitchen. "I've never...Why are you crying, Isabella?"

Charlotte answered for her. "She said that voice belonged to her uncle, then she burst into tears. She's afraid of him for some reason."

Through tears, Isabella muttered, "I need to find Kerley. Do you know where he went?"

"Calm down, honey. He said something about going to look at some ranch this morning, but I'm sure he'll be back soon." Willie Mae put her arm around her. "Now come sit down and tell us what's going on with you."

Isabella didn't tell them the real story, but said, "Uncle William doesn't believe Kerley and I are married, and he wants me to marry his neighbor."

Charlotte frowned. "That doesn't make any sense. He can't make you marry somebody else when you're already married."

Isabella changed the subject. "I can't believe he brought Aunt Vassie with him, but thank you for not renting them a room."

"I felt a little sorry for her, but I knew right off he wasn't the kind of customer I want here, and I figured his mouse of a wife wasn't enough to make me change my mind."

"Please tell us what's going on, Isabella." Charlotte touched her arm. "We want to help."

"Thank you, but I can't talk right now. I want to go to my room and wait for Kerley."

"But..."

"Let her go, Charlotte." Willie Mae picked up the cloth and handed it to her. "You go on to your room, honey. We'll make sure nobody bothers you until Kerley gets back."

"Thank you." On impulse, Isabella gave her a quick hug, then hurried to her room.

Charlotte turned to her mother. "I wonder what that's all about."

"I'm sure she'll tell us when she's ready. In the meantime, do you think Amos would know where Kerley is?"

"I thought he told you he was going to look at some ranch."

"He did, but I thought Amos might know which one. I'd like to get him back here as soon as we can. Isabella is awfully upset."

"Are you saying you want me to go to the office and see what Amos knows?"

"I'll go, if you'll stay here."

"No, Mama. I'll go. If Isabella decides to confide in anyone, I'm sure it would be you, and you need to be here."

"Thank you, honey. I know I can always count on my daughter."

Charlotte kissed her mother's cheek and smiled. "I'll come back and let you know what Amos said."

"Please, do."

~ * ~

Vassie dropped her carpet bag on the floor at the foot of the bed. "This isn't a bad room."

"It should be furnished in gold for the amount it's costing us. We need to find where those men are holding Isabella, pick her up and head back to Nebraska as soon as we can."

131

"I agree, William, but there's nothing we can do tonight. As soon as they bring the hot water up, I intend to wash up then rest for a while."

"I can't believe they wanted to charge me an extra dollar for a bathtub when a pitcher of warm water is supplied without cost."

"I agree with you. It is outrageous, though I would have liked to have a tub bath. But for that money, I can make do with a pan of warm water."

"Of course you can, woman. How often do you get in the bathtub at home?"

She sighed. "I admit, not very often."

There was a knock on the door.

"Who is it?" William shouted.

"It's your warm water, sir."

He opened the door. "Put it on the washstand."

"Yes, sir." The boy placed the pitcher of water on the table, then turned with a smile.

"Well, you've done your job. What are you waiting on?"

"Uh...Nothing, sir."

"Then get out of here."

The boy hurried out of the room.

"I think he expected you to give him a coin for bringing the water, William."

"How dare him expect such a thing. It's places like this that try to take all of a man's money. The sooner we can get out of this town, the better."

She sighed again. "I agree. Now if you'll go see if you can locate Isabella, I'll take my bath and see if I can get some of this grime off me."

"Sometimes I wish I hadn't insisted you come with me, Vassie. You've done nothing but fuss and complain. But when Fenton refused to come, I couldn't find anyone else, and I didn't want to make the trip alone."

She didn't answer, but waited for him to pick up his hat and leave the room. She then removed her hat and sat on the bed to remove her shoes. "You don't know how many times I've wished I had refused to come with you, William Greely. If I didn't believe the Bible verse that a woman should always do what her husband tells her to do, I wouldn't have come, no matter what you said or what you'd have done to me for refusing."

Fourteen

Kerley's heart pounded as he rushed upstairs. He didn't know what he'd find when he got to their room. He knew how terrified Isabella was of her uncle and how she had planned and plotted to get away from him. Now he was in town, and though Kerley knew she had nothing to fear, she wouldn't look at it logically.

Opening the door to the room, he was surprised to see her putting her few clothes in the bag she'd placed on the bed. Hurrying inside, he said, "Why in the world are you packing your clothes, Isabella?"

She dropped the yellow dress to the bed and ran to him. "Oh, Kerley. I'm so glad you're back. Hurry and help me get our things together. My aunt and uncle are here, and we have to get out of town before they find me."

He pushed the bag aside and sat on the bed, pulling her down beside him. "It doesn't matter if they are here or not, you have nothing to fear from them."

"But they'll make me go back to the farm with them."

"Listen to me, Isabella. You're a married woman. It doesn't matter what they want, they can't make you go anywhere you don't want to go."

"But…"

"No, buts, honey. As a matter of fact, if those men in jail tell the sheriff your uncle hired them to kidnap you, he'll be going to jail along with them."

She stared up at him. "Are you sure?"

"I'm positive. Now relax and put your clothes back in the wardrobe. We're not going anywhere."

"But, Kerley, he'll tell everyone about my marriage to Dale and the whole story will come out. Everyone will know my baby is…"

"Don't say it, Isabella. As far as anyone is concerned, you're having my baby."

"Then what will people say when he tells everyone about Omaha?"

"I've got that figured out, too."

"You have?"

"Yes. Now dry your eyes and we'll go downstairs and explain it all to Willie Mae. All you have to do is agree with what I say, and everything will be fine."

She looked doubtful. "I guess I don't have any choice except to believe you."

"That's right."

She gave him a small smile and moved to the water bowl to wash her face.

Downstairs, they found Charlotte and Amos had joined Willie Mae in the kitchen. Willie Mae jumped up and got cups for them. "I have the water hot for Isabella's tea and of course, you want your afternoon cup of coffee, don't you, Kerley?"

"You're a woman after my heart, Willie Mae."

She laughed. "Have a seat at the table and we'll talk."

In a timid voice, Isabella said, "Kerley said he thought you deserved an explanation of why I'm so afraid of my uncle."

Amos nodded. "I admit we're curious. When Charlotte came to the office to find out if I knew where you were, Kerley, she told me how upset Isabella was. Since I didn't know where you were, I decided to come back here to see if I could help."

Kerley said, "I'm glad you did."

Willie Mae served their drinks, then sat. "You don't have to tell us anything, but Amos is right. We sure are curious."

"We want to tell you." Kerley smiled at Isabella, then said, "It all started in Omaha where Isabella was staying at a boarding house her friend Kathleen ran. I had returned to my job as a Texas Ranger and had traced an outlaw to Omaha. It just so happened that my brother, Dale, was staying at Kathleen's boarding house. I got a room there and the minute I laid eyes on Isabella, I knew she was the woman I wanted to marry, and I found out she felt pretty much the same way. Within a week of meeting her, my brother helped arrange the nuptials and our wedding took place in the parlor of the boarding house. We had a three-day honeymoon, then I had to finish my job. I had arrested the outlaw and had orders to take him back to Galveston to stand trial. The whole thing took me almost three months." He paused to take a drink of his coffee, then continued.

"When I got back to Omaha, I found out my brother had been killed by a man who accused him of cheating at cards. Shortly after his death, Isabella's uncle had come to town and forced her to go back home with him where he'd arranged for her to marry a widowed neighbor because he found out she was going to have a baby.

"She kept telling him she was married, but he didn't believe her. He thought she'd had an affair with my brother, and he'd refused to marry her. Anyway, it took me another few weeks to track her down and when I found the farm, I learned Isabella had run away. When I finally caught up with her, we decided to go on to Texas where I planned to buy back the old family ranch. Because her uncle kept planting in her mind that our marriage probably wasn't legal, and since my brother had helped arranged our wedding by getting the preacher, we suspected her uncle could be right and decided to get married again. We liked this town, so we found Preacher Hall and said our vows again here. We had only been married for the second time for one day when those boys kidnapped her, and I guess you know the rest of the story."

"I think we do," Amos said.

"I think you have one of the most romantic stories I've ever heard." Charlotte smiled at them, then tuned to Amos. "Do you love me enough to marry me twice like Kerley did Isabella?"

He put his arm around her shoulder. "You bet I do, sweetheart."

"Well, Isabella," Willie Mae said, "after hearing Kerley tell your story, I don't think you need to be afraid of your uncle any longer. We'll all make sure he doesn't get anywhere near you while he's in town."

"Thank you, Willie Mae."

"I don't think you have a thing to worry about, Isabella. If what the guys in jail are saying is true, I may have to arrest your uncle."

"What are they saying?"

"That he paid them to kidnap you and send him a wire where he could come to pick you up and take you back to his farm."

Kerley reached over and took her hand. "Do you feel better now?"

"Much better. Thank you for telling them our story."

Willie Mae stood. "Well folks, I have a roast in the oven for supper. I need to cook some vegetables and see what kind of dessert I can whip up. I've already learned Kerley likes his sweets as much as Amos does. Why don't you young folks go to the parlor and let me get busy?"

"I appreciate it, but I need to get back to the office, Willie Mae. I have a stack of paperwork I need to do before my deputy decides to do it and messes everything up." He glanced at Charlotte. "We will come back for supper, if my wife wants to."

"Since I haven't cooked anything, we'll eat here. I'll help Mama finish cooking."

"I can help, too."

"No, Isabella. Since you've been so upset, you and Kerley need to spend some time together. Supper will be ready at six-thirty."

"But..."

"Don't argue with me. Now head on back upstairs with your husband."

Isabella blushed and muttered, "If you insist."

As Amos went out the back door, Kerley winked at Willie Mae and ushered Isabella out of the kitchen and toward the stairs to their room.

~ * ~

Amos decided he'd go to the office and question Spike again about Isabella's uncle instead of doing his paperwork. Though Kerley had explained about their marriage, the sheriff wondered if there wasn't more to the story. Pushing the door open, he nodded at his deputy, Brock Weathers, who was at the desk looking at wanted posters.

"Anything exciting happening in Edisonville this afternoon, Brock?"

"It's been pretty peaceful." Brock stood and moved toward the door. "Want me to go get the prisoners' supper before I head home to eat?"

"That'd be good. I'm going to bring the one called Spike in here and ask him some more questions. I think he knows more than he admits."

"Maybe you should question him in front of his friend, Billy Joe."

"Why do you say that?"

"I happened to hear them arguing. Billy Joe says he didn't want to grab the woman in the first place, and he thought he was going to make sure Spike didn't get any money from the uncle because he was going to tell the sheriff everything."

"What was he going to tell me?"

"I don't know. By the time I got in there, Spike had hit him and knocked him down. I put Clem in the cell with Spike and Billy Joe by himself. Then I tried to ask Billy Joe some questions, but he wouldn't talk to me. He laid down on the bunk and turned his back."

"Maybe you're right. I might ought to talk to them together." He frowned. "Or maybe I should talk to Billy Joe alone. He might be willing to tell me what's going on between him and Spike."

"Not a bad idea, Amos. I have one suggestion."

"What's that?"

"Bring him in here to have that conversation. I think he'll come nearer talking to you away from the cell, because all Spike has to do is give him a threatening look and the boy clams up. I don't know what kind of hold Spike has on him, but I gather he's afraid of the guy."

"Then we'll do it that way. You go on and get their supper, and while Spike and the other guy are busy eating, I'll bring Billy Joe in here and talk to him."

"Won't they suspect something?"

"While you're gone, I'll think of a way to do it so they won't know anything is going on."

Amos came up with the perfect plan. When Brock returned with the food, they took the trays into the jail area and gave Spike and Clem theirs. Brock then handed them each a cup of coffee. He turned to give Billy Joe his coffee, but as planned, he let go of the cup too soon and it fell on the cell floor and coffee flowed everywhere.

The two men in the other cell burst into laughter. "Look at that Clem. Billy Joe's still so clumsy he can't even hold on to a cup of coffee."

"I see what you mean," Clem answered as he crammed a forkful of potato into his mouth.

Amos shook his head. "Damn, what a mess, Brock."

"Sorry, boss. I thought the prisoner had it."

Still holding the tray of food, Amos shook his head. "Bring the prisoner in the office and he can eat his supper in there while you mop up this mess."

"Yes, sir."

In the office, Amos placed the tray on the side of his desk. "Pull up that chair and start eating and I'll get you another cup of coffee."

Billy Joe obeyed. "Thank you, sir."

Amos handed him a cup of coffee and poured one for himself, then took a seat behind the desk. "Hope you don't mind eating in here."

"I don't. This way nobody will stick his hand into my cell and take some of my food."

"Somebody does that?"

"Yeah. If there's somethin Spike likes to eat, he makes me give it to him. He says I don't need it and he don't have all he wants to eat."

"That doesn't sound fair."

"I'm used to it." He took a bite of his corn. "Ain't you eatin'?"

"I'll go home and eat later."

"Are you married?"

"I am. I'm also going to be a father soon."

"So, your wife is going to have a baby?"

"Yes, she is."

"Miz Isabella is going to have a baby, too."

"I know. I've met Miz Isabella. She's a nice lady."

Billy Joe nodded. "I like her, but Spike said I had to watch her. I did but I didn't let him hurt her, even if he wanted to."

"Oh. What was he going to do to her?"

"I guess what he does to that woman at Moll's Place."

Amos didn't have to ask what went on at Moll's Place. He knew it must be a house of pleasure. Instead, he asked, "I'm sure Isabella's husband was glad you protected her."

"I guess so." He frowned. "I'm confused, though."

"Why?"

"Spike said Miz Isabella was lying when she said she was married to that man. He said she weren't married. But I think he's wrong. She told me she was married, and I believe her."

"You're smart to believe her. She is married."

Brock came back into the office. "The cell is all cleaned up."

Billy Joe looked at Amos. "Do you want me to go finish eating in there?"

"Nah. No need to move. You might as well finish your meal here."

"By the way," Brock said with a laugh. "Your buddy Spike said to tell you not to eat all of your beef. He said he liked it and wanted some more."

Billy Joe's eyes got big. "But I done eat most of it."

"You need to eat all of it, Billy Joe."

"Oh, Sheriff, I can't. Spike will get mad at me and beat me up as soon as he can."

"Why in the world would Spike do such a thing to you?"

"'Cause I'm stupid and he has to tell me what to do. If'en I don't do it, he'll get Uncle Ollie to run me off and I don't have nowhere else to live."

"Do you live with Spike and your uncle Ollie?" When Billy Joe nodded, Amos added, "How long have you lived with them?"

"I don't know. I was a little boy. I think he said I was six or seven when I come there."

Brock got a cup of coffee and pulled up a chair. "Where are your folks, Billy Joe?"

"I ain't really got no folks. Uncle Ollie told me his sister brought me to him and his wife when I was a little boy. He said my mamma was a whore who didn't want me no longer, 'cause I was dumb, and I hurt her business. He said nobody knows who my papa was."

"What about your uncle Ollie's wife? Didn't she like having a little boy?"

"I don't remember her much, 'cause she died when me and Spike was still little."

Amos gave Brock a knowing look and joined the conversation. "So you lived with your uncle Ollie and your cousin Spike?"

"Yeah. They said as long as I done whatever they told me to do, I could live there. They said if I didn't, they'd throw me out of the house, and they didn't know what would happen to me 'cause I was too stupid to know how to take care of myself."

"So that's why you helped Spike and his friend kidnap Miz Isabella?"

"I didn't want to, but I had to let them do it. I knowed if I didn't, they would kick me out."

"I see."

A sudden look of fright crossed Billy Joe's face. "Oh, my goodness. Look what I've done."

"What have you done, Billy Joe?" Amos asked.

"I was talking and not paying any attention to what I was doing. I eat all the beef, and Spike's gonna kill me for being so dumb."

"I don't think so. I'll not have anybody killing someone in my jail."

"Thank you, Sheriff."

"You're welcome. Now I want you to tell me something, Billy Joe."

"What's that?"

"Why did Spike decide to kidnap Miz Isabella?"

"'Cause her uncle and the other man paid him to get her."

"What other man?"

"The one who said he was going to marry Miz Isabella."

Amos nodded. "I see. Do you know how much they paid Spike to grab Miz Isabella?"

"I don't know. They handed Spike some money and Spike said he'd get Miz Isabella if he paid us fifty dollars apiece. Then Spike give me a dollar and said that was my share and not to expect to get the next fifty. I didn't argue with him 'cause I knowed it wouldn't do no good. I don't know how much of the money Spike give Clem."

"Well, Brock, it looks like Billy Joe has finished his meal. How about taking him back to his cell and gathering the other trays?"

"Sure will."

"What am I doing to tell Spike about the beef?"

"Don't worry about it. Brock will tell him I wouldn't let you take any food back there."

"I hope he'll believe him."

Amos sat back and lit a cigar as they went into the cell area. When Brock appeared with the empty trays, he said, "McFarland's wife is right. Billy Joe doesn't deserve to be punished as much as the other two. He's more like a child who only does what Spike and his uncle tell him to do. They've told him so many times he's stupid he believes it."

"I wish there was something we could do to help the fellow because it seems his only crime is he isn't smart enough to think for himself."

"Probably was never allowed to do so."

"Probably not."

"I'm having supper at Willie Mae's tonight. McFarland and his wife are staying at the boarding house, and I think I might have an idea how we can help the boy. Of course, we'll probably need their help to pull it off."

"Do I need to ask what your idea is?"

"Not until I talk to McFarland."

Fifteen

The next morning, William turned to Vassie. "You've twiddled with your hair long enough. How much longer is it gonna take you to get ready? Do you realize how late it is?"

"I'm hurrying, William. I'll be ready in a minute."

"It's already seven o'clock. If we was still at home, you'd have already finished cooking breakfast and I'd be getting ready to go work in the fields."

"I'm about through pinning up this long hair."

"Make it snappy. I want to get out and find that feller Spike, so I can get Isabella and be on the that stagecoach when it leaves this awful town today."

"Are you sure there's a stage leaving later today?"

"For heaven's sake, Vassie, quit arguing with me. I've already wished a dozen times I hadn't brought you with me."

"I wouldn't have come if you hadn't said I'd have to look after Fenton's young'uns so he could come with you. I figured I didn't want to have to put up with them."

"I don't know if you having to put up with them would be any worse than me putting up with you and all your complaints."

Before she could stop herself, Vassie leaned back and crossed her arms across her chest. "If that's the way you feel about it, why did you bring me? Were you afraid to travel alone?"

Seeing the anger in Vassie's eyes, William took a deep breath. Though he knew he should probably back hand her across her mouth, he decided this wasn't the time to show her he was the head of their household, and he always would be. But right then, he wanted her to help him get Isabella home. Her punishment could wait until they got back to Nebraska. "Calm down, woman. I think I'm just afraid we won't be able to find our niece and get her home before Fenton changes his mind about marrying her."

Vassie relaxed. "I guess we're both nervous about that. I want to get her home as much as you do. The deal you made with Fenton Pyle affects me, too."

He nodded. "You're right. It shore does."

She put her brush down and stood. "Then I'm sorry I was being so lazy this morning. Let's go down and have some breakfast, then we'll see about finding Isabella. Somebody downstairs might even know where she is."

"Then let's go. I have a feeling this is going to be the day we find her." Yes, he was doing the right thing by not correcting his wife now. He'd take care of Vassie's standing up to him later. For the time being, he'd let her think she'd gotten away with sassing him.

But it didn't work out the way he'd hoped. After eating, he escorted Vassie to the general store where he allowed her to buy a handkerchief trimmed in purple pansies only because he wanted to gain the owner's confidence before he asked if he knew Isabella's whereabouts.

Disgusted because he didn't get the answer he wanted, he decided he would find his niece faster if he searched on his own. He sent Vassie back to their room and decided to try the other businesses in town. But he got the same answer at each one. Nobody knew an Isabella Greely or an Isabella McFarland, for that matter.

It was noon and he was hungry and tired. It was time to go back to the hotel and see if Vassie had obeyed him and stayed in their room until he returned. Stepping into the hotel, he walked up to the desk. "Is my wife still in her room?"

"I haven't seen her since you and she came in and went up earlier, so I assume she's still there."

William gave him a disgusted look. "Nobody in this town seems to know where anybody is. I've asked everyone if they've seen my niece, and it don't look like anybody's ever heard of her."

"I'm sorry, sir. Maybe she hasn't been in town."

"I'm sure she has. I got a wire from here saying she turned up here with a man. Of course, I'm sure she wasn't with him because she wanted to be. I'm sure he forced her to come with him."

Millard frowned. "Who is your niece, Mr. Greely?"

"Her name's Isabella Greely."

"I don't know anybody by that name, but Isabella must be a fairly common name."

"Why do you say that?"

"Mr. and Mrs. McFarland stayed here for a couple of nights. Her name was Isabella."

"I bet that's my niece." William became excited. "Where did they go?"

Millard was suddenly nervous. "I'm not supposed to talk about it. I guess that's why nobody in town knows anything about them."

"Listen, man. I came all the way from Nebraska to get my niece." He leaned over the counter and stared at the clerk. "Now, if you know, tell me where she is."

"But the sheriff told me not to say anything. I always do what the law says."

"I don't care what the sheriff said. I just want my niece."

Millard took a deep breath. "I will tell you this. Mrs. McFarland was abducted by some men and her husband rescued her. After they put the men in jail, the McFarlands left the hotel."

"Where did they go?"

"Unless they went to the boarding house a few streets over, I assume they left town."

"That fool. What are his plans for Isabella?"

"I wouldn't know that, sir, but I do know when she was gone, he said he'd tear this town apart to find his wife. He also said he'd kill the men if they'd harmed her or their baby in any way."

Though William wasn't a cussing man, he couldn't help saying, "Damn it! He's not her husband and that's not his baby."

Millard backed up. "If you say so, sir."

"I do say so." He turned toward the stairs without another word.

As he entered the room, he didn't lower his voice. "Let's go, Vassie."

Startled, she dropped the book she was looking at. "Where're we going, William?"

"Don't ask questions. Just obey me."

"Yes, dear."

~ * ~

The stage rumbled into Edisonville early in the afternoon. A tall, well-dressed, middle-aged man climbed out and picked up his carpet bag. He wondered if he should go directly to the Yellow Door Boarding House or if he should find somewhere to eat a late lunch before he contacted the sheriff.

The thought of Willie Mae Monroe's cooking won out. He figured if he told her he hadn't had anything to eat since an early breakfast at one of the stage stops, she'd find him something from the leftover dinner she had probably served to tide him over until supper. He didn't care what she gave him because he knew the upcoming supper would be a treat. Not many of the towns he traveled to had a hotel or a boarding house who had a cook to compete with Miz Willie Mae.

As he entered the door of the boarding house, Willie Mae stepped into the room from the direction of the stairs. A big smile crossed her face. "Well, hello there, Judge Julian Lansing. It's good to see you again."

"It's good to see you, too, Willie Mae Monroe. I hope you have an extra room for me."

"You know I'll always have a room for you, Judge. I'm just sorry to tell you the special room you like upstairs is rented to a lovely couple. But there is one down the hall that I think you'll find suitable."

"I'm sure it will be fine. In fact, I'd take a blanket and sleep on the porch swing just to get to sit at your table at supper today."

She laughed, then moved behind the desk and held the pen out to him. "If you'll be so good as to sign in, I'll show you to the room."

He took the pen and cleared his throat. "I hate to mention this, but I haven't had anything to eat since breakfast. You wouldn't happen to have—"

She waved her hand and interrupted. "Say no more. Follow me to the kitchen and I'll make you a plate to take to your room."

"Oh, Miz Willie Mae, you've just become my best friend for life."

She laughed. "Now, Mr. Julian, I think you told me that the last time you stayed here."

"Then I guess it must be true."

Laughing again, she took down a plate and filled it. "It's a good thing the food is still warm. I won't have to heat it up for you."

"I bet it would taste fine cold."

"Flatterer. Bring your plate and come along and I'll get you to the room. Then I have to start supper. From the way you look, I think I'll have to cook extra tonight."

When Willie Mae left the room, he put the plate on the table beside the window. She had been right. He did like this room. The big bed with its carved headboard and matching carved side table suited his taste, and the blue curtains and spread gave it a touch of softness without looking too feminine.

He was half through his meal when he saw the sheriff walk around the side of the house. He was sure the man was going to come in through the back door. This didn't surprise him because he knew Amos Reynolds had married Willie Mae's daughter. It would be convenient if they would be coming for supper. It would save him a trip to the office to see what trials he'd be presiding over while he was here.

When he finished his meal, he decided he'd take the plate back to the kitchen and see if the sheriff was still there. If he were, they could talk, and he could get his answers. As he stepped into the hall, the door of the big room at the end opened and a lovely young woman stepped out. He decided she must be half of the couple Willie Mae said was occupying the room he usually stayed in.

He nodded and wondered why she looked frightened. He smiled, hoping to let her know he was harmless. "Hello, ma'am."

"Hello," she muttered in a shaky voice.

He wondered why she was afraid of him, but he wanted to put her at ease. "I checked in after dinner and Miz Willie Mae was kind enough to fix me something to eat. I was going to return the plate to the kitchen and thank her again for feeding me."

When she nodded, but said nothing, he added, "I saw Amos come up the street and I was hoping to catch him."

"I'm sure he's already gone."

"Oh?"

"He came to get my husband and they left together."

"I see. I guess I'll have to see the sheriff later."

"If you like, I can take your plate to the kitchen." She took a deep breath. "I was going down to see if I could help Willie Mae cook supper."

He only hesitated a minute. "I would appreciate you doing so. That way I could rest up before the evening meal. That stage ride into town was rough today and I'm a little tired."

She took the plate and he turned back into his room, but not before he noticed how her body seemed to relax as she moved away from him.

Sixteen

"Are you about through cleaning my pants, Vassie?"

"I'm working as fast as I can, William. That sauce sure made a mess on them."

"I didn't mean to spill it. If that stupid waitress hadn't jostled my hand, I wouldn't have dropped the bowl."

"If you had let her put it on the table without reaching for it, this wouldn't have happened."

"How dare you talk back to me, woman!"

Vassie took a deep breath. Maybe she should change her tone. "I'm sorry, William. I suppose I'm still a little upset because we didn't get to finish our dinner and I'm still hungry."

"Well, get those pants clean, and after we go to that boarding house to confront Isabella, maybe I'll let you get something else to eat."

There was a sharp rap on the door. She looked around. "Who in the world could that be?"

"How should I know? Go answer it and see. I can't get up with no britches on."

She opened the door and her eyes got big when she saw two men standing in the hall. One of them had a sheriff's badge on his shirt. "Yes, sir," she said.

"Mrs. Greely. I'm Sheriff Amos Reynolds. Is your husband in?"

"Yes, he is."

"I'd like to speak to him."

"You'll have to come in. I'm cleaning his pants and he can't get up."

Amos looked confused but didn't say anything as he stepped into the room. Kerley followed him. Seeing the man sitting on the bed with the blanket across his knees, Amos said, "Mr. Greely?"

"That's me." William frowned. "Why do you need to see me, Sheriff?"

"I have some questions for you, Mr. Greely."

"Why?" He eyed Kerley. "You look like somebody I've seen before."

"You should remember me. I stopped by your farm to pick up my wife and you said she'd run away during the night."

"Now I remember. You said you wanted to water your horse, but you didn't say nothing about no wife at the time. In fact, when I asked, you said you didn't come from Omaha."

"I had a feeling something was going on when you said your niece had run away. Knowing my wife had been forced to go to Nebraska with her uncle, I put two and two together and figured she was trying to get away from you."

"She ain't your wife."

"She most certainly is."

Amos spoke. "We can get into that later, Kerley." He turned to William. "Mr. Greely, did you hire Spike Miller, his cousin, Billy Joe Miller and Clem Author to kidnap your niece and hold her here until you came to town to force her to go back to Nebraska with you?"

"I came to take my niece home where she belongs. I don't know nothing about no kidnapping."

"So you didn't send those young men here to hold your niece for you until you arrived?"

"I only asked them to help her escape this man who must have kidnapped her. She's a decent woman and I know she sure wouldn't be with a stranger on her own."

Kerley's eyes stared into his. "I'm no stranger. I'm her husband."

"Is he telling the truth, William?" Vassie asked.

"Shut up, woman. You know what he's saying ain't so. You know how she tried to tell us she was married to a man in Omaha, but then I found out later he was dead. I didn't believe her then, and I shore don't believe him now."

"That dead man in Omaha happened to be my brother. When you found out he was dead, you didn't bother to find out which one of us she was married to."

"Then why didn't you tell me you was her husband the morning you come by the farm?"

"Because you kept talking about her running away because she didn't want to marry somebody you had picked out for her. I wanted to know what it was all about before I told you who I was." He glared at William. "After I found her, she convinced me she never wanted to see you again and I told her she wouldn't have to."

"How could she do that?" Vassie said. "We're her only family and we care about the girl. We just wanted to see that her baby had a name. Our neighbors would never believe she was married."

"Her baby has a name. It's my name and that's McFarland."

William stuck out his chin. "I don't believe you no more than I do her."

"So," Amos said. "You didn't bother to find out if her story was true. You took it on yourself to try to force her to commit bigamy?"

"She wouldn't be doing nothing wrong because she was never married to this man or his brother or nobody else. Fact is, she never has been. We don't even know who that baby belongs to 'cause she keeps saying it's her husband's child."

"It is her husband's child, and that's me. But I'm tired of arguing with you. Isabella warned me about how hardheaded you are. But I thought you'd believe the truth when you heard it from me." Kerley turned to Amos. "Now do you understand why I married her again when we got to Edisonville?"

"I sure do. But the fact that you and Isabella are married doesn't mean these folks are not in trouble." He looked at William. "The men I arrested said you paid them to follow and grab Mrs. McFarland. Therefore, I have no choice but to arrest you for hiring those men to kidnap her."

William was eying Kerley. "What do you mean, married her again?"

"Isabella and I were married again here in Edisonville a few days ago."

Vassie wrung her hands. "Oh, my Lord, William. What's happening?"

"Shut up, Vassie. It'll be all right."

The sheriff took over. "You need to come with me, William Greely. Are you going to come along peacefully, or am I going to have to put handcuffs on you?"

"I ain't got his britches clean yet."

"Doesn't matter, ma'am." the sheriff said. "He can wear them dirty or he can walk down the street on in his long johns. Doesn't matter to me."

"William, can he do this to us?" She was becoming frantic.

"Calm down. I'm not arresting you, ma'am. Not at this time anyway. Right now, I just want to question your husband."

"But shouldn't I go with him?"

"Not now, Mrs. Greely. If I have to arrest him, I'll send the deputy to let you know. Then you can visit him at the jail if you want to."

"But what'll I do while he's gone?"

Amos shook his head. "Give him his pants and then you can go to the dining room and have some tea or something. I said I'd let you know what's going on."

William scrambled into his dirty pants. "Don't go to the dining room or nowhere else, Vassie. Just wait here in the room. I won't be gone long. This has got to be some kind of mixup. I'll make them understand we're only here to take Isabella back home where she belongs."

Amos knew better than that, but he only waited until William had his britches buttoned. Then he ushered him out the door, and Kerley followed.

Vassie stood there staring at the closed door, then without knowing why, she burst into tears. It was the first time she'd cried in a long, long time and she didn't know why she was crying now.

~ * ~

Isabella entered the kitchen and put the dirty plate in the sink. "I ran into a man in the hall upstairs and offered to bring this plate back for him."

"That is Julian Lansing. He's one of my regular guests. He stays here every time he's in town. I'm sure you and Kerley are going to like him when you meet him at supper."

"Maybe so."

"You don't sound too enthusiastic about the prospect."

"I guess after all we've been through, we're leery of strangers."

"I can understand that, but you'll soon learn Julian is different."

Isabella changed the subject. "I came to see if you'd let me help you cook supper."

"My dear, with the wonderful way you cook, you should know I'd never turn down your help."

Isabella smiled. "Then what's on the menu for tonight?"

"I decided to make chicken and dumplings. Julian likes them and I hope you and Kerley do, too."

"I do and I don't know of anything to eat that Kerley doesn't like. Want me to roll out the dough for the dumplings?"

"That'd be great. I'll start on the dessert. Julian always enjoys my chocolate pie. How does that sound for you and Kerley?"

"It sounds fine to me. As for Kerley, as long as it has sugar in it, he'll love it."

Willie Mae chuckled. "Sounds like most men. Never met one who doesn't like his sweets."

Soon they were working in harmony with little talking. Isabella wanted to ask Willie Mae about her friend, Julian, but she decided she would sound too nosy. Yet it bothered her a little that there was another boarding house guest. She'd hoped that as long as she and Kerley were in Edisonville, they would be the only ones staying there. Of course, that was probably hoping for too much. Willie Mae ran a business and to make money she had to rent the rooms. She had already turned down her aunt and uncle as guests this week. How could she be expected to turn down others?

"Willie Mae, may I ask you something?"

"Of course you may."

"I know this boarding house is your business, and to make money you have to rent rooms."

"That's right."

"Then why did you refuse to rent my uncle and aunt a room when they showed up?"

"That's a simple question to answer. I need to make a little money, but I don't have to make a lot, so I don't rent to anyone I don't like, and I didn't think I'd like your uncle on sight. When he spoke, I knew I was right about not liking him. In fact, I couldn't stand him. I judge all the people who stop to rent by one simple rule. This is not only a boarding house, but also my home. I don't let anyone rent a room I wouldn't invite into my home as a guest. I knew right away your uncle would never be invited here."

"That's a good rule, Willie Mae. If I ever run a boarding house, I'll remember it."

"Do you plan to run a boarding house someday, Isabella?"

"No. I'm sure I'll be a ranch wife, because Kerley wants to be a rancher."

Isabella hadn't heard the back door open, but she looked up when he said, "What's this about Kerley being a rancher?"

She laughed. "Willie Mae and I were talking about the future."

"I see." He grinned at them. "We'll talk about the future later. Right now, I'd love to have a cup of Willie Mae's good coffee, if that's possible."

"It certainly is possible." Willie Mae turned to the stove. "Sit down, I'll get you a cup."

He sat and looked at Isabella. "I have something I need to tell you."

"What?"

Willa Mae put his coffee in front of him. "Do you want me to leave the room while you talk to your wife, Kerley?"

"You don't have to," Isabella said. "If Kerley has no objections, I don't mind you hearing whatever it is he has to say."

"Then I'm just going to spit it out. Amos arrested your Uncle William today for hiring those young men to kidnap you and keep you here in Edisonville until he came to get you and force you to go back to Nebraska."

Her face fell. "Oh, no. Where is he?"

"He's in jail."

Tears filled her eyes. "Oh, Kerley. I'm causing so much trouble."

He stood and put his arms around her. "It's going to be all right, Isabella."

She leaned against him. "I hope so."

"Let's go to our room so you can cry it out."

He nodded at Willie Mae, then guided Isabella out of the room. His coffee sat on the table untouched, and her dough was still in the bowl. But that was fine. It was ready to be rolled out.

~ * ~

After the sheriff left with William, Vassie wandered around the hotel room and her mind darted from one thought to another. What was she supposed to do? What in the world had William gotten them into? She wished again she'd refused to come with him to this little Texas town to find Isabella. Why hadn't she refused, since a woman shouldn't take such a trying trip, even if her husband insisted? She knew full well a wife should always do what her husband told her to do. She had read the verse in the Bible and William had mentioned it to her often enough. But did that mean she should follow him any time he took some crazy notion that put them both in danger?

Oh, she had tried at first to get him to go on this trip alone when he said Fenton Pyle had refused to leave his farm. In fact, she'd tried to get William to forget the whole thing.

"Why don't we just forget about Isabella marrying Fenton, William?" she'd suggested the night he'd told her to start packing for the trip.

"Don't be a fool, woman," he'd said. "If Fenton don't get to marry up with Isabella, we won't never get that extra five acres with the creek on it for our farm."

"Maybe he'd sell you those five acres."

"Don't you think I've tried to buy them from him for years? He says the only way I can get that land is to get him a wife to raise his young'uns."

"But couldn't we find a woman here to marry him?"

"No, Vassie. Ain't no woman who knows him gonna marry him, no matter what we promise her. Isabella is the only answer, and we've got to go get her to do it, so stop arguing and keep packing."

Vassie had tried one more time. "William, have you ever wondered if Isabella is telling the truth? Could she be married?"

A dark look had crossed his face. "I know she ain't married now and it don't matter if she was. She needs a husband for that young'un and Fenton is willing for it to have his name. Now, I'm telling you one more time, stop arguing with me before I have to take my hand to you. Just get them clothes packed and keep your mouth shut about something you don't know nothing about."

Vassie had said nothing else. She knew she'd pushed him almost to his limit and she sure didn't want him to turn on her. She began taking clothes out of the drawer and breathed easier when he walked out of the room without saying anything else.

But now, here she was in this hotel room alone in this strange town and she didn't know what to do. The sheriff hadn't said anything when William had told her to stay there because he'd be back soon. But would he? What if they put him in jail for hiring those boys to kidnap Isabella? Should she go check to see what had happened to him? Should she go to that boarding house and see if Isabella would agree to go back to Nebraska without too much of a fight?

Even worse, what if that man who was with the sheriff was really Isabella's husband? What would he do to them for trying to take Isabella away from him?

Oh, William. Mama told me years ago I'd regret marrying you someday and I do believe I'm ready to admit she was right. What am I going to do?

Seventeen

Kerley looked across the table in their room where he and Isabella were having supper. "These dumplings are wonderful. Willie Mae said you made them."

She smiled. "I made up the dough, but she did the rest."

"They're good anyway."

She gave him a little smile. "I'm glad you like them. Now tell me why we're having supper in our room instead of in the dining room with everyone else."

"I did promise you I would tell you, didn't I?"

"Yes, you did. Please stop putting it off."

"All right, my persistent little wife. I might as well tell you and get it over with before you badger me any longer."

She made a face at him. "I don't badger. I just ask because I want to know. Besides, you said it affects me as much as it does you and that makes me nervous."

"I'm sorry, I didn't mean for it to upset you."

She sighed and bit her lip. "If you're going to tell me you made a mistake in marrying me and have decided to leave me alone, I want to know now so I won't worry about it."

He laid his fork down and reached for her hand. "I have no intention of leaving you, Isabella McFarland. Unless you leave me or run me off, the only way we'll separate is if God decides I've been on this earth long enough."

She looked surprised. "Really?"

He smiled at her. "Yes, really."

"Oh, Kerley. It makes me happy to know you feel that way. I want to be your wife and live with you for the rest of my life."

"I want it to be that way, too." He gave her hand a little squeeze and his face took on a serious look. "You know my goal has been to get to the old family ranch and try to buy it back from the bank and make our home there, but I think my goal has changed."

She frowned. "I don't understand."

"For the first time, two reasons have started me thinking with a clear head."

"What were those reasons?"

"One was something Amos said. While we were searching for you, we got to talking about our childhood. He told me he was from St. Louis where his grandfather owned a bank and had been someone the people could always count on to be honest and fair with the people. When his grandpa died, his father took over, but was not an honest banker like the grandpa had been. He said his father expected him to grow up and take the reins of the family business when he retired and run it the same way his father had. Amos said he couldn't see himself doing it his father's way and he decided he'd turn the bank back into what it had been in his grandpa's day. He said it took a while, but he realized that no matter what it did, the bank would never be the same. The remark he made was, 'I decided that no matter how hard I tried, I couldn't change the past, but I could control my future.' It was then he cut ties with his father and headed West. That's how he ended up here as a man who would never be rich like his father, but he would be one who would be happy with his decision for the rest of his life."

"That's a wonderful story and you only have to be around him and Charlotte for a short time to see how happy they both are."

He nodded. "The other reason I've been rethinking my goal is you, Isabella."

"Me?" She looked shocked.

"Yes, you. It occurred to me that you've had some hard blows, but you hadn't let them get you down. Your uncle had tried to control your life, so you ran to Omaha to live with your friend, then my brother deceived you. You had every reason to give up and let others decide your path for you. But you didn't. You accepted the fact you couldn't change anything that had happened to you, but you could certainly control what happened in your future. You even married a stranger to prove it."

She blushed, then stammered, "Well, I kind of liked that stranger."

He smiled. "I'm glad. I've taken long enough to get to the point of what I want to say, so here goes. I decided my wanting to get the old ranch back was only my way of thinking I had let my grandfather down. He's the one who started the ranch. When he died and my father took over, I was only eight years old. Things went along pretty good for a while, but it didn't take me long to see that my dad wasn't the man Grandpa Gary was. Dad was more like Dale. He didn't want to be a rancher. He tried, but if it hadn't been for Mama, it would've never worked. Then she got sick and died. Pa didn't wait long to marry Noreen and, a few months later, Dale was born. I could tell things weren't the same on the ranch, but as a kid I didn't worry about it. When I went away to school, I came home to find things were different. Oh, I went to work on the ranch, and I tried to get Dad to use some of the new things on the ranch I'd learned in college, but he refused to change anything. The day he told me if I didn't like the way he was running things I could leave was when I joined the Rangers. On a trip home, I met Betty Lou and it wasn't long until we were married. Then four years ago, Dad and Noreen had the accident that crippled him and injured her. I took a leave from the Rangers and went home to help, but then Dad died. Shortly after that, my marriage ended. Then I got the last blow. It wasn't long after that until Noreen let me know she'd inherited the ranch and she didn't want or need my help. I returned to my job, and, within a short time, the ranch went into foreclosure.

Again, I offered to help, but was told not to bother. It wasn't long until I got word Noreen had died and the ranch was gone. That was when I was on the trail of the outlaw that took me to Omaha where I found out about my brother's death. I think you know the story from there."

"I can imagine the rest, even if I hadn't met you in Omaha. I assume you came back after arresting your outlaw and found your brother had been killed."

"That's right. The one thing I got wrong was what the men at the saloon said about you. The bartender told me the woman my brother was living with had stolen his horse and left town."

Isabella stared at him. "So you thought I had stolen his horse and run?"

"I'm sorry to say that at first that is exactly what I thought. But I don't think so any longer. If I had taken the time to check you out while I was there, I would've learned the real story."

"I see."

"Anyway. I said all this to tell you that I don't feel compelled to go back to the McFarland ranch any longer. I think it's time I make a new life and stop trying to change things back to what they were when Grandpa Gary was alive. I've decided to let the past stay in the past."

She took a deep breath. "What do you plan to do, Kerley?"

"The other day, I found out there is a ranch for sale not too far from Edisonville. I rode out and looked it over and decided it might be a good place to raise a family. All I'd have to do is see if I could hire a hand or two to help me and maybe somebody to help you in the house."

"I'm confused. You mean you want me to live there with you?"

He gave her a strange look, then stood and reached out his hands and pulled her to her feet. "Isabella, for once and for all, get it in your head that we're in this together. I know I make decisions on my own from force of habit, but if you don't like something I've decided to do, please say something. That is the only way our marriage will work out in a way that we can both be happy."

Tears came to her eyes as she let him take her in his arms. "Oh, Kerley. I'm sorry I doubted you, but I'm so scared. I don't know what I'd do if I didn't have you."

He pulled her closer. "I think I told you that when we got married, I meant for it to be forever."

"You did."

"Now, it's your turn. Do you intend to believe me and admit you feel the same way?"

She nodded. "I do. I really do, Kerley."

"Then, let's not mention this again. Tomorrow I want to get up early and ride out and see that ranch again. I want you to go with me and if you like it, I'm going to talk to the bank."

"If you like it, I know I'll like it."

"You probably will, but I still want you to see it before I buy it." She nodded, and he went on, "Let me get these dirty dishes back to the kitchen, then we'll go to bed. I want to make love to my wife."

She blushed and he laughed.

"I also want to get to sleep so we can get an early start tomorrow. I'll tell Willie Mae we won't be here for breakfast."

"Thank you, Kerley. I'll be waiting for you."

He hugged her again, gathered the dishes and hurried out of the room.

Isabella began to undress, and for the first time, she wished she had one of those fancy nightgowns she'd seen in the stores. One she'd be proud to wear for Kerley.

~ * ~

At midmorning, the next day, Willie Mae was in the kitchen preparing a roast for the oven when she heard the bell to the front room ring. She laid her spices aside, wiped her hands and headed to see who would be coming to rent a room at that time of day. When she reached the entry, she was surprised to see a nervous woman standing there wringing her hands and looking as if she didn't know what to do.

Immediately, she recognized the woman as Isabella's aunt. She wondered where the obnoxious uncle was and secretly hoped he hadn't come with the woman.

"May I help you?" Willie Mae said, as she tried to keep her voice from becoming hateful.

In a shaky voice, Vassie muttered, "I...uh...I don't know...Maybe."

"Ma'am, you look like you're about to collapse. Please sit down, then we'll talk."

Vassie nodded and almost stumbled to the settee. "I am tired," she whispered.

"Is your husband with you?"

"No. I don't know where he is."

"Oh?"

"I just don't know what to do. I thought... Well...maybe Isabella would know."

"Isabella?"

Vassie nodded. "I came to talk to her, if you'll let me."

"Ma'am, Isabella isn't here." Remembering the woman's husband, Willie Mae wasn't about to tell her where Isabella was.

The woman looked confused. "But they said this was the only other place in town to stay."

"What I meant to say was that Mr. and Mrs. McFarland ate an early breakfast then left this morning. I'm not sure when they'll be back because they didn't say."

"Oh. I guess that means he's staying here, too."

Willie Mae frowned. "Of course, he is. Where else would you expect her husband to stay?"

"But William said they weren't married."

"I don't why he'd say that. He should be proud his niece married a wonderful man like Kerley McFarland." To keep Vassie from arguing with her, she added, "I'm surprised you came here alone. Where is your husband, anyway?"

She sighed. "The sheriff came and got him yesterday and I haven't seen him since. He told me to wait at the hotel, and he'd be back shortly, but he didn't come. The sheriff sent a man to tell me he would be in jail for a while. I waited up most of the night, but he didn't come back, and I haven't seen him since they left with him. I don't know what I should do next."

"And you thought Isabella could help you?"

"If she will, I'm sure she can. She's a smart person." Vassie grinned slightly. "She sure outsmarted William and Fenton Pyle when she ran away this last time."

"Who's Fenton Pyle?"

"The neighbor William said she had to marry."

"Doesn't William know that if Isabella had married this man, she would be committing the crime of bigamy since she was already married?"

"He said she was never married."

"Kerley said they were married, but since your husband had put the idea that the marriage might not be legal in her mind, he decided to marry her again to be sure. Reverend Noah Hall married them again in the church right here in town the other day. Now there is no question about their marriage and your husband might as well accept that."

"He's going to be mad, because now he won't get the five acres he wants."

Willie Mae frowned. "What do you mean?"

"Oh, it's some kind of business deal he and Fenton Pyle had and it all depended on Isabella marrying Fenton and raising his four young'uns."

Willie Mae could see Vassie was getting upset, so she changed the subject. "I was getting ready to do some cooking. Do you mind coming into the kitchen with me? I'll make you a cup of tea and we can have a talk. That is, if you want to wait a little while to see if Isabella comes back anytime soon."

"That would be very nice Miz...uh...I don't know your name."

"It's Willie Mae Monroe, but you can call me Willie Mae. Everyone does."

"Then you can call me Vassie."

"I'll do that." She stood. "Come along, Vassie. I might even find some of the leftover chocolate pie we had for supper last night to go with that tea."

"That'd be good. I haven't had anything to eat since dinner yesterday and I love chocolate pie." Vassie stood and followed a stunned Willie Mae to the kitchen.

~ * ~

Amos looked up when the jailhouse door opened. "Howdy, Judge. When did you get to town?"

"Came on the stage yesterday."

"You must be here for a rest since the trial is set for a day next week?"

"That, and the fact I decided I wanted to be here long enough to get my fill of Willie Mae's wonderful cooking."

"I know what you mean. She has Charlotte and me over to eat at least once a week. Sometimes more, since Charlotte doesn't feel like cooking sometimes now that it's getting closer to time for the baby to arrive. Of course, I enjoy Willie Mae's cooking, but to be honest, Charlotte cooks just like her mother. I never leave the table hungry at either place."

"You're a lucky man." He took the chair Amos indicated and pulled a cigar from his pocket. "I ran out of smokes and, while I was out replenishing my stock, I thought I'd drop by and see if there was anything you've added to the court docket since you wired me." He held out a cigar to Amos.

Amos took the cigar. "I haven't added another case, but I did add another man to be tried. He was the one who hired the men who committed the kidnapping in the first place."

"I see. Doesn't sound like this trial will last long."

"I'm sure you'll be out in time to have dinner with Willie Mae if we do it in the morning, or supper if we do it in the afternoon."

"Have you alerted the jury?"

"I've made a list and I plan to send Deputy Brock to inform them tomorrow or next day."

"Good. It shouldn't take long to get this one finished."

"I'm sure Kerley and Isabella have already told you they'll be glad to get it over with."

"Who are they?"

Raising an eyebrow, Amos said, "Isabella McFarland is the woman who was kidnapped. I figured you'd have met them at Willie Mae's place."

"She told me there was a couple staying there, but I haven't met them. They had supper in their room last night, and this morning, they had already eaten and left when I went downstairs."

"I see. Well, when you do meet them, I'm sure you'll like them and will be happy to deal out justice for them."

The judge frowned. "I'm not sure I should meet them before the trial, Amos. You know I try my best to be fair and impartial when I go into my courtroom. I know in some of these small towns it's almost impossible, but I try to stick as close to the way the law likes it as I can."

"I suppose you're right. Maybe I could ask them to move back to the hotel until the trial."

"I doubt that'd work. Willie Mae has been bragging about what a wonderful couple they are and how she loves having them at the boarding house. She'd be mad at me if they moved because of me being the judge, and the good Lord knows I don't want to move to the hotel."

"Though you haven't met yet, I don't see any way you can continue to stay away from each other unless one of you moves."

"We might be able to work it out."

The door opened and Russell Brevard, owner of Brevard's Mercantile, walked in. He had a tight grip on the arm of a boy who looked to be about ten or eleven years old. "Sheriff, I'm sorry to interrupt, but I caught this rascal busting up the pumpkins I had on a wagon in back of my store. I thought I better bring him to you instead of whooping him like I wanted to."

Amos shook his head. "Casey Randolph. I can't believe you're in trouble again. Didn't we have a discussion about your behavior only last week?"

"I didn't mean no harm, Sheriff. I was just having a little fun."

"So you think it's fun to destroy somebody else's property?"

He dropped his head. "I didn't hurt nobody. It was just old pumpkins."

"Do you know how many pumpkins he destroyed, Russell, or how much they were worth?"

"I'd say I saw seven or eight busted ones. At ten or fifteen cents each, that would amount to at least a dollar. There could have been more busted ones, but I didn't count."

Amos nodded toward Julian. "You know the judge, don't you?"

When Russell said he did, Amos went on, "Since he's here, I think he'll agree to have a little trial right here in my office. We'll see what he says should be done with young Mr. Randolph."

Casey's eyes got big. "I don't want to have no trial."

"Well, young man. It looks like it's too late for that now."

Julian nodded. "It is too late, so let's have the trial."

A scared Casey stared at him but said nothing.

Julian hit his fist on Amos's desk. "I call this court into session and as I decide this case, I'll have complete silence in this make-do courtroom."

He then looked at the shopkeeper. "Does this boy's folks have an account at your store?"

"His mother does, Judge."

"Then I think it would be proper to add a dollar and a half to her bill, plus another two dollars penalty for your trouble."

"No!" Casey's eyes got bigger. "Mama can't afford that."

"Then, do you have the three dollars and a half to pay this man yourself?"

Tears came to the boy's eyes. "No, but don't punish Mama. She ain't got no money to pay it and she'll be all upset, and she'll cry, and I don't like to see her do that."

"Maybe you could ask your father for the money."

Casey shook his head. "He can't pay it. He's in prison."

Julian looked at the boy for a few minutes, then said, "Then, Casey Randolph, I'm going to give you a choice. You can make your mother pay for your fun, as you call it, or if Mr. Brevard agrees, you can go to work for him doing whatever he needs you to do, until you've worked out the cost of those pumpkins. The other option is six months in jail."

"But I can't go to jail. I have to help Mama 'cause she ain't got nobody else to help her."

"You should have thought of that before you smashed those pumpkins."

Looking defeated, he glanced up at Russell Brevard. "I'll work it out if you'll let me."

Russell nodded. "I'll let you as long as you do like I say and not refuse to do what I tell you. Also, you better not destroy anything else in the mercantile."

"I promise, sir. I'll do a good job. I promise I will."

"Then, son, that is my verdict. You will work for Mr. Brevard until your debt is paid in full." Again, Julian hit his fist on the sheriff's desk. "In this case, I call this court adjourned."

They heard Casey say as he and Russell went out the door, "That judge is pretty smart. I'm glad Mama don't have to pay you."

"I'm glad, too, Casey. Now the first thing I want you to do is clean up the mess you made with all those busted pumpkins behind the store."

Their voices died away and Amos looked at Julian. "I agree with that boy. You are a pretty smart man. Having to help at the store might just straighten that youngster out."

"I'm glad I was able to help. I just wish all my cases were that easy."

"I wish all of mine were that easy, too. "I can't help but feel sorry for the kid. His pa was sent to prison last year for attacking the banker's daughter. It's a good thing she lived, or he would have hung."

"That wasn't one of my cases, was it?"

"No. It was Judge Raymer's. I think it was the last one before he retired."

"I remember him filling in for me. That was when I had broken my leg."

Amos laughed. "I remember how everyone kidded you when they heard you fell over a dog just outside the saloon in Lubbock."

"It did sound fishy, though it was the truth. I didn't even have the pleasure of going into the saloon. It tripped me outside." He stood. "And on that note, I think I need to get back to the boarding house. I bet Willie Mae is getting a good dinner ready and I don't want to be late for it."

"Don't blame you. I guess we'll be seeing more of you while you're here."

"You sure will. Tell that pretty wife of yours I'm looking forward to seeing her before I have to leave town."

"I will and I'm sure she'll be happy to see you, too. One more thing...I like the way you handled this case. We might want to rethink having a jury for the upcoming trial."

"I leave that up to you, Amos."

Eighteen

When Julian stepped into the boarding house kitchen, he was surprised to see a middle-aged woman in a drab gray dress sitting at the table with a cup of tea or maybe coffee sitting in front of her. He wondered if she had anything to do with the woman who had been kidnapped, but he didn't want her to know he knew anything about that crime. He cleared his throat. "How do you do, ma'am. I suppose you've checked in today while I was out. I'm Julian Lansing."

The woman glanced at him and muttered. "Hello, sir."

Willie Mae turned toward them. "This is Miz Vassie Greely, Julian. She came to see her niece who doesn't happen to be here at the moment, so I told her she could wait here in the kitchen while I finish up dinner. I'm sure Isabella and her husband will be back before too long."

"I haven't met your niece and her husband, Miz Greely, but Willie Mae says they're a delightful couple and I'm looking forward to making their acquaintance."

The woman nodded. "She told me that, too."

He lifted an eyebrow, but didn't say anything, though he couldn't help wondering why the aunt wouldn't know her niece was part of a nice couple. He turned to Willie Mae. "Is there anything I could assist you with in finishing up dinner, my good lady?"

"Thank you for offering, but no, Julian." She smiled at him. "Why don't you go into the parlor and relax until I let you know it's ready?"

He turned to leave, then heard the sound of horses outside. "Someone seems to be riding into your back yard. Isn't that unusual?"

"Most of the time it is, but not today. Isabella and Kerley rode their horses to wherever it was they went this morning. I'm glad they got back in time to eat with us."

Vassie's hand began to shake. "I hope Isabella will talk to me."

"Maybe it would be better if she didn't see you when she first walks in, Vassie. Why don't you go into the parlor and let me tell her you're here?"

"Maybe you're right." She stood and picked up her cup. "Do you mind if I take my tea in there with me?"

"I don't mind at all. In fact, you're shaking so much, why don't I carry the cup for you?" She glanced at Julian. "Get yourself a cup of coffee and have a seat if you like. I'll be right back."

Willie Mae walked back into the kitchen as Isabella came through the back door. Glancing behind her, Willie Mae asked, "Is Kerley not with you?"

"After we brushed the horses, he insisted I come inside. He's going to water them and give them some oats." Her eyes darted to Julian, but she didn't say anything.

"Honey, I hate to tell you this, but you have company."

"Me?"

"Yes. It's your aunt."

"Oh, no! Is Uncle...."

"No, Isabella. She's alone. I don't know what's going on, but she's upset, and she said you would know what she should do."

"I don't understand. Is Uncle William coming?"

"I don't know. Like I said, she only wants to talk to you."

"I guess I'll have to see her. Will you stay close enough to hear if I need for you to get Kerley?"

"Of course I will. Do you want me to go into the parlor with you?"

"Would you?"

"Of course." Willie Mae glanced at Julian. "I'll be right back."

~ * ~

Kerley finished with the horses and headed to the house. He wanted to make sure Isabella hadn't overtired herself. She had been a trooper today, although she had stayed at the ranch house with the owner's wife. She told him she had walked all around the buildings, the garden and yard, then she had toured the house. She admitted she was a little tired and he knew her riding Moonstar wasn't easy on her either. Now that they were back, he wanted her to eat a good meal, then go to their room and rest most of the afternoon. He felt she had to take care of herself because he realized if anything were to happen to her baby, she'd be devastated. And he had to admit, he didn't want anything to happen to it either.

Entering the kitchen, he saw the lone man sitting at the table drinking coffee. Perhaps this was the man Isabella told him she had run into in the hall yesterday. He nodded and said, "Hello."

"Greetings. Since you came in through the back door, I'm assuming you're Mr. McFarland." Kerley nodded and he went on, "I'm Julian Lansing and I'm glad to meet you."

Kerley extended his hand. "Likewise. Willie Mae said you were a good friend of hers and you always stay here when you're in town."

"I do. I've never been able to find another place that serves the delicious food Willie Mae puts on the table."

"I agree with that." He looked around. "Where is she, by the way?"

"She escorted a lovely young woman, who I'm guessing is your wife, to the other room. She said she'd be back shortly."

"Maybe I should..."

Willie Mae came into the kitchen. "Hello, Kerley. Why don't you get a cup of coffee and have a seat at the table?"

"I think I should check on Isabella first."

"No, Kerley. She asked me to tell you to wait here until she calls you. Now, do like I say. Have a seat and I'll get you some coffee, then I'll explain what's going on."

After he was seated and he had the promised coffee, Willie Mae sat beside him. "Isabella's aunt showed up here wanting to talk to her..."

"I better go..."

He started to get up and she put her hand on his arm. "No, Kerley. Isabella doesn't want you to go into the parlor yet. She said she'd call if she needed either of us, and I'm sure she will."

"But what is that woman doing here?"

"I don't know, but whatever reason she has, the woman is scared and upset, and she says Isabella is the only person who can tell her the right thing to do."

"I'm not sure this is something I should be witnessing. Maybe I should leave," Julian said.

Willie Mae shook her head. "I think it's too late for you to go, Julian."

Kerley frowned. "I don't want to be rude, but what does he have to do with it?"

Neither spoke for a minute, then Julian said, "I'm not here for just a visit, Mr. McFarland. I'm a judge and I'm here in Edisonville to hear the court case about your wife's kidnapping. When I arrived and checked into The Yellow Door Boarding House, I had no idea you and your wife would be staying here."

Kerley stared at him a moment, then said, "Should we even be talking?"

"Probably not, but since we're both staying under the same roof, I think the wise thing to do is to agree not to mention the trial when we're together."

"I agree with that."

"Well, now that you fellows have agreed, I'm going to put dinner on the table. I'm a little hungry and I bet you are, too."

"What about Isabella?"

"She'll need to come eat, too, and if I'm not mistaken, so should her aunt. The poor woman told me she hadn't eaten all day." She stood. "Now you fellows talk about horses or cows or anything except the upcoming trial. When I need you to carry plates to the dining table, I'll let you know."

~ * ~

Isabella looked into her aunt's eyes. "Now that you're calmer, please tell me what you came here to say, Aunt Vassie."

"I'm so confused, Isabella."

"I'm confused, too, but we need to get to the bottom of why you're here."

"I didn't want to come to this town. I've never been this far away from Nebraska, and everything is strange here. The land doesn't even look the same." She sighed. "But when Fenton refused to come with him, William made me come."

"Where is Uncle William?"

"I don't know. The sheriff came to the room yesterday and took him away so he could ask him some questions. I ain't seen him since and I don't know what to do." Her eyes filled with tears again. "Tell me what to do, Isabella."

Isabella sat back and looked at the woman before her. Not only was she growing old, she looked like she'd been lost for a long time. Taking a deep breath, she said, "All right, Aunt Vassie, I'll tell you what to do. First you have to dry your eyes and stop feeling sorry for yourself. Then we'll talk."

Vassie pulled a handkerchief from her sleeve and dabbed her eyes. "I'm all right now, Isabella."

Isabella couldn't help being shocked at how quickly Vassie recovered, but she didn't mention it. Maybe it was because she was used to being told what to do, then doing it. "Now, tell me why you and Uncle William came all the way to Texas to get me."

"He said you had to come home and marry Fenton."

"I've told you over and over that I was married. How could I marry another man?"

"But William said he was dead."

"What difference did that make? I was carrying a baby. You both should have respected me and my coming child enough to let me have my baby in peace."

"But William said you needed a daddy for the baby."

"My baby has a daddy. He'll be in the house in a minute and there's no way he'd ever let me, or my child go back to Nebraska and marry a horrible man like Fenton Pyle."

"I know that now," Vassie whispered.

Isabella lifted an eyebrow. "You do?"

"Yes. He was with the sheriff, and he said he was your husband, but William said he wasn't. He said you had never been married. But since I've been thinking about it, I believe that man is your husband."

"That's good, because he most certainly is. Now, we have to find out where Uncle William is. Are you staying at the hotel?"

"I can't."

"Why can't you?"

"The man said unless I paid for a room I had to get out. I don't have any money. I didn't know what to do, so I packed my clothes and came to find you."

"Where are your clothes?"

She nodded to the small bag beside her feet. "Right there."

"Is that all you have?"

"William said I didn't need nothing but a change of unmentionables and a nightgown."

"Does Uncle William tell you everything to do, Aunt Vassie?"

"Of course he does. He's my husband, and the Bible says a wife must obey her husband."

Isabella frowned. "So you turned your back on me because he told you to."

"I didn't want to, Isabella. I didn't want him to make you marry Fenton Pyle so he could get the five acres of land with the creek, but I didn't have a choice. I had to obey him."

Isabella stared at her aunt for a minute, then called, "Willie Mae, has Kerley come in yet?"

Kerley appeared at the door. "I'm here, honey."

"Come in, Kerley. I want you to help me decide what to do about Aunt Vassie."

Nineteen

It was mid-afternoon when Willie Mae stepped out on the front porch and found Julian sitting in one of the rockers. He didn't turn when she came out and he looked as if his mind were a million miles away. "My goodness, you look like you have the weight of the world on your shoulders."

He whirled around. "I didn't hear you, Willie Mae."

"I didn't think you did. Is everything all right?"

He sighed. "I don't know."

"What do you mean by that?" She moved to the rocker beside him and sat.

"I've always prided myself on the fact that I went into every case that came before me with an open mind and a determination to be completely impartial."

"I understand that. That's why you're such a good judge."

"I don't think I'll be very good this time. After meeting the McFarlands and watching poor Miz Greely at dinner today, I figure my mind is already made up about how this case is going to turn out, and I haven't even heard any of the testimony."

"Sometimes a person can't help knowing what to do when the right thing is so obvious."

"Oh, Willie Mae. How did you come to be so smart?"

She grinned. "I'm not so smart. I always make up my mind about a person when I look into their eyes and hear them speak. For instance, when this judge I know showed up at my door about four years ago, he didn't think his life was worth living. He was ready to give up and bury the rest of his life in a bottle, but there was something behind his haunted eyes that told me he was worth the effort to save him. And if you could meet him now, you'd say he's one of the finest men who walks this earth."

"Has it really been four years?"

"Seems like yesterday, doesn't it?"

He smiled at her. "It does. It was also the most important day of my life. If it hadn't been for you and this boarding house, I'd probably be dead. But now, thanks to you, I'm looking forward to a lot of life left to live."

"I'm glad I could help."

"Help." He chuckled. "Lady, you saved my life. You took the time to show me I could go on living, though my family had been wiped out by an escaped prisoner. It was only after I finished the case and left here and then had to return in a few months for another one, did I learn that my first visit had only been a couple of weeks after your husband's murder. Something that would have devastated most women, but not you. You had decided that instead of drowning in your own sorrow, you'd help me cope with mine."

"I think we helped each other. It was good for both of us."

"Since I've been sitting out here thinking, something has occurred to me, Willie Mae. The Yellow Door Boarding House is not just a place to rest your bones for a night. It's a place for people who are sad and weary to come to heal."

"That's a wonderful thing to say, Julian."

"I mean it, my dear. If I had my way, I'd move in for good."

"I've never considered having a permanent resident here."

"Well, you may not know it, but I've been thinking about retiring from the courts and finding a new line of work. Edisonville might be a good place to do that."

"I admit, it's a good town to live in. I wouldn't want to live anywhere else."

"That's what I thought."

She frowned. What did he mean by that? She wasn't sure she wanted to know, so she changed the subject. "Didn't you think it was sweet of Kerley and Isabella to insist on renting Vassie a room here?"

He chuckled. "I assume by that remark you want to change the subject."

"I think I do. I want to digest what you've said before I render an opinion on it."

The door opened and Isabella came outside. "I wondered where everyone had disappeared to."

Willie Mae smiled at her. "Come on out and join us. Where's Kerley and your aunt?"

"Aunt Vassie was so exhausted from no sleep last night I persuaded her to take a nap. She is sound asleep in her room. Kerley went to the hotel to make sure she didn't owe anything more and to see if there was anything she had left there."

"Good for him." Willie Mae stood. "Isabella, I know you said there was something you wanted to talk to the judge about before the trial. I'm going to get us a glass of lemonade and give you that chance to talk to him in private."

She turned and left the porch before either of them protested.

~ * ~

Isabella licked her lips. "I'm not sure I should say anything, Mr. Judge, but I did want to talk to you about Billy Joe."

Amused at her reference to him as Mr. Judge, he tried not to smile. "Billy Joe? I'm not sure I know who he is."

"He's one of the three young men who my uncle sent to grab me."

"And you want me to know something about him that you don't want to say at the trial?"

"Kerley said he thought you would understand and that was before he met you. After meeting you here, I think he's right."

"I appreciate that. So what do you want me to know about this Billy Joe?" He hoped she wasn't going to tell him the man had mistreated her horribly or worse, molested her.

"Billy Joe didn't want them to kidnap me but was forced to do so."

"Forced?"

"Well, Judge. I guess you'd have to get to know Billy Joe. He was orphaned as a little boy and he was sent to live with his mother's brother, who had a son a few years older than Billy Joe. He told me that after his aunt died, his uncle said he could continue to live with them as long as he did everything his cousin Spike told him to do. He told me he always listened to Spike, because when he didn't, either his uncle would whip him or his cousin would beat him up. He said that at one time Spike beat him so hard, he ended up with a broken arm. He was also told he was too stupid to make decisions on his own and they had to do all the deciding for him. They've told him that for so long he believes he'll have nowhere to go if he doesn't listen to them."

"Does he have a feeble mind?"

"I don't think he does, but as I said, he's been told he's stupid so long he believes it."

"So, what does this have to do with them kidnapping you?"

"Billy Joe was the one who guarded me most of the time and I got to know him pretty well. He was also the one who was the nicest to me. He always left me untied and he made sure I had food. He was even kind enough to be discreet when I had to take care of my personal needs. In fact, I think he was on the verge of letting me go, though he knew Spike would beat him for doing it."

"Are you asking me to give him a lighter sentence because you like him?"

"I don't know what should be done in his case. I'm just afraid he'll never survive in prison, if that's where they all go. I'm sure he'd be separated from Spike, and he'd be lost."

"What about the third member of this group?"

"I'd never seen him until he snatched me at the hotel. All I know is he's a friend of Spike's."

"I see. Then you've given me something to think about, and I promise you, I will think about it."

"Thank you, Judge."

Willie Mae came out with a tray containing four tall glasses. "I saw Kerley putting his horse back in the barn, so I brought him a glass of lemonade, too."

Isabella smiled. "You're spoiling him, Willie Mae. I hope he doesn't expect me to wait on him the way you do when we leave here."

"I'm not worried about him. I can tell he has a wife who'll always look after him and in return, he'll take good care of her."

"No longer than I've known them, I agree with you, Willie Mae. As for my way of thinking, that's the way it should be between a couple who seem to be as much in love as they look like they are."

"You're right about that, Julian."

Isabella didn't say anything, but she did smile.

~ * ~

Kerley reached over in bed and took hold of Isabella's arm. "I can't help noticing how quiet you've been since we came to our room. Is something bothering you?"

"I need to tell you something and I'm not sure how I should start."

He frowned into the dark. "What in the world have you done?"

"You've done so many nice things for me, like getting Aunt Vassie a room here without question, going to settle things for her at the hotel, and—"

He interrupted. "Isabella. I'm your husband. I'm supposed to take care of things for you."

"I know." She sighed. "I'm going to say it. I may have done something wrong and I'm afraid you'll be upset with me."

Sliding his arm around her shoulder, he said, "I promise you, no matter what you tell me, I'll try my best not to get upset."

She sighed again. "I went out on the porch while you were gone, and the judge was out there. Willie Mae went inside to get us something to drink and that's when it happened. I know I should have talked about something besides the kidnapping, but I didn't. I told him all about it, and especially about how I didn't want Billy Joe to be punished as severely as the others."

"What did he say?"

"Nothing much. Willie Mae came back outside and began talking about something else. As soon as I felt I could, I told them I needed to go check on Aunt Vassie and I didn't go back out there."

Kerley pulled her closer to him. "My sweet Isabella, I don't think you did anything wrong and, for heaven's sake, don't ever think I'd be upset with you for doing something so minor. You're a special lady and the longer I'm around you, the more I realize that."

"Oh, Kerley. Do you mean that?"

"I thought you knew me well enough to know I don't say things I don't mean."

"I'm learning to know you...and..." her voice trailed off and she put her head on his shoulder.

"And what?"

She muttered something, but he didn't understand. "What did you say."

She whispered, "I'm also learning to like you more and more."

He held her tight. "I'm glad because I already like you more every day."

"Really?"

"Yes, really." He took hold of her chin and turned her face up to his. In a moment, his lips covered hers and in a matter of minutes they were lost in a world of their own.

~ * ~

Clinging to Isabella's arm, one could see how nervous Vassie Greely was. Looking up at her niece, she said, "I've never been inside a jail house before, Isabella."

"To be honest, neither have I. But Willie Mae assured me that we wouldn't be uncomfortable in this one. She said her son-in-law made sure the place was clean and tidy for any lady in town to visit whenever she needed him."

"What if he puts me in jail?"

Though she tried, Isabella couldn't suppress the laugh. "He's not going to put you in jail, Aunt Vassie. Please relax."

"But I knew William hired those boys to come get you and hold you here until he came to collect you and take you home."

"Do you think you should have told him not to do it?"

"Of course not. I did tell him that maybe you were married, and he might ought to forget making you marry Fenton, but he told me he'd beat me if I didn't shut up. I didn't say anything else about it."

"So he wouldn't take your advice?"

"Oh, no. William would never listen to me. He always yelled at me and sometimes hit me if I made him mad enough. Then he'd do whatever he wanted to do, so I quit telling him to do anything."

Isabella frowned. "He actually hit you?"

"Yes, but I knew I always deserved it. You know the Bible says that a wife must obey her husband and if she doesn't, he has the right to discipline her."

"I know the Bible says a wife should obey her husband. I also know it says a husband should treat his wife the way Jesus treats his church. I sure don't think the Bible says anything about a man hitting his wife."

"But William says when she doesn't obey, that gives him the right." She gave Isabella a strange look. "Hasn't your husband ever hit you?"

"Of course he hasn't. Furthermore, he better not."

"Oh my, Isabella. Aren't you afraid he'll throw you out if you don't listen to him and take whatever punishment he thinks is necessary?"

"Aunt Vassie, we'll probably never agree on this matter, so let's just say my husband respects me enough that he'd never raise a hand to me, and therefore, I respect him enough to listen to all of his suggestions of what we should do. So far, he's made good decisions concerning me and our marriage and I expect him to continue to do so. As long as he does, I won't argue with him about them." She took her aunt's arm. "The jail is just down the street, so let's drop the subject. I'm sure Amos will tell us what's going on with Uncle William's arrest. We'll know what we should do after we learn his fate."

Vassie sighed and nodded, but she didn't say anything until they reached the door of the jail. "I hope he's not too mad at me."

Isabella didn't answer as she opened the door and ushered her aunt inside.

Amos looked up from his relaxed position at the desk, then stood when he saw them. "Hello, ladies. Please come in and have a seat."

"Thank you, Amos. This is my aunt, Vassie Greely. I've brought her to see her husband."

"Yes. Kerley came by and told me you'd be coming in this morning. I decided since there are so many prisoners in the cells, I'd bring Greely in here to speak with his wife."

Isabella had hoped she wouldn't have to see her uncle, but she supposed it would be best for the two of them to talk there. Grabbing a bit of hope, she said, "Would you like me to step outside?"

Before he could answer, Vassie blurted, "No. I want you to stay with me."

"All right, Aunt Vassie. If the sheriff doesn't disagree, I'll stay."

"It'll be fine if you stay here, Isabella." He stood, picked up a ring of keys and headed to the area where the cells were located. "I'll be right back."

In a matter of minutes, William Greely preceded the sheriff through the door. His eyes seemed to light up and he said, "I can't believe it, wife. You got Isabella, so maybe you're not as stupid as I thought you were."

He then looked at Isabella. "I don't know how she did it, but I'm glad you came to your senses and decided to come get me out of here so we can all go back to Nebraska. Fenton will be happy you decided to marry him after all."

From the corner of her eye, Isabella saw Amos frown. She shook her head. "I'm sure my husband would object to the idea of me marrying another man, Uncle William. Therefore, I'm not going anywhere with you."

His eyes narrowed. "So you're going to keep telling that story, when everybody knows you're not married."

"I understand now," Amos said. "You're the man who keeps trying to make your niece commit bigamy. For your information, I happen to know that not only is she married, but she's married the same man twice just to let people know you've been spreading lies about her marriage."

"I don't believe it. When I get her back to Nebraska, she'll be married to a man who will give that baby of hers a name and everything will be fine."

"I'm not going back to Nebraska or anywhere else with you!"

In a weak voice, Vassie said, "She is married, William."

"Shut up, before I backhand you, woman!"

"There'll be no backhanding anybody in my jail unless you want to add to the possible crimes you've already committed."

"It's not a crime to hit your wife, Sheriff. The Bible says a wife must submit unto her husband."

"Maybe so, but I don't think the Bible says a husband should beat on his wife just because she disagrees with him now and then."

"No wonder men in this day and time have such a problem with their women. They've forgot how to be a man and show them who the boss is."

"Don't worry, Greely. Plenty of men think the way you do, and it's a shame because that's why most of them are so unhappy in their marriages." He shifted his position. "Now, if there's nothing else you want to discuss with your wife, I'll take you back to your cell."

"What do you mean, take me back? Vassie came to get me and I'm ready to go."

"You're not going anywhere until the judge hears the case against you, Greely."

"But..."

Amos turned to Vassie. "Is there anything else you need to tell your husband, ma'am?"

"I want to know what he wants me to do."

"You heard her. What do you want her to do?"

"Just stay at the hotel until I get out of here."

"I'm staying at the rooming house where Isabella and her husband are staying."

William wrinkled his brow. "I told you to stay at the hotel. Why did you disobey me?"

"I didn't mean to, William, but they wouldn't let me stay there because I didn't have any money to pay them."

"I can't believe that rude woman at the boarding house is letting you stay there free."

"She's not. Isabella's husband paid for my room."

"Then he can keep paying for it."

"I don't think so. Let me see what you have in here." The sheriff opened a drawer in his desk and took out a cloth bag and looked inside.

"Don't you dare give her my money!"

"She's your wife, isn't she?"

"You know she is."

"Then you have the obligation to look after her." He took a worn wallet from the bag and handed it to Vassie. "Here you go, ma'am. I think there might be enough here to pay for whatever you need."

"Don't you dare spend any of my money, Vassie! You'll regret it if you do."

"Ignore him, Mrs. Greely. You use any or all of the money you need. You have a right to do so."

"Are you sure?"

"I'm positive, ma'am."

"I'll get you for this," William bellowed.

"Just so you know, I'll be adding the fact that you threatened a law officer to your list of offenses, Greely. Now, unless Mrs. Greely has any more business with you, I'm taking you back to your cell."

She shook her head and he stood, took William's arm and led him toward the back.

When they were alone, Vassie leaned toward Isabella and whispered, "I can't believe this."

"What do you mean?"

"I've never met any men who are as nice as this sheriff and your husband."

Isabella patted her hand. "There are more of them than you think, Aunt Vassie. Now, when he returns, we'll bid Amos goodbye and head back to the Yellow Door. I'm sure Willie Mae will have a good dinner and I'm beginning to get hungry."

Vassie smiled. "Believe it or not, I am, too."

Twenty

It was evening and Isabella sat in front of the dresser mirror brushing her hair. Kerley stood behind her and put his hands on her shoulders. He was grinning.

She smiled back at him. "So what you're telling me is that you now own the ranch?"

"No, Isabella. What I'm saying is that *we* now own the ranch. You do remember telling me that you thought if it was the ranch where I thought I'd be happy and the one I'd like to run for the rest of my life, that I should buy it, don't you?"

She put her brush down and turned to face him. "I do remember that, but I guess I'm not used to a man listening to me or remembering what I say."

He laughed. "You need to get used to it, because from now on, you and I are in this together."

"You're such a good man, Kerley McFarland."

"I'm glad you think so." He held out his hand and she stood.

They moved to the two chairs in front of the window, and she gave him a timid smile. "Now that you say the ranch is ours, when will we be moving out there?"

"I gave them a week to get packed up and moved. I thought that would give me time to hire a couple of men."

"Are their hired hands not interested in working for you?"

"Two of the hands are staying. The other three hands were their sons."

"I see."

"I also want to look for a cook."

"I can..."

He stopped her. "No, Isabella. I don't intend for you to do the cooking for all those men. You'll only be cooking for you and me."

"Really?"

"Yes, really."

She cocked her head to the side. "Why are you so good to me?"

He shrugged. "Beats me."

She laughed. "Do you know when I first met you, I thought you were the most arrogant and rude man I'd ever met?"

"So, have you now changed our mind?"

"Yes, Kerley. I changed my mind some time ago."

"To tell you the truth, I've changed my mind about you, too."

"Oh?"

"Yeah. The first time I looked at you I thought you were mighty pretty, but I didn't let that sway me to change my mind that you were a scheming little crook who had taken advantage of my brother and stolen his horse."

"If my looks didn't change your mind, what did?"

"Getting to know you changed it." He winked at her. "Of course, your looks didn't hurt."

She laughed, stood, and patted her stomach. "I'm getting sleepy and since you've been so kind as to compliment this fat woman's looks, I'm going to bed and think about when I was slim and could be considered a little attractive."

He stood and took her hand. "I agree. I'm sleepy, too. Of course, I'm still pretty slim and I'm hoping there's somebody out there who would consider me kind of attractive."

They went to bed laughing and Isabella couldn't stop the idea that slid across her mind. She was no longer falling in love with her husband. She was already there.

~ * ~

The next day at noon, Willie Mae was putting dinner on the table in the Yellow Door Boarding House when the back door opened and Judge Julian came through, followed by Sheriff Amos Reynolds. "It looks like I timed getting back perfectly. Everything smells wonderful."

Willie Mae grinned. "There you go flattering me again, Julian Lansing."

"I agree with him, Mother-in-law. Since I told Charlotte I'd grab a bite in the cafè today, I might just change my mind and eat here."

"Of course you will. You two go on into the dining room and have a seat. I'll call Isabella and her aunt."

"Here we are, Willie Mae," Isabella said. "We'll help you put the food on the table."

After the food was brought in and everyone had taken seats, Amos asked, "Where's Kerley?"

"He had some business at the bank this morning," Isabella said as she passed the platter of ham. "I thought he'd be back by now, but it must be taking longer than he thought."

"Maybe he'll get here before you finish eating," Willie Mae said.

"If not, Isabella can tell him why I came by."

"Why's that, Amos?"

"Julian and I have been talking. We thought it'd be a good idea to push the trial for those kidnappers up since he got to town early. We decided the day after tomorrow would be good."

"That'll be great. I just want to get it all over with so we can move into our new place."

Amos raised an eyebrow. "I'm sure you'll be glad to go, but we'll miss you around here."

"I'm sure you'll be seeing a lot of us."

He frowned. "I don't see how we could visit very often. Kerley said his family ranch was about a hundred miles from here."

Isabella smiled. "Didn't he tell you?"

"Tell me what?"

"He decided not to go back to the family ranch. He's buying one that's around four or five miles out of Edisonville."

"The Avery place?"

"I think that was the name."

"Well, well. Wait until I tell Charlotte. She'll be thrilled because she likes being friends with you and I know Willie Mae is glad about it."

"I sure am. They've already promised that they'll come for supper here at least once a week."

After the discussion of the McFarlands' plans waned, in almost a whisper, Vassie spoke for the first time. "What'll happen to William and me?"

"A lot of that depends on what Isabella wants to happen, Mrs. Greely. The judge always wants to know what the injured person wants."

"All I want is for him to go back to Nebraska and never contact me again."

After a slight silence, Julian said, "Maybe that can be arranged."

~ * ~

The courtroom was packed the morning the trial was to take place. Isabella wanted to stay at the boarding house, but Kerley insisted she attend with him. "You might have to be a witness," he'd said.

Now, there she sat in the front row of the make-do courtroom in the Pickle Barrel Saloon. Kerley sat on her right and Vassie on her left. Willie Mae and Charlotte were on the other side of Vassie. The rest of the chairs were full of people, and there were several standing around the walls. She didn't know any of them, with the exception of the man who ran the hotel.

The chatter in the room dropped to a loud buzz when the judge walked in and took his seat at the table that had been set up in the front of the room. He looked over the crowd but said nothing.

In a minute, the side door opened, and Amos and Brock came through, leading Spike and Clem.

Instinctively, she reached for Kerley's hand.

He gave her hand a squeeze, then leaned over and whispered, "Relax. It'll be fine."

She didn't have time to answer because Judge Lansing slammed his gavel on the table and said, "Quiet in the courtroom."

Silence followed, then he said, "What's the first case, Sheriff Reynolds?"

"The case of Spike Miller and Clem Author, who are jointly charged with kidnapping Mrs. Isabella McFarland."

"We didn't kidnap nobody," Clem blurted.

"Quiet," the judge said. "Have a seat at that table there. You'll get your chance to tell your side of the story." He looked at Amos. "Why were these two men charged with kidnapping, Sheriff?"

"A month ago, I met Kerley McFarland at the hotel where he was frantically looking for his wife. Her bags were scattered in the hallway of the hotel and the door to the room they shared was open. She was nowhere in sight. McFarland is a former Texas Ranger, and we followed the tracks of the person who had taken his wife. It took two days, but we did find Mrs. McFarland, and she told us these were two of the three men who had abducted her."

"Where is the third man, Sheriff?"

"Because of the circumstances, he was charged with a lighter crime, Your Honor. He'll be tried later."

"I see." He looked around the courtroom. "Mr. McFarland, would you please come forward?"

Kerley squeezed Isabella's hand again and whispered, "I'll be right back."

After Kerley was sworn in, the judge said, "Now, Mr. McFarland. Would you please tell me what went on the day your wife was abducted?"

After telling the story very much like Amos had done, he added, "It's a good thing the sheriff was with me when I went to confront the men. If I'd gone alone, I might be on trial for murder."

Several mummers in the courtroom agreed with him and the judge banged his gavel. He then asked, "Was your wife harmed in any way, Mr. McFarland?"

"She said she was fine, but since she is having our first child, I wanted to make sure. I took her to Doctor Stoddard. He said she wasn't physically hurt, but it would be good if I got her away from the hotel where she'd been terrorized so she could come to grips with what had happened to her. We moved to the Yellow Door Boarding House, and we've been there since."

"Thank you, Mr. McFarland. You can go back to your wife. I'll call you again if I need to ask you anything else." He looked at Spike and Clem. "I'll start with you, Spike Miller. What do you have to say for yourself?"

"It's all just a big mistake. Her uncle told us she had run away from home, and he wanted her to go back to marry his neighbor."

"But Mrs. McFarland is already married."

"Her uncle said she lied about being married, and since she was going to have a baby, this fellow in Nebraska was willing to marry her so she could help him raise his brood of young'uns. We thought he was telling the truth and she needed to go back home with her family."

"Did he pay you to bring her home?"

"He give us thirty dollars and said he'd give us the rest when we got her."

The judge looked at Clem. "How about you? Do you agree with what Spike said?"

"I weren't there when they made the deal with Greely. Matter of fact, I hadn't met the man until he was put in jail beside us."

"Then how did you get involved?"

"Spike come to me and told me him and Billy Joe was going to track the woman and rescue her for her uncle. He said I was a better tracker than him and I could make fifty dollars, so I come with him."

"Did Billy Joe help you take Mrs. McFarland?"

"He didn't even want to come with us, but Spike made him."

Spike broke in. "I had to make him, Mr. Judge. Billy Joe is an idiot, and he don't know how to do nothing but what I tell him to do. He couldn't make it without me."

"Since Mrs. McFarland was with her husband, didn't that give you a clue that her uncle was wrong, and she was a married woman?"

"We thought he was just some man who she had took up with to get away from her uncle."

The judge shook his head. "Is there anyone else here who would like to say anything about this case?"

When nobody answered, he glared at Spike and Clem. "Doesn't look to me like Billy Joe is the only stupid one of you and maybe he's the smartest. Stand up. I'm ready to pronounce your sentence."

When they stood, he went on, "Spike Miller and Clem Author, I sentence you to six months in the state prison for abducting Mrs. Isabella McFarland. I wish I could sentence you to an additional six months for being stupid enough to do it in the first place, but there is no penalty for being stupid. I will add to your sentence if either of you ever sets foot in the state of Texas again. You will be arrested and immediately put back in prison for an additional five years." Slamming the gavel, he added. "This case is closed, and this court is in recess until one o'clock this afternoon."

~ * ~

The food looked and smelled good in the Edisonville Café but Isabella didn't have much of an appetite. The way Vassie was pushing her potatoes around on the plate, it didn't seem she had one either.

Kerley looked at them. "Is there something wrong with the food?"

"The food is fine. I'm just too nervous to eat."

He reached over and took her hand. "Isabella, please try to relax. It will all be over in a little while. Then we'll be able to get on with our lives."

"I understand, but it's not easy for me to hear what everyone is saying and to know this is my first introduction to the people who live in this town."

"The people of this town are on your side. Haven't those who have spoken to you said so?"

"You're right. I should be more concerned about Aunt Vassie."

"Don't worry about me, honey. I don't know what will happen, but I want you to know that I'm sorry William's actions have put you through this."

"What about you, Aunt Vassie? If the judge puts Uncle William in prison, what will you do?"

"I have no idea."

Kerley smiled at his wife. "Let's not borrow trouble. Besides, if your uncle does have to serve some time, we'll see that your aunt is taken care of."

Vassie looked stunned. "Would you really?"

"Of course we would. Now, please try to eat a little. I don't know how long the next trial will be, but I don't want either of you getting hungry while it's going on."

A few minutes before one, they went back to the courthouse and to the same seats they had before, which had been reserved for them. In a minute, Charlotte and Willie Mae joined them.

Leaning over her mother and Vassie, Charlotte whispered to Isabella, "I'm sorry we couldn't eat dinner with you, but the judge wanted to join Mama and me, since Amos was busy getting the other two prisoners on the prison wagon. Julian said that wouldn't be a good thing if he was seen eating with you and Kerley and your aunt."

Isabella nodded. "I understand."

Before they could talk further, Julian Lansing rapped the gavel on the table and called the court to order. Then the side door opened, and Amos escorted William Greely into the room.

"Your Honor, this is the case of William Greely, who has been charged with hiring three men to kidnap his niece."

"I didn't hire them to kidnap her. I hired them to find her."

"Take a seat at that table and be quiet, Mr. Greely. You'll get your chance to speak later." After Greely was seated, the judge asked, "Now, Mr. Greely. You've heard the charges against you. How do you plead?"

"I'm not guilty."

"All right. Tell me why you're not guilty."

"I went to Omaha and brought my niece home and learned she was going to have a baby. I knew there would be a scandal if she had the child without a husband, so I arranged for my neighbor to marry her. He wanted to get married 'cause his wife died a couple of years ago and he had four young'uns who needed a mama." He pointed a finger at Isabella. "But that ungrateful woman didn't want to marry him and give her baby a name and a father."

"Why didn't she want to marry him?"

"She said she was married, but I didn't believe her."

"Why didn't you believe her?"

"The man she was with in Omaha had died."

The judge raised an eyebrow. "He looks pretty much alive to me."

"That ain't the man. He says the dead man was his brother and he was the one who was married to Isabella. I don't believe him, either."

"Didn't you see him in Omaha?"

"No. Somebody has since told me he was a Ranger, and he'd gone to capture somebody. Sounded like another lie to me."

"So you forced your niece to go back to Nebraska with you, though she told you she was married and didn't want to go?"

"Like I said, she was lying." He leveled his eyes at Isabella. "See her sitting there with him acting like they've been married for a long time."

The judge ignored him. "Did you hire Spike and Billy Joe Miller and Clem Author to kidnap your niece, and hold her here until you could come and get her again?"

"I just hired them to find her and let me know where she was. She didn't have no business running away when I had everything planned for her to cover up her sin."

"I didn't know it was a sin for a married couple to have a child, Mr. Greely."

"She ain't no married woman. I told you she and him was lying."

"So you still don't believe they're married?"

"No. I think she could've hired him to pretend to be her husband. That way she wouldn't have to marry Fenton Pyle."

"Who is Fenton Pyle?"

"My neighbor."

"Why do you want her to marry Pyle?"

"'Cause he needs a wife and she needs a husband."

"What about the five acres of land Pyle promised you when your niece marries him?"

William looked shocked. "How'd you know about that?"

"It doesn't matter how I know. I just know it."

"Well, that ain't got nothing to do with it. The Bible says a woman must submit to a man and it's time Isabella learned that lesson."

"If I'm not mistaken, that Bible verse pertains to husbands and wives, not nieces and uncles."

"It means any woman and any man."

"Mr. Greely, I've heard enough from you. I'm ready to pronounce my sentence."

"Are you going to make her go back to Nebraska with me?"

"No, I'm not. I'm afraid her husband would shoot me if I tried, because unlike you, I know your niece is married to Kerley McFarland and has been for some time. I also know she is about ready to present him with his first child."

"I'm telling you, it ain't his child."

The judge shook his head. "Like I told the men before you, I don't have the authority to sentence you for your stupidity, and that seems to be your biggest problem. I have no choice but to let you go with one stipulation. You are to leave Edisonville today, and if you ever set your foot in Texas again, I will have you thrown in prison for the rest of your natural life. Court is now adjourned."

"I can't believe you're doing this to me," William yelled.

"Shut up and get the hell out of my courtroom." Turning to Amos he added, "Get him out of here, Sheriff, or I'll send him to prison just because he's making me mad."

William shook off the hand Amos put on his arm and started down the aisle between the row of chairs. Spying Vassie, he yelled, "Come on, woman. We're getting out of this evil town."

Trembling, she stood.

Isabella reached for her hand. "You don't have to go with him, Aunt Vassie."

"Oh, yes I do, my dear. It's my duty."

Glaring at Isabella with hate in his eyes, he grabbed Vassie's arm. "I said, let's go."

Isabella watched them leave but knew there was nothing she could do to stop them.

Twenty-one

After the trials ended, Charlotte and Willie Mae insisted on introducing Isabella and Kerley to several people. They said since the couple was going to become a part of the community, people needed to meet them. Isabella was pleased by the way people seemed to welcome them. It made her look forward to settling on their ranch and making more friends.

Finally, the crowd thinned, and Kerley left with the judge and the sheriff. She knew he was going to listen to Billy Joe talk to the judge. She only hoped Julian would take into consideration and remember what she'd told him when they talked on Willie Mae's front porch.

When the three women headed toward the Yellow Door, Isabella left conversation up to Charlotte and Willie Mae. She couldn't stop her mind from replaying what was said in the courtroom and on the verdicts the judge had rendered, though she tried to focus. She kept hoping the right thing would happen with Billy Joe. Kerley had told her Judge Lansing was going to try him at the jail and the judge had asked him to be there. She wished he could be with her, but she knew it was important that he handle the situation. She understood, but hoped he'd come along soon and let her know what had gone on there. Her mind was so absorbed in woolgathering she jumped when Charlotte put her hand on her arm.

"I'm sorry. I didn't mean to scare you. Are you all right?"

Isabella laughed. "I'm fine. I was so lost in my thoughts I forgot where I was for a moment."

"That's fine. Mama and I were just wondering if you think your aunt and her husband would be at the boarding house for supper."

"Oh, my goodness. I hadn't thought of that." She looked at Charlotte and her eyes got bigger. "I don't think I can stand to be in the same room with him ever again."

"Don't worry, honey." Willie Mae moved beside her and took her hand. "We'll see that the old codger doesn't bother you."

"I think he and your Aunt Vassie will probably be gone. I think he took the judge's words to heart and was in a hurry to get away."

"Charlotte's right, but to be sure, here's what we'll do." They looked at Willie Mae and she went on. "When we get there, I'll hang around the desk in the parlor in case he hasn't taken your aunt and left. Charlotte will go to your room with you to make sure you don't come out until she and her husband are gone."

"To make doubly sure they won't give you any trouble, when you go into your room, I'll knock on Miz Vassie's door and check on them," Charlotte added.

"I don't know how I'll ever be able to repay you two for all you've done for me."

"Friends don't pay friends back and we consider you a friend, don't we, Mama?"

"We sure do. I knew the minute they walked into my house that we'd be friends."

"I just want you both to promise me something. When Kerley and I move to the ranch, you will visit often."

"I sure will, and I'll also expect you to keep your promise to show up to my house at least once a week for a meal. I think that husband of yours likes my cooking."

"He loves your cooking, Willie Mae, and so do I."

"I'll come to see you as often as I can, and you have to come to town. Our babies are going to be close to the same age and I want them to grow up together."

"That would be wonderful. I like that idea, too."

They reached the house, and without saying anything else, Isabella and Charlotte headed up the stairs. As they had planned, Isabella went to her room and Charlotte paused at Vassie's room.

Isabella had only stepped into her room when Charlotte screamed. Rushing back into the hall, she hurried to her aunt's room. Going in, she saw blood on the floor and Charlotte was kneeling beside her aunt's form. Rushing to them, Isabella cried out, "What's happened?"

"I don't know, but your aunt is alive. Stay with her and I'll get Mama."

Dropping to the floor beside Vassie and taking her hand, Isabella burst into tears. "Oh, Aunt Vassie, did Uncle William do this to you?"

Though Vassie was unable to answer, Isabella knew he had. Jumping up, she grabbed a pillow off the bed and put it under her aunt's head. "I'm afraid to move you, Aunt Vassie, but I'm going to get some water and see if I can get some of this blood off your face."

Charlotte came back into the room. "Mama went to get the doctor and I'm going to get Amos. Will you be all right here alone?"

"I'll be fine. Just tell Kerley I need him."

"Don't worry, I will," she said as she went out the door.

Isabella didn't reply as she got a pan of water and a cloth to work on Vassie's face. As she wiped away the blood as gently as she could, her continual prayer was that her aunt would survive this awful attack, and that her uncle would pay for putting his wife through such a horrible beating.

~ * ~

Billy Joe's eyes got big as Amos led him out of the cell and into the jail office where he saw four men in the room. He recognized Miz Isabella's husband and the deputy, but he didn't know the other two. He wanted to ask who they were and why he had to see all of them, but he knew from experience he needed to keep his mouth shut and they'd tell him what they wanted him to know.

The sheriff spoke. "Billy Joe, I know you know the deputy, but let me tell you who these other fellows are."

"I know Miz Isabella's husband, too. I remember when you and him come and took her home and brought me to jail."

"So, you do understand that McFarland is married to Isabella?"

"Sure. She said he was her husband and Miz Isabella wouldn't tell a lie." He looked at Kerley. "Is she still all right?"

Kerley nodded. "She's fine, Billy Joe."

"Good. I like Miz Isabella. She never talked mean to me like Spike does."

"Have a seat in that empty chair, Billy Joe. The man in the corner is a friend of Mr. McFarland and the other man is Judge Lansing. The judge has some questions he wants to ask you."

Billy Joe did as he was told and looked at the judge.

"Billy Joe, tell me about why you came to Edisonville with your friends to kidnap Miz McFarland."

"I didn't have no choice. Spike said I had to come, and Uncle Ollie told me I had to do what Spike said. I'm glad I did come, though."

Julian lifted an eyebrow. "Why are you glad?"

"'Cause Spike and Clem let me be the one to guard her. I like her and she knowed I wouldn't let nobody hurt her."

"So, you didn't do it for the money?"

He shook his head. "I don't know nothing about no money. Spike did tell me he might give me a dollar, but I told him I didn't want no dollar because I liked watching Miz Isabella. She's nice."

"Why wasn't he going to give you more than a dollar?"

"I don't know, unless it's because he knows I'm too stupid to handle more than a dollar."

"Maybe you're not as stupid as you think you are."

"That's what Miz Isabella told me. She's a nice lady and she told me lots of things." He grinned at Kerley. "She even told me she loved her husband and didn't want to go home with her uncle. She ain't gonna have to go, is she?"

The judge shook his head. "No, Billy Joe. She's not going home with her uncle."

"Good. She told me he didn't believe her when she told him she was married. But she is. She told me she was, and I believe her."

"I'm glad you believed her, Billy Joe, because she was telling the truth," Kerley said.

"I know that, Mr. McFarland. She told me somethin' else, too."

"What was that?"

"She told me she loved her coming baby and her husband, and she couldn't wait to be back with him again. Now she is, and I'm glad."

The judge cleared his throat. When they all looked at him, he said, "Billy Joe, you know you're going to have to be punished for what your cousin and his friend have done, don't you?"

"Yes sir. I don't mind. I'm used to people punishing me."

"I have already sentenced the other two kidnappers to six months in prison and told them they can never come back to Texas again."

"And they said they'd do it?"

Julian couldn't hide his smile. "They don't have a choice. When a judge sentences a criminal, he or he has to do what the judge says."

"So I guess I'm going to have to go to prison, too."

"No, Billy Joe. You didn't plan to kidnap Mrs. McFarland, and you were good to her. I don't think you need to be punished as much as your cousin and his friend. In fact, Mrs. Isabella McFarland asked me not to punish you as much as I did them."

"She done that?"

"Yes, she did, and I've made up my mind what your punishment is going to be." He took a deep breath. "My decision is that you will be released under the following conditions: You will find a job and prove that you're able to pay your own way. You will also agree to live in this area and never return to live with your Uncle Ollie Miller and his son Spike."

Billy Joe looked scared. "Oh, Mr. Judge, I ain't got nowhere to go except Uncle Ollie's house."

"You do have somewhere else to go, Billy Joe." The judge looked at Kerley. "Would you please explain what we've decided on, Mr. McFarland?"

"I'll be glad to." He gave Billy Joe a smile. "Isabella told me how good you were to her, and she asked me to make sure you had a job when the sheriff let you go. I have bought a ranch near here and I need men to work on that ranch. I've talked it over with the judge and the sheriff, and they've agreed that I can hire you to work on my ranch. In fact, that man over there in the corner is Dax Spivey. He's here to take you out to the ranch and show you around and introduce you to the other man who'll be working with you. The people there will be moving out in a few days. Then Isabella and I will move in. Of course, I'll be out there tomorrow, and we can discuss any questions you have about your new job."

The boy stared at him. "Are you sure? Spike says I'm stupid and I might mess up. You won't beat me too hard when I do, will you?"

Kerley shook his head. "We all mess up at times, Billy Joe. As long as you don't deliberately do something to cause harm, you'll have time to learn and correct your mistakes."

"What will Uncle Ollie say? He expects me to come back so I can do all the cooking. Him and Spike don't like to cook."

Before Kerley could answer, the judge said, "Your uncle will have nothing to say. He will no longer be in charge of what you do, young man. You will have to take your orders from Mr. McFarland and his wife."

"So you can cook?" Kerley asked.

"Yes, sir. I'm a good cook. Even Miz Isabella said I was."

"Then I may hire you as my bunkhouse cook instead of just a cowhand." He turned to the cowboy in the corner. "Are you ready to take him out to the ranch and show him the bunkhouse, Dax?"

"I sure am, boss."

"Then it sounds like everything is under control and I call this case settled."

"Thanks, Julian." Amos stood. "I'll get your stuff out of the drawer, Billy Joe. You didn't have much. Just a knife and a dollar and an old pistol."

"Spike said I might shoot myself if I had a good one."

"We'll have to do something about that. Every man on the ranch needs a good gun," Kerley said. "You do have a horse, don't you?"

"If Spike didn't sell her, I do. She's old, but she's a good horse."

"I leave you in Dax's hands, Billy Joe, and I'll see you tomorrow." Kerley nodded to Julian. "Are you ready to head to the boarding house?"

"I sure am. I hope Willie Mae has…"

The door slammed open, and Charlotte ran into the office. "Amos, you need to come to Mama's place. Vassie Greely's husband has almost beaten her to death."

"Where's Isabella?"

"She's with her, Kerley."

"I've got to get there. Take care of Billy Joe, Dax." He didn't wait for an answer.

"Should I get the doctor?" Amos asked.

"Mama went to get him. You need to find that awful man."

In a matter of minutes, they had all scattered, leaving Brock to take care of things at the jail.

~ * ~

If William Greely had a twinge of guilt as the crowded stagecoach rumbled out of Edisonville, he didn't realize it. He decided things were going to be fine. Whenever Vassie realized she'd pushed him too far, she'd get herself together and come back to Nebraska. It didn't occur to him she would take the whipping he'd given her to make her to realize she would be better off without him. Neither did it occur to him that she had no money to pay for her trip home. If it had crossed his mind, he'd probably have said let that obnoxious man Isabella claimed she had married pay for it.

He jerked back into reality when one of the painted women sitting across from him shoved his leg and snapped, "Unless you're willing to pay me for the privilege, you better watch where you put those knees, you dirty old man."

William glared at her. "I can't believe I would ever hear such evil words come from a lady's mouth."

"Honey, what gave you the idea I was a lady?"

The two women beside her giggled and the man beside him said, "Honey, when we get to the stage stop, I'm willing to pay you well if you'll take a walk with me."

"Oh, you sweet man. It'd be my pleasure to take a walk with you."

"What about me?" the brassy blonde beside her asked. "I'm sure I'll be ready for a walk when we stop, too."

"Don't worry, honey. I can handle two women." He gave her a toothy grin. "Probably three, if your friend there wants to join us."

The third woman grinned and winked at him.

William frowned. What kind of people was he traveling with? Didn't any of them know the rules of acting decent in front of other people? Somebody should show them what a lady's place in this world is. It would take a man with a strong will and a strong hand, but it could be done. After all, they were only women, and a woman had to be shown how to act. Why, he wouldn't put up with Vassie acting this way in front of other people for a minute and it wouldn't take him long to make her realize what her place is.

Before he could think further, a shot rang out and the stage sped up. "Oh, my lord, what's happening now?"

"Might be a holdup. You better get out your gun," the man said.

"I don't have a gun."

"Then you better hope the driver can outrun the outlaws."

But the driver wasn't able to do that. The stage soon pulled to a stop and almost instantly, the door was jerked open.

"Get out here!" a masked bandit demanded.

The man beside William went first, then the women. He got out last.

There were five outlaws and they all started whistling and muttering as the women disembarked.

"Settle down," the one riding a black horse yelled, and surprisingly the men did. "Now, let's take care of business.

He pointed his gun at the driver. "Throw down the money box."

The driver complied.

He turned to the people standing on the ground. "Now, folks. Open up those wallets and take out the money. Also take off your rings and watches and any other valuables you have on you and put them in the sack my man there is going to pass around."

William looked at him with a frown. "Who do you think you are?"

"I'm the man who will shoot you if you don't do like I say."

"You better shut up and listen to him," the painted woman said.

He ignored her. "I will not give you my hard-earned money. Why don't you get a decent job to make money instead of taking what other people have spent their lives working for?"

The robber shook his gun at William. "As I said, put your money in the sack or I'll put a bullet between your eyes."

"You wouldn't dare shoot an unarmed man."

That was the last thing William Greely ever said. He fell to the ground and the robber calmly said, "Go through his pockets and get what he has. The rest of you start filling the sack."

They didn't hesitate to start scrambling for their money.

Twenty-two

Several hours had passed since Doctor Basil Stoddard had come and seen Vassie Greely. "I've done what I can for her," he'd said. "Her heart seems to be strong, but the rest of her body is in bad shape. I'm not sure how long it will be before she wakes up. Right now, being unconscious is her body's way of trying to repair itself. Just keep an eye on her because she may be confused when she wakes up. Of course, feel free to call me anytime if you need me again."

Isabella had nodded and Kerley had said. "Thank you, Doctor. We'll do that."

Stoddard shook his head as Kerley walked him to the door. "Whoever beat her in this brutal manner should be locked up, if not hanged."

"I agree with you."

When Kerley returned, he saw Isabella had moved to the small settee, dropped her head to her hands and began to cry. He went to her, sat and put his arm around her. He wished he could do more to comfort her, but he wasn't sure what. She didn't seem to want to talk, so he didn't say anything. He only held her in his arms and let her rest her head on his shoulder.

They had been in this position for some time, and he wondered if she had drifted off to sleep. He didn't want to disturb her if she had, so he shifted a little to make her more comfortable. She spoke and it startled him a little.

"Why, Kerley?" Her voice sounded like that of a scared child.

"I don't know, honey. I don't understand it either."

"Would you ever beat me like that?"

He looked down at her. "Of course not. Whatever gave you such a crazy idea?"

"Uncle William always said a man had a right to hit his wife whenever she needed correction. He said the Bible told him so."

"I don't know what Bible he's been reading, but it's sure not the one I'm familiar with."

She raised up and looked at him. "So you wouldn't beat me?"

"No, Isabella. I would never beat you. I agree with what the doctor said before he left. A man who would do this to the woman he's supposed to love should be locked up for the rest of his life, or better still, hanged for it."

"Oh, Kerley. It means a lot to me that you feel like that. You're such a good man. It's no wonder I'm falling in love with you."

Those words startled him in a different way. He had felt Isabella was beginning to like him, but it never occurred to him she could be falling in love.

Before he could say anything, there was a soft knock on the door and Willie Mae walked in with a tray of food. "I knew Isabella wouldn't come downstairs to eat, so I brought her some supper. I'm going to stay with her while you go downstairs and eat."

"But..."

"Don't argue with me. Amos is downstairs and he needs to talk to you."

He looked at Isabella. "Will you be all right?"

She nodded. "Go on. I'll be fine."

He kissed her forehead and stood. "I won't be gone long."

Willie Mae was setting the food on the table beside the settee. "Take your time. We'll be fine."

Kerley left the room, hoping Amos had caught William Greely and had him locked up in jail. As important as that was, his thought lingered on the fact Isabella had said she was falling in love with him.

He entered the dining room and saw Amos, Judge Julian and Charlotte at the table. She smiled at him. "Come on in, Kerley. Mama put you a plate here and everything is ready to eat."

"Did your mother eat?"

"She said she took two plates and enough food for her and Isabella."

"I see." He sat in the chair beside Julian, and they began passing him food. "Have you caught William Greely?"

"Greely's dead, Kerley."

Kerley raised an eyebrow. "What happened?"

"I sent a wire to the sheriff in Nixxon and told them to hold him there because he'd committed a crime here in Edisonville, then I took off to see if I could catch the stage. I didn't, but I found Greely's body on the side of the road about six miles out of town. There were a lot of tracks around where I found him. I figured there had been a holdup and his belligerent mouth got him shot. After I brought him back and left him with the undertaker, I sent another wire to Nixxon and told them what I thought had happened. I haven't heard back, but I'm sure Sheriff Wilson will let me know if something happens there."

Kerley said, "I dread telling Isabella about his death. In one way, she didn't think much of the man, in another, she still cared for him."

"I understand. One can be conflicted about their feelings where relatives are concerned."

"They sure can."

"How's Mrs. Greely doing?" Julian asked.

"She's still unconscious and I don't know what's going to happen there."

Charlotte spoke up. "I've been praying Isabella doesn't lose her aunt, too. They seemed to be getting along so well while she has been here."

There was a noise in the front of the house and Charlotte stood. "Mama must have forgotten to lock the front door. I better go see if it's someone wanting a room."

"Want me to go with you, honey?" Amos asked.

"No. Continue eating. I'll yell if I need you."

She was gone only a few minutes. When she returned, she handed the folded paper to Amos. "It was a boy bringing this from the telegraph office."

Amos took the wire and read it. "It looks like Wilson got my wire in time to arrest the stage robbers. They had hit the saloon there and were living it up. Now they're all in jail. One of them had a sack full of items they had taken from the passengers and among the loot they found a wallet with William Greely's name in it."

"So they'll have to pay for killing William as well as the robbery."

"Looks like it."

"I hope that makes Isabella feel better when I tell her about his death."

Nobody said anything, but he could tell from their faces they all understood how hard his talk with Isabella was going to be.

~ * ~

At three o'clock the next day, Isabella stood beside Kerley as her Uncle William's pine coffin was lowered into the ground in the community graveyard on the edge of town. Besides the Reverend Noah Hall and his wife, Charlotte and Amos were the only other funeral attendees. Isabella knew they had come to support her, and she appreciated it, though it hadn't been necessary. Knowing they cared was enough, but when they insisted, she accepted their offer. The fact that Willie Mae had volunteered to sit with the still unconscious Vassie, and Julian had said he'd stay in the parlor in case someone came by wanting a room helped, too.

But the main reason she felt the most grateful was the fact that Kerley had handled all the arrangements for the burial. She hoped that someday she'd be able to repay her wonderful husband's kindness. A husband she knew she'd love forever. It didn't matter that he'd never said anything about loving her. She loved him so much that just being married to him made up for it. He liked her, and that was enough.

The preacher finished his final prayer, then he and his wife walked over to her. "If you need me or my wife, please don't hesitate to call."

"Noah is right, dear." Martha Jane patted her hand. "We feel that you and Kerley are special."

"She's right." He smiled. "You're the only couple I've ever married who were already hitched."

"You may not believe this, Preacher, but we both feel like you were the one who officiated at our real wedding."

"That's a nice thing to say, so from now on I'm going to tell people I'm the one who married you two so it would stick." He shook Kerley's offered hand and gave Isabella a serious look. "I saw this morning when I came by that your aunt is still unconscious. I just want you to know that when you have to tell her about her husband's death, you can call on me if you want to. I'd be more than happy to be there to support you."

"Thank you, Preacher Hall. That's very kind of you, and I may call you."

After they left, Amos and Charlotte joined them, and they went back to the boarding house together. Vassie Greely was still unconscious.

~ * ~

Two days later, Isabella sat in the settee drinking her usual cup of afternoon tea when a low moan came from the bed. Setting the cup aside, she jumped up and ran to check on her aunt.

Vassie's eyelids fluttered, and Isabella grabbed her hand. "Are you waking up, Aunt Vassie?"

The only response was another moan.

After watching her aunt for a few minutes, Isabella ran to the door. Opening it and running to the top of the stairs, she called, "Willie Mae. Aunt Vassie is waking up." She then turned back to the room.

It wasn't long until Willie Mae appeared in the room. "Is she awake?"

"Not yet, but she's moaning and she's beginning to move some, and she even squeezed my hand,"

"Relax, honey. I sent Julian to get the doctor. I'm sure they'll be back shortly."

"Thank you."

Willie Mae patted her arm. "You know you don't have to thank me. Now I'm going to run back downstairs. I'll be in the entry, so just call if you need me."

"I will."

As Willie Mae left, Vassie moaned again. Then her eyes fluttered open. She didn't say anything, but she stared at Isabella and squeezed her hand again.

"Oh, Aunt Vassie, you're coming back. I've been so worried about you."

Though Vassie didn't answer, Isabella kept talking to her. "I love you and I'm so sorry this happened to you. I've been praying and my prayer has been answered. I know you're going to get well, and things will eventually be all right. I just know they will be."

Shortly the door opened, and the doctor said, "I hear we have a patient that is coming around."

"Oh, yes, Doctor Stoddard. She actually smiled at me one time, but she then went back to sleep."

"That's to be expected." He moved to the bed and sat set his bag on the table. "It may be a while before she's completely conscious, but this is a wonderful sign that things will work out."

When Vassie became completely conscious, she almost panicked because she didn't understand why William hadn't come to check on her. Then, when she was told she had been unconscious for over a week, she didn't understand why William would have left her in this town alone. She kept muttering, "He's going to be furious if I don't come home."

It took almost all day to convince her there was no way she could travel as far as Nebraska and then the inevitable happened. Vassie asked Isabella to send a wire to William telling him she would be home as soon as she was able to travel.

Isabella knew there was no way she could avoid telling her aunt the truth any longer. She took a deep breath. "There's something I have to tell you, Aunt Vassie."

"I know, dear. You don't think I should go back to William after what he's done to me. But I'm sure he's sorry he was so gruff. I must have made him madder than I usually do, and he thought it was right to punish me harder than usual. I'm sure he won't do this again."

She took another breath. "You're right. He won't do it again."

"So send the wire in the morning."

"He won't be there to get it."

Vassie frowned. "Why not?"

She took a third deep breath. "Uncle William is dead, Aunt Vassie."

Vassie stared at her a moment, then said, "How do you know?"

"After we found you, the sheriff decided Uncle William needed to be arrested for attempted murder. Knowing he'd left on the stage, Amos followed it to arrest him."

"Did the sheriff kill him?"

"No. It turned out the stage had been robbed, and they killed Uncle William. The sheriff found his body on the side of the road."

"Oh, no. Where is he?"

"We had no choice. Kerley made the arrangements, and we buried him in the cemetery here." She patted her aunt's hand. "You would have been pleased with the service. The Reverend Hall and his wife attended, and he did a wonderful eulogy."

Tears began rolling down Vassie's cheeks. "Would you please leave me alone for a little while?"

"Aunt Vassie..."

"Please, Isabella. I need to think alone."

Though she didn't want to, she stood. "I'll be in my room and all you have to do is call."

Vassie nodded but didn't answer.

~ * ~

Kerley put his arms around Isabella. "Honey, try not to fret."

"But, Kerley. I've looked into her room three times and each time she's waved me away. I'm worried about her."

"I don't want you to get upset, so I'm going to take over."

"What do you mean?"

"You go ahead and get ready to go down to supper. I'm going to talk to Vassie."

"But..."

He put his finger across her lips. "Don't worry. I'll tell you everything."

"But..."

"Shush." He leaned over and kissed her. "I'll be back shortly."

Before she could protest, he went down the hall and into Vassie's room.

"I don't want any company," Vassie muttered.

Kerley ignored her and pulled a chair up beside her bed. "You may not want company, but you need it and I'm not leaving until I have my say."

"Then say what you have to and leave me alone."

"You do know Isabella loves you and wants to help you cope with what has happened."

"There's nothing she can do. This is a problem on my shoulders. For the first time since I was a young woman, I don't have a husband to tell me what to do."

"That may be true, but you do have people who care about you and want to help."

"How can they help, Kerley? I'm alone and unable to look after myself. I don't have any money. I'm living here and you're probably paying for it. It would be better for everyone if I joined my husband in death."

"You're talking foolishness, Vassie. Are you deliberately trying to hurt Isabella?"

"Of course not."

"Then quit talking like that. You're not the first woman who has lost her husband and had to live on her own, and I'm sure you won't be the last."

"It's not that. I know I'll get by if I have to go to the poor house."

"Then what is it?"

"It's the sin I'm committing."

Kerley frowned. "What are you talking about?"

She gave him a sad look. "Other than a few tears when Isabella first told me, I haven't been able to cry for William. I know that's wrong. A woman should mourn her husband's passing, but I just can't seem to do it and I know people will blame me."

"The man almost killed you, so how could anyone blame you for the way you feel?"

"But he had a right. The Bible says…"

"I know what the Bible says, Vassie. I also know it doesn't mean a man has a right to beat his wife to death."

"Are you sure?"

"Positive. Now what else is bothering you?"

"I don't know how I'll ever be able to pay you back for paying my bill here."

"There is no bill to speak of. Willie Mae refuses to charge for your room, but she does let me give her a little extra for the food she prepares. It's not enough to even think about."

"But I still owe you for it."

"No, you don't. Hasn't anyone ever told you that family takes care of family?"

"But I'm not related to you. In fact, Isabella was William's niece, that's why I became her aunt, so I'm not blood related to her."

"That doesn't matter. As far as she's concerned, you're her aunt. I'm her husband, so in a way that makes you my aunt, too. Now, is there anything else you need to be straightened out on?"

"Will you tell me what I'm going to do when I get better?"

Kerley smiled. "I will. I don't know if you know it or not, but I've bought a ranch a few miles out of town. Isabella agrees we're going to live there and raise our children. Though I have to go out there to work, Isabella will stay here with you until you're better. I've already talked to the doctor, and he said as soon as you were able, you'll be moving to the ranch with us."

Her eyes got big. "Are you sure?"

"Yes, I'm sure. Now, will you quit worrying about what's going to happen to you, and let my wife come back in to see you? She's worried sick about you."

"Yes. You can also tell her I'd like her to bring her supper up here and eat with me if she'd like."

Kerley winked at her. "I'll do that. I might even come with her. and we can have a family meeting about moving to the ranch."

~ * ~

Later that evening, as Isabella's head was on his right shoulder, he was surprised when she said, "All right, husband. I think it's time you confessed."

He frowned. "Confessed what?"

"How you did it."

"Did what?"

"Charmed my usually shy and retiring aunt to become your avid admirer."

He laughed. "She's a nice lady and she has a good taste in men."

Isabella laid her hand on his naked chest and ran her fingers through the hair there. "I think I have good taste in men, too."

A little taken aback, and not wanting to get into the subject of their feelings, he said, "I have something I need to tell you, but I don't think we should tell Vassie yet."

"What?"

"Julian told me he'd taken it on himself to check on the Greely farm in Nebraska. It turns out the farm came from Vassie's family. It seemed her father gave it to William for marrying his daughter. He also had a stipulation that if William died before she did, the farm would revert back to her."

"Do you mean she owns it?"

"Yes. I thought we'd talk to her later about what she wants to do with it."

"I'm sure she'd want to do whatever you suggest she do. I'm almost sure if she were younger, she'd fight me for your attention."

He laughed. "Oh, Isabella. You confuse me at times."

She removed her hand from his chest and sat up. "What do you mean?"

"I never thought I'd be able to trust another woman again, but I'm beginning to trust you."

"Of course, you can trust me. Why would you think you couldn't?"

"I never intended to tell you this, but here I am opening up about it." He reached for her arm and pulled her back down beside him. "You knew I was married, and I was finishing up my cases with the

Rangers so I could move back to the ranch, not only to help my invalid father, but to settle down with my wife. I thought to finish the last case I had, I'd be gone a couple or maybe three months or more, but it so happened I had some breaks and finished in one month. I headed back to the ranch, where Betty Lou was staying with my dad and his wife. I had plans of building a house for us on the ranch and living there the rest of our lives. Getting home early and in the middle of the night, I decided to slip into the house and surprise her, but I was the one who got the surprise. I got to our room and found her in bed with a man. I threw them both out of the house. I later found out that the man was my step-mama's cousin who was visiting, and he and Betty Lou had been having an affair almost from the day he arrived. I swore I'd never trust another woman."

"Oh, Kerley. I'm so sorry. You must have been heartbroken."

"It hurt at the time, but I think I was angrier at myself for being such a fool." He pulled Isabella closer to him. "Now look at me. Here I am with another wife who I can't help but trust and I keep waiting to see if she will betray me, too."

"I would never betray you, Kerley. I know you married me to give my baby a name and to keep me safe from my uncle, and I appreciate that. And maybe at the time, I married you for the same reason. But that's not true now and I want you to know that I've fallen deeply in love with you. It's the man you are that made me love you. If either of us is ever betrayed, I assure you, it won't be you."

"You won't be betrayed either, Isabella. Though I tried not to let it happen, sometimes there are things you can't control. In spite of everything, I've fallen in love with my wife."

She flung her arms around him. "Oh, Kerley. I love you, too. I know I always will."

He pulled her to him and kissed her with passion.

In moments they were lost in their own world of love.

Epilogue

Fall turned into winter and the Avery Ranch was now known as the McFarland Ranch. Kerley and Isabella had settled in and as soon as she recovered, Vassie insisted on being their cook and housekeeper. After learning Billie Joe was good at preparing food, Kerley assigned him the job of ranch cook. Isabella shared some of her knowledge of the use of spices, and his skills improved so much the hands seldom went into town for a meal.

As Isabella grew bigger with child, her aunt and husband insisted she not do as much housework. She didn't agree, but finally gave in.

The McFarlands had become a respected and accepted part of the town. Kerley was often called upon to help out when there was trouble, and Isabella was always invited when there was a gathering of women to make quilts or to attend a special tea to celebrate some event. They also became members of the church where they made more friends.

Because of his connections, Judge Julian Lansing took it upon himself to check into the Greely farm in Nebraska. It turned out that Vassie's father had given the farm to William Greely on the condition he marry his daughter. He did put the stipulation on the deal that if Greely preceded her in death, the farm would revert back to his daughter.

When she learned this, Vassie pursed her lips. "Now I know why William was so mean to me all those years. He didn't love me at all. He only wanted the farm. Sell the place. I don't want it."

Fenton Pyle bought the farm and the judge made sure he paid a fair price for it. As for Pyle, if he ever found some woman to marry and help raise his children, nobody knew and nobody cared. Julian handled the sale, and when he returned to Edisonville, he opened a bank account for Vassie. After that, she seemed to walk with her head held a little higher.

That wasn't the only change that Julian was involved in. He retired as the judge of the territory and decided to settle down in Edisonville. He moved from the Yellow Door Boarding House to the hotel because he said he intended to be Willie Mae Malone's only escort in town.

Nobody was surprised when the boarding house sign came down and the place closed its door to paying guests to become a personal home again. The wedding was planned to take place after Charlotte's baby was born, because it was getting near, and Willie Mae said she'd not be on a honeymoon while her first grandchild was entering the world.

The only other big happening was when Ollie Miller showed up to demand Billy Joe go back to the town of Gomer with him because he was tired of eating his own cooking. Though nobody interfered with Billy Joe's choice, he'd gained confidence in his own decisions since he had been shown by the McFarlands, the hands, and even the town's residents that he was capable of deciding for himself. Ollie went back to Gomer alone, because Billy Joe said he *was* home, and he had no intentions of living anywhere else for the rest of his life.

After that encounter, things settled down until the morning Isabella came into the kitchen and reached for her coffee cup to fill. She didn't make it to the stove, as she let out a little cry and the cup fell to the floor.

Vassie came running into the room. "Are you all right?"

"I don't think so. Get Kerley."

Confusion reigned for a little while as Vassie got Isabella to bed and Kerley sent one of the hands for the doctor. He sat beside his wife's bed until the doctor and his wife arrived and ran him out of the room.

He didn't like sitting alone in the parlor and waiting to hear that Isabella was all right. It seemed like hours had passed, but he wasn't even sure. That was why the sound of horses in the front yard was a welcome sound to him. He hurried to the door as soon as he heard a buggy pull up outside. He grinned when he saw Julian help Willie Mae from the back seat and Amos helped his big pregnant wife to the ground. Stepping out on the porch, he called, "Come in, friends. I can't believe you came out on such a cold day."

Amos shook his head. "When these women heard the doctor was sent for because Isabella was about to give birth, there was no way Julian and I could keep them in town."

"Of course not," Charlotte butted in. "Isabella is my best friend. What would she think if I wasn't here for the birth of her baby?"

"And she is like a second daughter to me," Willie Mae added. "You know I had to be here. Besides, with the weather looking like it might turn nasty, I wasn't about to let Amos bring Charlotte out here alone in her condition."

Kerley stood back and held the door open. "Come in and warm up. I've got a good fire going."

"Has anything happened yet?" Julian asked.

Kerley shook his head. "I can't believe it takes so long. I've been waiting for hours. I just want Isabella to be all right."

"Don't worry, Kerley. She'll be fine." Willie Mae patted his arm as she passed him. "When we get inside, I'm going to take over your kitchen, because I bet Vassie has been too busy to cook."

"She did make a pot of coffee, but I think I've drunk most of it."

Billy Joe appeared at the end of the porch. "I heard the buggy and thought I'd check to see if anything has happened, boss."

"No, Billy Joe. Miz Isabella hasn't had the baby yet."

"I don't mean to bother you. I guess I'm anxious."

"I understand that. I'm anxious, too. I promise I'll let you know as soon as she has it."

"Thank you," he muttered and disappeared back around the house.

"Looks like Isabella has an admirer," Amos said.

Kerley nodded. "He's certainly devoted to her. In fact, it's almost like he thinks she's his mother."

Amos laughed and when they got inside, they saw Charlotte had already started up the stairs.

Willie Mae was hanging their coats on the hall tree. "You men have a seat, and as soon as I check things in the kitchen, I'll go up and check on Isabella."

"I'd appreciate that, Willie Mae. They won't let me back in the room and I don't know what's happening to my wife."

Willie Mae grinned and left the room.

In a matter of minutes, she returned with three mugs of coffee. "I've put a new pot on, and it'll be ready by the time you have to warm yours up. I also put a roast on and I'll fix some vegetables later. Now, I'm going to check on your wife. I'll let you know how she's doing."

"I appreciate that, Willie Mae."

Before she could get out of the room, the doctor's wife came down the stairs. "Willie Mae, will you please hurry upstairs? We need you."

Kerley's heart seemed to drop, and he blurted, "What's wrong?"

Emma Stoddard shook her head. "Nothing's wrong, Kerley. Isabella is fine and I didn't mean to scare you. We just need her help getting some clothes."

Kerley seemed to relax, but Amos frowned. "Why in the world would they need clothes?"

"Doesn't make a lot of sense, does it?" Julian took a drink of his coffee.

"I guess it's not for us men to understand. I haven't had a hint of what's happening in there since they threw me out. It's almost like it doesn't have anything to do with me."

Amos laughed. "I guess at this point, it doesn't have anything to do with you."

Both men laughed at this, and it wasn't long until they fell into general conversation.

Thirty minutes passed before Willie Mae appeared back in the room. She was all smiles. "Kerley, I want you to know that Isabella is doing fine, and it shouldn't be too much longer. Now, drink another cup of coffee and see if you can help Julian calm Amos down."

Amos frowned. "Why should I be calmed down?"

"Charlotte got up from the chair beside Isabella's bed so the doctor could check his patient's progress. When she did, water covered the floor from under her skirt."

"What does that mean?"

"It means there's a chance Charlotte could give birth before Isabella does."

Amos jumped up. "Where is she? I've got to see if she's all right."

"We have her in bed in the guest room, but if you want to see her, you've got to calm down, son-in-law. You have to sooth her because she's as surprised as we all are."

Julian looked at Kerley. "Now I guess he knows how you feel."

Kerley nodded. "It's kind of strange it happened so fast for Charlotte. It's taking Isabella forever."

"Must have been the buggy ride out here." Julian stood. "I'm going to get another cup of coffee. Do you want a refill?"

He held out his cup. "I might as well."

But before Julian could leave the room, the sound of a baby's cry filtered down the stairs.

Kerley jumped up and met Emma coming down the stairs. "Is Isabella...?"

"Isabella is fine, Kerley. A as soon as we get them cleaned up, you can come upstairs to see your wife and meet your son."

A huge grin crossed his face. "Isabella said she thought it'd be a boy."

"Yes, Kerley. You have a son."

"Are you sure Isabella..."

"Isabella is exhausted but, as I said, she's fine, and I know she's anxious to see you."

"Can I come go up now?"

"In a few minutes. Now go sit down and I'll call you as soon as we get them ready." She turned and headed back to Isabella's room.

"Congratulations, Kerley," Julian said as Kerley came back into the parlor. "I bet you're glad to have a son."

"Isabella said it would probably be a boy." He shook his head. "I just want to see her and make sure she's really all right."

"Relax. I'm sure it won't be long before they call you to go up."

In about fifteen minutes, Vassie appeared and told him Isabella was ready, though it seemed like an hour to him. "I think it's time."

She smiled at him "Relax, Kerley. Some things take a little time."

He hardly heard her because he was rushing up the stairs. All he wanted to do was make sure his wife was as fine as they said she was.

His heart was beating twice its normal rate when he opened the door. Isabella lay in the bed with her blond hair pulled back and tied with a ribbon. Her green eyes glowed when she looked at him.

Rushing to the bedside, he asked, "Are you sure you're all right?"

"I'm a little tired, but otherwise, I'm fine. How are you?"

"Now that I see you are doing well, I'm fine." He pulled the chair beside her bed and leaned over and kissed her forehead. "I'm sorry you were in such pain. I never dreamed you'd be in such agony."

"It's normal to have some pain." She looked down at the bundle in her arm. "Would you like to see him?"

He nodded and she unwrapped the baby. Kerley stared at him, then said, "He's awfully little."

"We all start out that way, Kerley."

"I suppose you're right."

"He's been fed and he's asleep. Would you like to put him in his bed?"

He wasn't sure he wanted to, but he nodded. "I'll try not to hurt him."

She smiled. "He won't break, Kerley."

He felt awkward with the baby in his arms, and he didn't know what to say. He thought Isabella expected him to speak, but words didn't come. He swallowed and looked down at the helpless child and tried to think of something, but he didn't have to speak because the door opened and an excited Vassie stuck her head in.

"Sorry to interrupt, but thought you'd want to know Charlotte just had a little boy, too. Amos is beside himself, just like Kerley. Isn't it wonderful?"

"Oh, yes." Isabella became excited. "I hope that means our sons will be friends just like their papas are."

"I'm sure they will be. Now I'll leave you two alone with your son." She closed the door.

He turned back to the bed, and he had a sudden realization. The most wonderful woman he'd ever known was looking at him as if he were the most important man in the world. The man she'd given her heart and not only depended on him to take care of her for the rest of her life, but the man who would raise her son and take care of him as well. He glanced down at the baby in his arms and his thought turned to, *No, he's not just her son. He's our son and he always will be.*

He walked back to the bed and sat down in the chair. "Do you mind if I hold him a bit?"

"If that's what you want to do, of course I don't mind." She gave him a puzzled look.

"Have you named him yet?"

"No. I was thinking about it, but nothing sounded right."

"I have a suggestion." When she only looked at him, he went on. "I always thought if I ever had a son, I wanted to name him Gary after my grandpa. I also remember that's what you said your brother's name was. I think that would be a good way to honor those we loved."

"Oh, Kerley. That's a perfect name. Are you sure? After all, the baby's not..."

He interrupted. "Don't say it, Isabella. I'm the one who has helped his mother get through those rough days of being pregnant. I'm the one who sat downstairs and listened to her cries as she brought him into the world. I'm the one who'll be here to help her raise him and who he'll call Daddy. So don't you or anyone else ever say he's not my son. From this day forward, Gary is not just Isabella's baby. He's Kerley and Isabella McFarland's son."

A tear came into her eye. "Oh, Kerley. I didn't think I could ever love you any more than I did already, but you've just proved me wrong. You're the most wonderful man in the world."

He winked at her and stood. "Let me put my son in his bed, then I'm going to come back and hold his mother in my arms and kiss her until she says she doesn't want to kiss me anymore."

"Hurry, Kerley. I can't wait for those kisses."

He grinned as he put the sleeping baby in the bed beside theirs. "I'll hold you again soon, son, but right now I've got to get to the most important woman in our lives. Don't worry. We're not going to ignore you long. In fact, if she's willing, we may eventually give you some brothers and sisters to play with. But you must remember, you're my first son and that makes you the one to set an example for the others."

On impulse, he kissed the baby's head. He then turned and grinned again because Isabella was sitting up and holding her arms out to him, arms he knew would always be open for him. Kerley McFarland knew at that moment he was not only the happiest man in Texas, but the luckiest one as well.

Meet Agnes Alexander

Agnes Alexander has published hundreds of short stories and articles and has had over 50 books published. In 2011 she decided to concentrate on writing what she most likes to read: Western Historical Romance. *Isabella's Baby* is her seventh Western book with Wings.

A lifelong resident of North Carolina, she counts traveling as one of her passions. She has visited 48 of the 50 states and says Alaska and Hawaii are on her bucket list, but she says getting older has slowed her traveling somewhat. Of course, she loves to read, but tries to limit herself to one or two books a week. Besides traveling and reading, Agnes enjoys jewelry making, watching old movies, playing with her cat, Victoria, and spending time with her family.

Other Works From The Pen Of
Agnes Alexander

Valissa's Home – After her brother gambles away Heartsong, Valissa's home, she learns a giant of a cowboy now owns it and expects her to move out in three weeks.

Opal's Faith - Though her family has been forced to move to Arizona, Opal has faith that her father, with the help of a hired hand, will make a home for them out of the rundown ranch.

Ulla's Courage - After losing her home and the mercantile, it takes courage for Ulla to give up her life in Independence and marry a stranger who is headed to Oregon with his two children.

Zelda's Guilt - Feeling guilty because an accident took her father's life and left her stepmother disabled, Zelda tries to care for her siblings and save their small ranch.

Nelda's Homecoming - Thinking her husband has a mistress, Nelda returns to her hometown planning to get a divorce, but she doesn't count on him being determined to stop her.

Wilma's Outlaw - Sparks fly between them when Wilma helps a reformed outlaw fight for five orphans.

Letter to Our Readers

Enjoy this book?

You can make a difference

As an independent publisher, Wings ePress, Inc. does not have the financial clout of the large New York Publishers. We can't afford large magazine spreads or subway posters to tell people about our quality books.

But, we do have something much more effective and powerful than ads. We have a large base of loyal readers.

Honest Reviews help bring the attention of new readers to our books.

If you enjoyed this book, we would appreciate it if you would spend a few minutes posting a review on the site where you purchased this book or on the Wings ePress, Inc. webpages at:
https://wingsepress.com/

Thank You

Visit Our Website

For The Full Inventory
Of Quality Books:

Wings ePress.Inc
https://wingsepress.com/

Quality trade paperbacks and downloads
in multiple formats,
in genres ranging from light romantic comedy
to general fiction and horror.
Wings has something for every reader's taste.
Visit the website, then bookmark it.
We add new titles each month!

Wings ePress Inc.
3000 N. Rock Road
Newton, KS   67114